Exceptions & Deceptions

(Short Stories)

CLIFF BURNS

Cover art: "Balloon Suspension" by Joslyn Cain

Cover design: Chris Kent

Interior Design & Layout: Daniel Middleton, Scribe Freelance

Printed by: Lightning Source

Published by Black Dog Press, 2013 (*blackdogpress@yahoo.ca*)

ISBN: 978-0-9694853-8-4

ALSO BY CLIFF BURNS:

Stromata: Prose Works (2012)
New & Selected Poems: 1984-2011 (2012)
The Last Hunt (2012)
So Dark the Night (2010)
Of the Night (2010)
Righteous Blood (2002)
The Reality Machine (1997)
Sex & Other Acts of the Imagination (1990)

"The unknown is an exception,
the known a deception."

Francis Picabia
("F.P. Who knows nothing, nothing, nothing.")

Acknowledgements

"Boys" appeared in *Prairie Fire* (Canada)

"Daughter" appeared in *Crimewave #4* (U.K.), *Markings* (U.K.) and aired on *Gallery* (CBC Radio)

"Surrealist World" appeared in *On Spec* (Canada)

"Facing Mrs. Abercrombie" aired on *Gallery*, CBC Radio (Produced by Kelley Jo Burke)

"Matriarchy" aired on *SoundXChange*, CBC Radio (Produced by Kelley Jo Burke)

"Harold Stensrud Watches the Olympics" appeared in *The Dalhousie Review* (Canada)

"Femme Fatale" appeared in *The Timber Creek Review* (USA)

"Printed Matter" appeared in *On Spec* (Canada)

"The Daddy Monster" appeared in *The Nashwaak Review* (Canada)

A number of the stories in this collection were originally posted on the author's blog, "Beautiful Desolation" (http://cliffjburns.wordpress.com).

for my family

Contents

* Previously unpublished

Boys

I WAS UPSTAIRS, IN the bedroom, and thought I heard something outside.

From the window in the spare room I could see that one of the big garage doors was three quarters of the way open, which explained the racket. I went downstairs, not hurrying, taking the time to go to the closet and get my nylon bomber jacket, zipping it up on the way out. I didn't bother grabbing the slivery wooden bat I keep by the back door in case of housebreaks or disagreements with neighbors. I guess when it comes right down to it I'm just not a very violent person and, anyway, I was pretty sure I wasn't dealing with any big time desperado.

By the time I got out there he'd already wheeled the barbeque over to the open doorway and had a couple of *humungous* porterhouse steaks sizzling away on the crusty grill. I was surprised he'd had the presence of mind to allow for proper ventilation. He was drunk as a skunk; you could smell the booze from three feet away, which was about as close as I intended to get.

"Hey, Donnie."

He was in rough shape: he hadn't shaved in a couple of days and was sweating profusely, like he'd just run a mile. He looked like a man in the midst of a serious bender, red-eyed and wolverine mean, and I decided to make a conscious effort not to provoke or antagonize him. I didn't want to tangle with someone in that condition. I wasn't sure if he'd had his shots.

"The steaks smell good." He still wasn't into the whole verbal thing and glared at me through the blue, fragrant smoke. Taking regular pulls at a can of beer—Coors—drinking to maintain an even keel, staving off an epic-sized hangover. "Is there any more beer?" He went into the garage and retrieved two Silver Bullets from our antique Co-op freezer, considerately lobbing one in my general direction. "Thanks. Good to see you too, man."

He sniggered, snapping open his beer. "Fuck, Terence, you haven't changed a bit, you know that? Still as big a pussy as ever."

"Fuck you," I replied good-naturedly, "I'll fight you to the death for one of those steaks." I took a long drink while he watched with gloating approval.

"Nice barbeque." And it was, a deluxe Weber unit with all the bells and whistles. "You could cook a fuckin' water buffalo on this thing."

"Jesus, how many times does a guy have to say 'thanks' before you're satisfied?"

"Best fuckin' wedding gift you ever got." He dribbled beer on the steaks and flames went *fwooosh! fwoosh!* I backed off another foot or two.

"Maybe I should get my garden hose—"

"Don't be such a wimp," he growled, "everything's under control here. Why don't you go inside and hustle up some plates. Salt and pepper, steak seasoning...you got HP Sauce?"

"How about utensils?" I asked. "Oh, I see you brought your own."

He ignored me, using a blade on his multi-tool to prod the slabs of cow. "Hurry up, for Chrissake, I'm starving. I crave food, but I also *insist* on the proper condiments."

By the time Marnie got home, around four, I was pretty much in the bag. There were squashed beer cans strewn on the driveway; she drove over one as she pulled up.

I could see her face through the windshield of the Century. She didn't look impressed. But, what the hell, I was pissed and feeling like *I'm the king of this particular castle* so her sour puss had little effect. I waved at her, adding insult to injury.

I'd only managed to eat half my steak. The partially digested meat sat in my gut like lead shot. I'm not usually much of a meat-eater. My system would be *weeks* flushing itself out.

Marnie opened the door and popped the trunk. "Lo, Mo!" Donnie yelled. He knew she'd hate that.

She brushed him off like a gnat. "Hey, Donnie," she called back, "Wanda get smart and divorce you yet?"

I winced and Donnie looked like someone had hoofed him in the balls. He should have known better. The gal had a tongue on her that could crack granite. And, of course, they had a history.

"Need any help?" I offered, looking for any chance to make up lost ground.

"No, thanks," she said brusquely, grabbing three bags of groceries and banging the trunk shut, "you boys keep right on doing what you're doing."

Oh, she was mad. And you could see her point. Here it was, four o'clock on a Saturday afternoon, her man is blotto and, guess what, his drinking buddy is a no-good bum she's known since *kindergarten*, the two of us acting like a couple of first-class fools. And not only *that*, it was mid-November and bloody cold, what were we doing barbequing in the first place? What would the neighbors think?

"Good to see you again, Mo!" Donnie hollered and she paused. For a second I thought she was going to turn around and let him have it...but she pushed through the gate, heading for the house. Donnie seemed inordinately pleased with himself, grinning at me like a maniac.

"There she goes." He couldn't wipe that demented smirk off his face. "Still the biggest bitch on God's green earth."

I started to get mad but then I thought about it and I could see his point. One of his favorite lines was about how she'd broken his arm in grade three and his heart in grade eleven.

I turned my attention back to the barbeque. It was definitely a fine appliance, top of the line, undoubtedly toting a hefty price tag. But, then again, Donnie knew people. He would have gotten it at *cost*.

It was a call I dreaded making.

"Hey, Wanda."

"Well, well, what do you know. I figured he'd either end up there or else jail. Is he drunk?"

"Like W.C. Fields only not as funny and twice as mean."

"You can tell that chickenshit from me that it's time he stood up and started acting like a man. Quote unquote."

"—and that you still love him and miss him and can't wait 'til he—"

"No way, *uh uh*, forget that shit. He walked out on me, T.J. Abandoned me in my hour of need and I'm not about to forget that. We have ourselves a situation here—" But then she started crying and I missed the rest of it. She ended up hanging up at me, not wanting to embarrass herself, or maybe thinking ol' T.J. wouldn't understand, even after all the years we've known each other. I was hurt by her lack of faith in me...but I guess in her eyes I was just another man, with all the weaknesses and defects that implied.

In the meantime, I had an irate wife to placate and a drunk in my upstairs shower, probably passed out and drowning for all I knew (or cared).

First things first.

It turned out Marnie wasn't nearly as angry as I thought and even expressed some sympathy for my predicament. She wanted to know how Wanda was holding up and speculated on what had set him off this time. Mid-life crisis got her vote. Some sort of "male identity problem". Whatever that was.

"All I know is that Wanda sounded *extremely* pissed off. And, man, when that woman gets mad, look out."

Her lips twitched, an almost smile. "Does he still call her 'Wicked Wanda, The Wanton Woman'?" she asked, averting her face.

"Frequently," I confirmed. "But the strange thing is I think he genuinely loves her and wants to—"

"That's very touching." Deftly snipping that conversational thread. "But what are we supposed to do in the meantime? He's been in the shower for *ages*." She shuddered. "I'll have to bleach it. Or burn it…"

"Something's happened. Maybe Wanda's pregnant again—"

"Can't be. She made him get fixed a few years ago. One near miss too many."

"I didn't know that," I groused, "apparently you're more up on these things than I am. Whatever it is, Donnie's on the run and Wanda's tired of picking up the pieces."

"Does she want him back?"

"That remains to be seen."

"*I* wouldn't."

"That goes without saying."

Marnie brewed some extra strong coffee, then went outside to make sure the pair of us hadn't set fire to the garage. A few minutes later I heard her start the car and back out. I guess she forgot something at the store.

Donnie had shaved and washed his hair but hadn't sobered up much. He was still none too steady on his feet and his hand shook when he accepted a mug of coffee. It was scalding hot but he drank it down like cold fruit juice and croaked for more.

After his second cup, he appeared to swoon, lolling back in his chair and I thought for a minute he'd finally passed out. But then he rallied himself: "*Enough*," he said, pushing away the cup. "Now we need more beer." I'd brought in the pack while he was showering, got us each a can. "Any cigars? Some of those Meharis you like?"

"Nope."

"Jesus." He was incredulous. "What sort of lousy host are you?"

"What sort of guest shows up pissed as a newt and insults the woman of the house—"

"Hey, I was trying to be *nice*—"

"—and soils her clean bathroom with his polluted body and makes a general fucking nuisance of himself, and for *what*?"

14

"There's a reason," he insisted, no longer interested in sparring, sagging from some slow, inaudible leak. "There's always a reason, you know that."

"What, the pressures of life got you down again?" I was thinking about Wanda, alone against the world. And here he was, hiding out and ducking responsibility while she shouldered the load. "Maxed out the VISA, blew the kid's scholarship fund on hookers and lottery tickets—*what*? What is it, Donnie? Tell me, I'm dying to know. Jesus Christ, every time you do this you leave poor Wanda hanging out to dry and I'm telling you, she's sick of it." I really let him have it, not pulling my punches, hitting to *hurt*.

Because I couldn't count how many occasions I'd gotten up and discovered the back door open and him crashed out on the couch or in the kitchen, making microwave popcorn at four in the morning *in his underwear*. And each time I'd catch three kinds of hell from Marnie, who really *liked* Wanda and couldn't understand why I stayed friends with the guy and put up with his bullshit.

"Hey, man..." I was astonished to see *tears* in Donnie's eyes. "I have to forgive you because you don't know what you're saying. You don't know what kind of heavy shit I'm, y'know, trying to cope with right now."

"Fair enough. You got troubles, I got troubles and so we—" I was about to give him the standard 'Life sucks but dying is probably worse' spiel when he jumped partway out of his chair, banging his fists on the table.

"No, goddamnit, *NO*!" He bellowed, his eyes *spooky*, and it wasn't just the booze, there was something else, something eating away at the glue holding him together. "*I can't deal with it.* If it was just me I could, I swear to God I could, but this is my *kid*, man, my fuckin' *kid*..."

I wondered why Wanda didn't tell me. Why I had to hear it like this. "What's wrong with Allan?"

"*We don't know.*" He was pouring sweat again, burning up, a smoldering pyre moments from flashpoint. "Remember how he's always been weak on that one side?" I nodded. "Well, this summer it got worse and at first we were worried it was some sort of blood clot or...maybe he even had a stroke." I was horrified—*did*

15

Marnie know about this? "But we had tests done and nobody's sure *what* it is. Last week one of these specialist guys tells us it could be M.S. or something like that. Remember all those kids in Special Ed., the spastics and the freaks we used to laugh at? That could be my Al in a few years." He closed his eyes but couldn't escape the sight. "And who would have to take care of him, who'd have to be there for him and look after him for the rest of our lives?"

I didn't blame him for pounding the table. I wouldn't have blamed him if he'd pummeled it into sawdust and splinters. He was justified. I couldn't help thinking about Allan, someone I'd known almost since birth and watched grow into a sweet, ungainly boy who was always tripping over things, a menace on two legs, a lurching, windmilling horror. A kid with the disposition of a teddy bear and more soul than a Motown reunion album.

"But maybe the doctor's wrong. Maybe—"

"Wanda says we'll make do." Donnie shook his head. "It makes you wonder if she realizes what it's going to take."

"But you've got friends and family. Lots of them. If you need help—" It sounded feeble and half-hearted and he saw through it in a second, focusing on the stark reality.

"Allan is *our* problem. Mine and Wanda's. When it gets right down to it, we're the ones responsible for him." He went to the fridge, returning with the last beer "I don't suppose you have any more."

"I think there might be some cooking wine Marnie uses…"

He made a face.

The beer wasn't half gone before he was making preparations to be on his way. I didn't exactly try to discourage him.

"Thanks for, y'know, being there for me, man. Appreciate the hospitality."

"Please tell me you're on your way back home to Wanda." He wouldn't meet my eye. "But you will eventually."

He shrugged. "Sure," he allowed, "eventually."

16

There was no big emotional send-off or anything, no display of male bonding. He even managed to scrounge twenty bucks off me for gas money. Can you believe it?

After that, it wasn't hard saying good-bye. Donnie was a bad influence, plain and simple, he brought out a side of me that was probably best left behind double-locked, steel-plated doors.

I waved from the front walk. He turned his Dodge around in the middle of the street and announced his departure with a long blast on the horn that brought my neighbors to their windows. At least he remembered to put his lights on.

The booze was wearing off and a fist-sized area at the back of my head was pulsating like a big vein. I started back to the house but then Marnie tapped her horn. I walked over to the driveway and waited for her to get out.

"You look like crap," she said, by way of greeting.

"Head ache," I muttered.

"Hangover," she retorted and we left it at that.

Once inside, I got some Tylenol from the medicine cabinet. Marnie stood in the doorway. She wanted to know what happened with Donnie.

I told her about Allan and neither of us said anything for awhile. Finally, she stirred. "Mostly I feel sorry for Wanda." She did an about face and left.

I, of course, mostly felt sorry for *myself*. My head was pounding but I knew if I laid down and closed my eyes all I'd be able to see would be Allan and his goofy, Howdy Doody grin: "*Hi, Unca Terry!*".

Two in the morning, Donnie called from a stripper bar in Plentywood. He was drunk and abusive. I lost my temper, said a few things and we hung up on each other. About an hour later the phone rang again and I let the machine answer, the volume turned low. Marnie and I listened to the frantic, whispery message. I tried to make out if he was still angry or, far less likely, the slightest bit contrite.

"Asshole," Marnie murmured and soon went back to sleep.

But I had a hard time settling down again. I couldn't shake this feeling of dread, a sense that something was looming, a catastrophe of life-altering proportions. I suppose I could've woken Marnie and tried to talk about it but she'd likely be grouchy and, anyway, she didn't really know Allan, not like I did.

I remembered looking after him when he was really little and I waited and waited but finally I *had* to change his diaper. And it was an important rite of passage for me. But, Marnie, well, she'd have a hard time understanding something like that.

Marnie didn't much like kids, didn't think they were worth the trouble and grief they put you through. I wondered what Donnie and Wanda would say about that. For the rest of the night, lying there next to her, I tried to imagine what that conversation would sound like and whose side I would end up taking.

Daughter

JASPER COMES IN JUST as supper's nearly ready. The rest of us pick up on his mood right away and it gets really quiet in the kitchen, everyone waiting.

"We're moving out, Family," he says, trying to make like it's no big deal but meanwhile we're all looking at each other and thinking 'here we go again'.

So we start packing everything up, supper and all, doing our best to ignore our growling stomachs.

Everyone has their job and hops to it. Faye takes care of the kitchen and Little Todd and me load everything we own—which ain't much—into the one box we're allowed between the two of us.

"Quick, quick, my lovelies," Faye calls, but by now she should know better. Little Todd is only six but works as hard as anyone and I'm already finishing up in the bathroom, grabbing the shampoo, Jasper's razor and whatever else in there that's worth taking.

Jasper waits beside the car, taking stuff as we bring it out to him, cramming most of it into the backseat. The trunk is full of his things but, like I said, none of us has much anyway.

"All aboard," Jasper calls, pleased with how smooth everything goes, how soon we're backing out of the driveway and heading down the street, putting our troubles further behind us with each passing block.

I don't look back and feel no regrets about leaving. We never stay any place long enough to form attachments. That old house was just somewhere to live and after a few more moves I bet I'll hardly remember it.

Faye hands me some chicken, still warm. I peel off a piece and offer it to Little Todd. Faye flashes me a nice smile for being such a good sister to him but I can see from her eyes how tired and frazzled she is. And I'd say by the way Jasper keeps checking the mirror that he's jumpy too, only trying not to let on because, after all, we're God's chosen ones, His anointed flock and, therefore, protected from earthly danger and tribulation.

Or so Jasper says and tonight, more than any other night, I sure hope he's right.

It's a long drive but Little Todd and me have plenty of practice when it comes to sleeping on the road. Jasper never tells us where we're going and sometimes I get the idea he isn't sure himself, he's just following his nose or whatever. He says we go where we're guided and it's hard to argue when he puts it like that. And it wouldn't do you any good if you tried. He can quote chapter and verse and loves to hear himself preach. Sometimes when he's drunk he makes us get up and listen to him "prophesize" even if it's, like, three in the morning. It's scary because he speaks in different voices. Usually he ends up nodding off and drooling down the front of his shirt. Faye says it's part of being in the Spirit and sends us back to bed so she can deal with him.

Jasper asks her to sing to him and Faye, tired as she is, is happy to oblige. Usually it's a song of praise but sometimes she surprises us. For instance, it's no secret that Jasper just *loves* Bob Dylan. We know "Like A Rolling Stone" by heart. I guess you could say it's kind of our theme song.

We drive through the night and on into the next day. Finally, in the early afternoon, Jasper gets the word (or whatever) and we turn off the highway into a town that looks exactly like the one we just left, same color and everything. He stops at a telephone booth near a gas station, looks through the Yellow Pages and makes a few calls. Then he hops back in and we're off again, Jasper getting us to help him follow the signs until we're pulling into a parking lot in front of an ugly, grey building with slits for windows. Jasper goes inside to arrange things while the rest of us are left to wait, sweltering in the sun. Little Todd is dozing so we have to whisper:

20

"What's the name of this town again?"

"Manley," Faye says, yawning, "just across the state line." Giving me another one of her soft as a feather smiles. "You tired of all this driving, Miss Jo?" Knowing how much I like it when she calls me that. I stretch, jostling Little Todd's head in my lap—he grunts like a piglet but doesn't wake up.

"I'm okay," I answer because in this Family we don't whine, whinge or complain. She reaches back and runs her fingers through my hair.

"Have to give you a trim. You know Jasper doesn't like long hair on girls."

"On *anybody*," I correct her, indicating Little Todd's bristley skull.

Not much later, Jasper comes out, followed by a fat man in a wide, blue suit. The two of them shake hands. They're both smiling but neither of them means it. The fat man bends down so he can see through the windshield and waggles his meaty fingers at us. I politely wave back but Faye can't be bothered.

Not only does Jasper have keys, but also a hand-drawn map to our latest home.

"Any trouble?" Faye asks him and Jasper grins.

"The Lord is our Shepherd and provider," he says. "And not only that," he adds, waiting for us to join in, "—He deals in cold, hard cash."

Thanks to Jasper, devoted servant of our Lord and Redeemer, the Family's needs are always provided for. He's real good with his hands, Jasper is, in more ways than one. He can work construction, he can cut glass and fix almost anything except a broken heart (*ha ha*). And, as he himself puts it, he can steal like a heathen. See, as long as it's for the good of the *Family*, stealing is allowed. Since it's serving a higher purpose or what have you. I'm using Jasper's words because I've never figured out why it's bad for everyone else and yet all right for us. Jasper'll give you a dozen different reasons, depending on which day you ask him, so I guess it's okay (but deep down inside I still think a sin is a sin, no matter who commits it).

I hear Jasper say he paid the fat man for the first three months' rent in advance and I have to grin because if we stayed anyplace for three months it would be some kind of world record for us.

When he stops in front of the house it's not bad. No broken windows or beer bottles in the front yard. Matter of fact, it looks quite decent and respectable, a house any ordinary family would live in. Jasper looks at Faye, waiting to see what she thinks and she leans over and kisses him. "Aw, honey," she says, "it's *perfect*."

Later that afternoon, after putting away my things (which, let's face it, doesn't take long), I'm sort of wandering around the backyard…and I see her.

She stands on the sidewalk beside her house, wearing one of those backpack things, watching me, just staring kind of rude like. I pretend not to notice her. She must get the message because when I look again, she's gone. Then I feel bad for chasing her away. And wonder how I ever got to be such a weird, screwed up kid.

I think in my heart I already know what's going to happen. I know that Jasper will see the girl and want her. She's nothing like Andie but she's pretty and perfect like Andie was. A living doll.

Do you know the difference between a little girl…

Good old Jasper.

It's like somehow he knew she was going to be here.

Jasper comes in to say good night and right away I tell him about the girl next door, thinking to myself, *well, he was gonna find out sooner or later…*

He asks a few questions and keeps his eyes on mine the whole time I'm answering. Neither of us mentions Andie's name but she's there in the room with us, hovering in the air like clear smoke.

After she died we all became different people, smaller and meaner than we used to be. We each had our separate reasons for missing her. She was *his* special girl and *my* best friend. The closest thing to a sister I'll ever have.

Andie and me used to talk after everyone else was asleep. She was a year and a half older, nearly ready for a bra and easily the wisest, coolest person I've ever met. Like she always knew when Jasper was about to start drinking again and what nights to make sure she slept with jeans on under her nightie. Sometimes, during the worst of it, I'd hear her praying, but so softly I could never make out what she was saying.

After Jasper leaves I lie there listening to Little Todd snore. Somewhere in the house Faye and Jasper are talking, maybe about that girl next door. I'm glad she doesn't look anything like Andie. And I'm glad I already don't like her. If she was more like Andie it would make it harder...because then it would be like she never actually got away, never gave up, never died, never *won*.

"How come you don't go to school?" Melissa asks me. We're sitting on the swings in her yard, dangling our feet, still getting acquainted. I'm working hard to make her like me so I put up with her questions, at least for now.

"Faye—my mother teaches me."

"Is that *allowed?*"

I bunch my shoulders. "I guess."

"What does your dad do?"

"Fixes stuff."

"Like what?"

Another shrug. Already bored with her. "Everything." Then it's my turn. "How old are you?"

"I'll be ten this December." Andie's birthday was April 29th.

"That's good."

She doesn't ask about *my* birthday. Actually she's quite stuck up and I don't like her at all. She's going to have some hard lessons ahead and a totally different idea about what being in a *real* Family is all about.

"Ya wanna go inside and play XBox?" It's the fourth time she's brought up her stupid, fancy video game.

"Sure." We leave the swings and head toward the house.

23

"Where did you come from? Are you staying in town long?"

I smile at the back of her head but she doesn't feel it. "Long enough," I tell her, and that's pretty much all I'm going to say on that particular subject.

Our Family doesn't have an XBox or even a microwave oven. I have one pair of shoes and two pairs of pants. I really like reading but only own two books, *Little Women* and *Harriet the Spy*. Little Todd can't read and doesn't seem much interested in learning. He has a couple of trucks and a bag of marbles and that's good enough for him. See, the Family doesn't care about *things* and we pretty much spend whatever money Jasper brings home on food and bills. The rest we save for rainy days. When he can't find good, honest work, Jasper sells something out of the trunk. Once it was a brand new computer, still in its original box, and that was because we needed new tires for the car.

In no time at all I become Melissa's new best friend and pal. Pretty soon she's telling me stuff about her life, things even her *mom* doesn't know. Or so she claims.

Of course, I never let on that I couldn't care less about what's going on in her creepy little world. And just to get even, I tell Jasper *everything* she says. He seems really pleased with me lately. One night he tries to give me a whiskery kiss but I hold up my stuffed frog between us and we both act like it's a joke.

I don't like the lovey-dovey stuff but it's good that he trusts me again. Ever since Andie died I've had the feeling he's been *watching* me, though I guess it could be just my imagination. So I'm really giving it my best with Melissa, showing him that I'm still Family, ready to do whatever I'm asked with no questions or back-talk. With Jasper, you don't want him thinking any different. 'Cause, you know, as far as he's concerned, there's *Family* and then there's everybody else in the world.

Faye and me are working in the kitchen when there's a knock on the door. We give each other a quick look to make sure we both heard it, then I go see who it is.

Melissa is home from school early and wants to visit. Stands there with that look on her face, waiting to be asked in. So I guess I don't have a choice, do I?

But Faye and me pretend like it's the most natural thing in the world and invite her in for tea. Melissa immediately starts checking everything out, naturally seeing the boxes and the fact that we have hardly any furniture or knick-knacks.

After we finish our tea and cookies I try to get her to go outside but instead she decides she wants to see my room, so off we go. She stares at the sleeping bags on the floor and bare walls and Little Todd in his underwear, gaping at her, hardly believing his eyes. There's no clothes, no computer, no dresser, no *nothing*.

"Are you really, really *poor*?" she goes, once we're safely outside and perched on our swing seats.

"Not really. It's not that we can't afford things, it's just that we don't *need* them." Standing up for the Family like I've been taught to.

"But you don't even have a *TV*." Making it sound like child abuse.

Before I can answer that, Jasper comes along, whistling to himself and, of course, he sees the two of us or, anyway, he sees *her*. "Afternoon, ladies," he calls, walking over for a closer look. "So you're Melinda, are you?" Acting really friendly and smiling with his eyes. "How do you do?" Melissa ducks her head and Jasper gives me a quick nod. Right then it's settled.

From that moment on, it's only a matter of time.

Andie worried about what would happen if Jasper ever found out I helped her. Not that I did much. Basically, all I had to do was wait and watch (which was hard enough). I remember I held her hand. Once it was done I had to crawl back into bed and try to *sleep*, for God's sake, behave like I had no idea what I would be waking up to.

Andie never read *Little Women*. She told me the title alone scared her off. She asked me once if I knew the difference between a little girl and a little woman. Then, without waiting for an answer, she said: "The difference is, little *girls* don't understand..."

* * *

Jasper says there's no such thing as luck, that the good Lord Himself takes a personal interest in our Family. Well, I guess the good Lord must have been looking the other way last night because, guess what, Jasper finally gets busted and we wake up to cops at our door at eight in the morning.

Turns out they're both young and really nice and polite, telling us that Jasper has been arrested and there are a number of charges. The bail isn't going to be too high, nothing our secret stash can't handle. The cops don't say much, just that Jasper was spotted creeping around a lumber yard after closing and a sixty-six year old security guard put the grab on him. They've impounded the car and are getting a warrant to search it. Faye plays it cool, like she's sure there's been some kind of mistake, wondering if they could maybe recommend a good lawyer here in town...

She even lets the cops come in for a quick look around. Not that we have anything to hide. After they leave, she calls the lawyer and gets the ball rolling. By the time she hangs up it sounds like Jasper is as good as sprung, but the price is going to be steep. Faye takes the shoebox out from under the sink, grabs a wad of bills and gets me to call her a cab.

I suspect we won't be hanging around Manley much longer, so after breakfast I start Little Todd packing in our room while I box up the kitchen stuff, piling everything by the door. It takes us 'til noon but we just about finish the whole house. I'm sitting on the back step, having a much-deserved break, when Melissa comes home for lunch. She waves at me from the other side of the fence...but then she sees the boxes beside me and catches on to what's happening.

"Are you *leaving?*" she asks, hanging her arms over to the fence and looking pouty.

"Yeah," I say, not bothering to lie because what's the point.

"Did your dad get a job someplace else?"

"He *ain't* my dad." She stares at me and I decide to cool it. "He's...kind of my step-dad, y'know?" She nods.

Just then her mom calls out the window: "Melissa? Ask your friend if she wants to join us for lunch." I can hear it in her voice: good ol' Melissa has been telling her how bad off and starving we are and now mommy wants to play the Good Samaritan and maybe pump me with a few questions besides.

I hear a car pull up out front and right then and there make the decision, no time to think about it, hardly any time at all—

"You better go inside," I tell Melissa. "And tell your mom we ain't poor, we're just not stuck-up snobs like you people." I can see I've hurt her feelings but maybe not enough. "Don't you understand?" I snap at her. "I can't be your friend any more, okay? We're never gonna see each other again so just...*go away*, will you? Get lost, you spoiled little brat." She stumbles back from the fence and halfway to the house has to cover her face with her hands. Once she's inside she must really cut loose because through the open window I can hear her mom asking *what's wrong, honey, what's wrong.*

Faye and Jasper come walking around the side of the house, talking, laying plans for our daring escape. He nods at my hard work and gives me the car keys so I can start loading.

Now that I know Melissa won't be coming with us I feel a lot better about things. I have to admit, sometimes it gets lonely and it would be nice, you know, to have someone to hang out with and talk to. But then I think about how hard it would be for her, getting used to a whole new Family, living an entirely different life, everything else becoming just a dream.

I wonder if her parents would ever stop looking for her. I wonder if they would ever forget their precious daughter. I wonder if they would still be able to recognize her, years later, and call her by her real name.

Matriarchy

AFTER THE SERVICE AND interment, we drove back to the church for the reception. Stood in a receiving line, mourners shaking our hands and mumbling words of sympathy while we did our best to look suitably solemn. The church basement was airless, musty and full of old bones. Not unlike mother's coffin, I thought, and had to cough to cover an unseemly smile. A giddy, inconsiderate moment; I chalked it up to grief.

I endured the well-wishers for as long as I could—it was a geriatric crowd, comprised of brittle, dew-lapped dowagers, most of whom I'd known all my life. Some of them looked inclined to tousle my hair or chuck my chin. At one point I caught Edward's eye and nodded toward the exit. He took the cue and soon we made our escape, adjourning to a nearby bar to compare notes.

"Aunt Miranda still scares me," he confessed. "Her most of all. She was the only one who actually hit us." He reached for his pale ale, one of those watery micro-brews I detest. I remain a staunch Guinness man.

"You always blow things out of proportion. Miranda wasn't that bad."

He chuckled. "Right, Sonny, whatever you say."

I flared. "Don't call me that."

"Why not? It was always *Sonny* this and *Sonny* that. You were their favorite, let's face it. The golden boy." He sipped his beer. "Never acting up or giving them any trouble. And it was pretty clear you were mom's favorite too." He lowered his eyes. "It was you she wanted around at the end."

"Ed, it wasn't like that," I lied. "She asked for you repeatedly. I called, left messages—"

"I was out of town. Buying trip to Chicago."

I wasn't sure I believed him. A deathwatch is a terrible thing, long hours spent counting each shallow breath, wondering if *this* is the last one. "Let's forget it. She's gone now and none of that's important any more."

I was glad neither of us had the energy to pursue the argument. Drained by our mother's death and the ridiculously Anglican funeral rites. *Psalm 100* and the Aunts, dressed in black, sitting in a row, not even bothering to move their lips.

As if reading my thoughts, he said: "The sisters. Still an intimidating bunch. Remember how they took over after Pop left? He *begged* to come back, you know. Uncle George told me once when he was really juiced. And I think mom would've forgiven him…only they wouldn't even let her *talk* to him. Can you imagine having that kind of power over someone? Those old bitches completely took over her life and never let up, not to her dying day."

I couldn't help glancing around, an involuntary reaction, ingrained by habit. "They'll be looking for us. Mad we didn't stick around with the old fogeys. Must keep up appearances."

"Yeah," he allowed, "they're big on that. Aw, to hell with them. I'm not going back. They don't even bother hiding the fact that they hate my guts. I'm too much like dad. That's, like, a cardinal sin in their eyes."

"You're ducking out? Leaving me to deal with them? Thanks a lot, brother dear." I glared at him.

"I'll see them at the lawyer's." He glanced at me slyly. "While we're on the subject, I have to confess I've been a tad curious about the, ah, state of the estate, so to speak. Can you—"

"You'll find out soon enough." I don't know why I was goading him. Sibling rivalry, I suppose. Plus I wasn't exactly enamored with the notion of returning without him.

He grimaced. "C'mon, man, don't bullshit me. I…have to know," he added belatedly.

"Business a bit slow?" I teased. "Feeling the pinch?"

I saw from his reaction I'd guessed correctly. "Retail is tricky right now. Between the bloody internet and the dollar, it's a real crap shoot. I go from day to day not knowing if I'm going to lose a supplier or one of my managers is gonna take off for greener pastures." He shook his head. "Let's not get off topic. What's the word, money-wise? The old girl must have had a fair amount squirreled away."

"You've been accommodated for," I assured him. "Though not, perhaps, to the extent you might expect."

He regarded me warily. "What does that mean?"

"I *mean* in her final months our dear mama added a few new provisions to her will, including a healthy bequest to the city humane society."

My brother looked like he'd swallowed a bug. "*What*? How could you let her…we'll fight it, damnit. Claim she was senile, losing it. Diminished capacity. Have the whole thing annulled or whatever. We'll say they threatened her with a rabid pitbull or something. We'll—ah, *Jesus*, Derek." He slumped in his seat. "How long have you known about this?"

"Since last week. After the second stroke when I knew…she wasn't coming out of it. I started going through her things. That was tough." I decided against a second beer. Instead, surreptitiously popped a breath mint.

"You don't seem very bothered." He frowned at me.

"She did love her pets."

"More than us."

"Now, now."

Something occurred to him. "Do the sisters know?"

I tried to hide my smile but wasn't altogether successful. "Not yet."

"In that case," he stated, raising his glass in a mock toast, "I'm *really* looking forward to the reading of the will."

He couldn't be persuaded to return to the church with me. We stood outside the pub, hardly meeting each other's eyes. "I'm disappointed, I won't bother denying it." He kicked a loose stone. "A parent has a responsibility to her children."

"She did her best, Ed. I know you won't accept that but it's true. The Aunts controlled her and messed things up royally but when all is said and done she still deserves—"

"What? *What* does she deserve?"

"To be forgiven, I guess. Damnit, Edward, she was the youngest, the rest of them always lorded it over her and once Pop was out of the way there was nothing holding them back."

"But she *let* them take over her life. And when they'd punish us, she'd just stand there. Remember Miranda, those big rings of hers and the way she'd lay into us? Anywhere she could hit and Mom never *once* stood up for us."

"And Pop abandoned us. Don't forget that." A couple passed between us on their way into the bar. "You weren't the only victim, you know. You took off out east but *I* stayed. And I made my peace with her. Especially these past few weeks."

"Good for you."

I gave up. "I'm going back."

"The dutiful son."

"Yeah. Whatever." I started away but he reached out, forestalling me. "*What?*"

"You're right. Staying was the hard part. You were the better son."

"No, I wasn't."

"Better than me." He seemed genuinely choked up. "I appreciate that you were there for her. And I honestly couldn't get away." He let his hand drop to his side.

"Okay, Edward."

"You believe me?"

"Of course." I even managed a smile. "You wouldn't lie to me, man. You're my *brother*."

I hurried back to the church, worried I'd been missed. Aunt Sheila was stationed right outside the big front doors. She flicked a cigarette away, crossing her arms as she waited. "Where were *you?*"

"Taking Edward back to his hotel. He was pretty devastated. He told me to tell everyone—"

She interrupted me. "Miranda's looking for you." Her eyes narrowed. "Have you been *drinking*, Sonny?" I shook my head vigorously. Before she could pursue the point further, I moved past her, into the church. I made a beeline for the basement, nearly bowling over my cousin Frank and some woman I vaguely recognized.

"*Oops*. Sorry, Frank."

"No problemo, Sonny," he responded, jovial as ever. "We were going out for some air. Kind of stuffy down there." He leaned closer. "And I don't mean the surroundings." I had to grin. I've always liked Frank.

The woman, Amy or Andie—we'd been introduced but I'm terrible with names—leaned forward, eyes huge and woeful. "It must be awful losing a parent."

One of those remarks that's so dumb you don't know what to say. "Well, she's not really *lost*."

"Excuse me?"

"We know where she is, right?" She recoiled from me. "Sorry, bad joke."

"It's a tough time," Frank broke in, trying to salvage the situation. "We all have our ways of dealing with it, right, Sonny?"

"Absolutely." Amy or Andi wasn't mollified but she'd get over it. "Uh, Frank, you haven't seen Aunt Miranda around, have you?"

"Back there." He pointed down the stairs. "I think she's giving the priest hell. Poor bastard."

"I thought it was a lovely service," Amy/Andie opined.

"That doesn't matter," Frank said. "Not to Miranda."

"Is she the one—"

"Built like Khrushchev, acts like Hitler," Frank replied, slipping me a wink as he said it.

I chuckled but the woman appeared unimpressed by our levity. He led her away while I descended, steeling myself for the ordeal to come.

"Sonny." Miranda was an imposing woman, nearly as tall as I was, her eyes clear and sharp and penetrating. "I've been looking for you." She clasped a small purse in her hands. She had big hands. I remembered them well. And she still favored heavy rings, topaz and some brown and yellow stones I couldn't identify. "I could have used your help with that oaf of a minister."

"I heard someone saying how much they enjoyed his—"

Her contempt was palpable. "He didn't know Dorothy. I'll bet he's given that speech a hundred times." She looked past me and I saw Sheila and Sally approaching. "He actually brought up his fee, the cretin. The nerve of the man."

"I'll take care of it."

"You mean the *estate* will take care of it," she corrected me.

"Yes," I conceded. "That's what I meant."

"I suppose you know she left you the house." Her siblings had joined us, ringing me, hemming me in. "It should fetch a pretty penny, if you play your cards right."

"I hadn't considered selling it."

"One mustn't be sentimental about these things," Sheila spoke up.

"No, I suppose not."

There was a lull in the conversation. I saw them looking at each other. "We were by the house earlier," Sally said. "We thought you might need help getting things squared away."

"Mother was quite good about organizing her affairs."

"Ye-es," Sally allowed. "But we thought, well…"

"We were looking for the will, Sonny." Miranda got to the point.

"I assume that lawyer of hers, Johnson or Jackson—"

"We know she wanted you to have the house," Sheila patted my shoulder, "and that only seems right."

"But as to the other arrangements…" Sally prompted.

I was starting to weary of the interrogation. "It's all with the lawyer, I'm afraid."

"You keep bringing up this lawyer," Miranda snapped. "But surely you must know—"

"Nothing." As a child I'd learned to feign ignorance and that old ruse served me well once again. They had a dim view of men and I played the part to the hilt. "Honestly, Aunties, I'm in the dark as much as you are." I edged away. "I guess we'll just have to wait until Monday."

They weren't pleased with me but at that point I no longer cared.

My new dress shirt was soaked through. Forty-one years old and they still made me sweat like a pig. I glanced back and saw them huddled together, Miranda doing most of the talking. They'd squeezed me and gotten nothing for their trouble. Now they were discussing tactics, preparing a united front. Miranda giving terse instructions, Sheila and Sally nodding as they received their marching orders. Clearly, plans were being made and something was afoot.

But mother was beyond their reach now and no amount of scheming on their part would bring her back. In life, she'd never defied her sisters or acted contrary to their wishes. When I read her will, I wept for the first time in a long while. Not because of her passing, I was glad her suffering was over. I cried at the effort she'd expended to hurt them and because I knew she did it for us.

Partners

for Stacey

SHE WAS A PRETTY DECENT pool player, I'll say that much for her. A nice, smooth stroke combined with a good eye, although she tended to be a bit streaky. Nail three or four balls in a row, then blow what amounted to an easy tap in.

"Sorry," she muttered after one such miss. "I make that and I can just about run the table. Must be getting too cocky or something. *Shit.*"

"It's not like I'm setting the world on fire," I reminded her. "You're doing a lot better than me." Which was true, I was playing dismally, unable to even fluke one in. And I was trying too hard which didn't help matters any.

"You're great on the break," she offered helpfully.

It's easy, I wanted to tell her, *I just picture my ex-wife's face*. That likely wouldn't go over very well. Women nowadays have this sisterhood thing going and close ranks the minute they hear cracks like that. Their version of "all for one and one for all", I suppose.

She and I hadn't lost a game so far. We'd partnered up casually, nodding to each other as I plugged my change into the table. She had her quarters ready, intending to reserve it when I was done. I think I was playing more out of boredom than anything else. Needing to hit something that wasn't likely to hit me back.

I was about to ask her to join me for a friendly game when a young guy lurched up to the table, nearly falling across its worn, green surface. He was with the big wedding party I noticed arriving earlier. Turned out he was the groom and after accepting my mumbled, half-sincere congratulations, he made his intentions clear.

"I wanna play," he announced, with drunken bravado verging on belligerence. "Me 'n my buddy," he gushed, leaning in close and grinning like a Halloween pumpkin. "Us two against you 'n the lady. Waddaya say?" The woman didn't seem averse to the idea. She wanted to play pool and wasn't choosy about the arrangements.

The groom's pal wasn't in any better shape than he was. We had to keep telling them if they were shooting solids or stripes. At one point the woman caught my eye and smirked. I noticed she was pacing herself, her waitress friend bringing her the occasional drink, something with Kahlua in it. I favor either beer or scotch so I can never remember what you call those mixed concoctions.

After the groom and best man, we made short work of a couple of tipsy maids of honor. Those gals were anything but maids. One of them had big, jiggly boobs that kept spilling out of the scoop-necked shirt she was wearing. Her irrepressible mammary glands proved so distracting I actually made a good shot purely by accident.

"Nice one," my partner complimented me. "Or should I say," eying the baubles in question, "nice *ones*."

"Sheddup," I said and she blinked innocently at me.

The groom and best man kept coming back for more. We must have whupped those poor guys five or six times at least. They were good sports about it though. The groom latched on to me for some reason. As I waited my turn to shoot, he started telling me his life story (the long, dull, unedited version).

He was only twenty-one and already had a two year-old son with his fiancé. They were one of those couples who are constantly on the verge of breaking up but never quite manage to pull the trigger. Getting married was probably their last shot at it. They had come to a mutual decision that if it didn't work out in a year or so, they'd pack it in and go their separate ways. He just hoped that afterwards she'd let him see his son on at least a semi-regular basis.

Listening to the guy, I almost had to laugh. It took me back twelve years: Bonnie and I were going to make it work this time. Bonnie was a great gal, my high school sweetheart. We were made for each other. We weren't a statistic. It was true love.

His buddy kept nudging him every time a good-looking woman walked by. They weren't picky, anything in a tight pair of jeans drew their scrutiny. At one point the groom's mother, an attractive older lady, came up, took her son to one side and tried to read him the riot act.

He wasn't having any of it. "Fuck that, ma," I heard him say, practically hissing at her. "I'm getting *married* tomorrow. Tonight I'm havin' *fun*."

The best man scratched on the eight ball. It was the closest they would ever come to beating us and they knew it.

"Fuck, R.J.," the groom complained, "a drunk monkey coulda made that shot. Wassa matter with you?"

"Bring on fuckin' monkey, asshole, let's see what he's got."

"How could you miss, dude?"

"'Cause I'm *hammered*, okay? I can't hardly see the end of the table." They giggled and ended up in a rough, sloppy embrace.

"Hey, remember how smashed we were at that Ozzy concert?" The groom was wearing the tour shirt. They had driven blind drunk to Edmonton and got there only minutes before the show started.

It was the best concert *ever*, I was assured over and over again.

I said I preferred Ozzy in his Randy Rhoads days but they didn't know what the hell I was talking about. "Whatever, man. I'm telling you, this guitarist he had was awesome. The best *ever*."

"What was his name?" I asked foolishly and they looked at me as if I'd just flashed them.

"I dunno." They shrugged simultaneously. "Ronnie!" The groom howled. "*Ronnie!*"

"What?" A big, blond lug at their table hollered back.

"Who's Ozzy's guitar player?"

"*What?*"

"Who's Ozzy's guitar player!"

"Zakk Wylde!"

Their faces lit up. "Right! Fuckin' Zakk Wylde! He was smokin', man."

Okay, maybe I'm exaggerating. Were they as dumb as that...or just awfully, terribly *young*? A couple of kids already up to their necks in life and still learning how to swim. That was the gist of what I told my partner during a break in the action but she wasn't having any of it.

"They're *losers*. Complete scumbags, both of 'em." She pronounced sentence like a hanging judge, leaving no room for mercy or an appeal on compassionate grounds. I didn't like that. How certain she was. How quick to write them off.

"C'mon, they're just boys. Got a lot of growing up to do, that's all. They'll learn."

She acted like she couldn't believe her ears. "*Them*? They'll never learn and they'll never, ever grow up. That would require courage and effort." She laughed at the thought. "The trouble is, women know what they want a lot sooner than men do. You guys spend all your lives trying to catch up with us."

I told her my ex-wife would probably agree with her. "But just because you know what you want doesn't mean you automatically get to have it," I added, pointing out what I thought was a flaw in her argument.

She nodded, looking at me with new appreciation. "That's right," she confirmed, "you don't. And that's something else women know before you do."

Her waitress friend Lucinda snuck us one last drink even though technically it was past last call. I was so tight by then the effect was minimal.

The wedding party was gone, the place nearly deserted. An old George Thorogood song was playing from overhead speakers, the volume turned down. To tell the truth, I've never been a fan of George's. Everything he does sounds exactly the same to me. Tired ass country blues.

You could see the woman still felt unstoppable, riding high on the wave of her victories. The best pool she'd ever played, she told me, touching her glass to mine in cheerful salute.

I was pretty beat at that point. I'd started drinking right after lunch. Not heavy, but steady. I had that scraped out feeling. Some food would help.

It got on my nerves the way she kept picking up the money and flipping through it.

She shouldn't have taken it. Everyone in the wedding party had thrown in a buck, two bucks, five bucks, some of them even more. The groom and best man against the reigning champs, winner take all.

I tried to back out but the woman was keen on the idea and they shook hands on it, made me shake too and we were on. We let them break and they got nothing. I had what looked like a wide open shot but I put too much on it and missed by a hair. The woman gave me a funny look but it wasn't like I screwed up on purpose. Honest.

When it was her turn, she went on another one of her runs, knocking balls in right and left. As she lined up the eight ball we had most of the people in the bar gathered around the table. She potted it as cool as a cucumber.

Then she walked over and gathered up their money. Sixty or seventy bucks, nothing really, hardly anything in the grand scheme of things.

She tried to offer me half but I declined. Didn't make a big deal about it, just said no. Nobody seemed mad at the outcome and the groom and best man laughed it off like it was nothing. But they didn't stay long after that. The groom just about had to be carried out. He was going to have a bitch of a hangover for his wedding ceremony.

Not an auspicious beginning to a match made in heaven.

Then again, what the hell did I know?

"You didn't like it when I took their money."

We were standing outside, wondering if we were going to end up spending the night together or if we even *liked* each other. I was so strung out by that point it honestly didn't matter to me one way or the other.

"You could have let it go. Told them to forget about it." I was surprised at how angry I sounded. "I thought we were playing for fun."

She snickered and lit a cigarette, another turn-off. "Call it revenge." She pointed back inside. "Seven years ago I married an asshole who could've been his big brother. No good sonofabitch left me high and dry. I mean, nothing but the clothes on my back. Maybe I figured Junior had it coming to him."

"Lady, you got a hard way of looking at the world. Must be nice to be so perfect and flawless." I was blowing it but my head was starting to throb so I wasn't in what you would call a conciliatory mood. "You're one of those folks who like to fit the rest of us into convenient slots. Winners. Losers. The good, the bad and the ugly. There's a word for people like you…"

"Where does that put you?" Flicking ash off her cigarette. "In what category?"

"According to your high standards, I suppose I'd have to say I'm a loser."

"At least you acknowledge it." She grinned. "So am I. Believe me, the blade cuts both ways."

"What happens when a person doesn't measure up in their own eyes?"

She got that tough look back, the one she was wearing when she swept those bills up off the pool table. "You get used to it. Don't tell me you haven't figured *that* out."

I had to admit she had me there.

I don't recall at what point it was decided that she was coming with me. I wasn't, strictly speaking, fit to drive but I managed to get us back to the hotel all right.

There were plastic shopping bags on the bed. T-shirts, underwear and a couple of mystery novels. I cleared everything off and made drinks. "Sorry, there's only scotch."

"Beggars can't be choosers." She asked what I did. I explained I was a consultant on contract to the town water department. I was supposed to inspect their facilities and write a detailed report about what I found. Strictly confidential, of course. I had another two days to go, then I was driving back to the city. To my so-called life. I kept it short and sweet and unlike the kid I didn't editorialize.

She sipped at her drink. She was sitting on the bed but it wasn't an invitation—I could tell by her body language. I straddled the only chair in the room, trying to keep up my end of the conversation while carefully avoiding any exposed nerve endings.

I knew she'd been married.

I gathered things hadn't gone too well.

I assumed that as a result she likely didn't have real positive feelings toward men in general and therefore I better watch my step. This could end up in a passionate clinch or a nasty row. Was it worth it? For either of us?

I freshened our drinks and she raised her glass. "To my partner. The best damn partner a girl could hope for. Well, compared to the rest of that crowd anyway."

I toasted her right back. "And a helluva lot of good I was."

She crawled up further onto the bed until she was right against the headboard. "You did all right. You kept things interesting. Your problem is, you lack self-confidence. Did your wife get your balls in the settlement too?"

I laughed. It was a good line, although it cut awfully close to the bone. I could see her point; I didn't appear to be in any big rush to join her on the bed. "I was taking it easy on those boys. Trying to make you look good...as if you needed any help. You're a *shark*, lady."

"If you only knew." She rolled her eyes. "Seems like I've spent half my life in places like that. Only the names have changed. But it's always the same lousy pool table with those small, shitty pockets." She set her drink on the nightstand, covering her mouth with her hand as she yawned. "Yep, over the years I've had plenty of practice..." I waited but she seemed to be done. When I couldn't hold it any longer, I got up to use the bathroom. It felt like a week's worth of booze came gushing out of me. I turned on the tap to hide the noisy torrent. Washed my hands, splashed water onto my greasy face.

Tried not to look in the mirror, remembering what Bonnie said the last time I went by to see her:

"Christ, I hardly recognized you. You've really let yourself go, Glenn. You look like a *slob*."

When I came out, she was asleep. Not putting on an act, snoring like a trooper. I found room on the opposite side of the bed, laid down with my clothes on, using the comforter for cover. The room still seemed strange to me. An annoying fan kept cutting in and out and the elevator was just down the hall. The air dry and chilly. She had both pillows so I rested my head on the crook of my arm. The mattress was hard and uncomfortable as hell.

I slept like a baby.

In the morning it was awkward, both of us wooly-headed and self-conscious. She didn't stay long, politely but firmly refusing my invitation to breakfast. I offered to go for a walk so she could shower and clean up. She just wanted to be *gone*.

I gave her one of my cards. Stupid thing to do. After she left, I found it on the desk beside the bed, along with thirty-seven bucks in bills and loose change.

My cut.

Angie. I think she said her name was Angie. It was either Angie or Carrie…

She had introduced herself but it was noisy and I wasn't sure I'd heard right. Just to be on the safe side, I never called her by name. I guess I was afraid of offending her.

Something told me she wasn't a person you'd ever want to cross. I had a hunch that, like a lot of the women I tended to get involved with, she nursed old injuries and grievances and wasn't the type to forgive and forget.

Surrealist World

"Isn't it true, after all, that man is no more than an offshoot of solar matter cast over with a gadfly shadow of free will?"

—Rene Char

ANTONIN A EXPLODES HIMSELF all over the foyer of the Hotel Magritte, making a pretty mess. It is a protest against the recent renovations to the beloved landmark, a witless concatenation of dull, complacent colors and an ersatz rain forest of plastic plants. The panorama of blood and offal is photographed for exhibit by one of AA's accomplices, using an old style box camera. Sepia carnage.

The group had determined that a grand gesture was required, Monsieur B giving his blessing to the venture with a slight, almost imperceptible dip of his over-large, leonine head. Antonin A volunteered for the assignment, knowing it would guarantee him a spot in the pantheon beside Vache, Desnos, Rimbaud and a select few others.

The rebuff is accompanied by a hand-lettered manifesto, found on what remains of AA's shattered torso. The hotel management is warned that further reprisals can be expected if any attempt is made to clean up the statement. The tableau of gore is to be left as is, a potent symbol of what's in store for reactionaries and aesthetic miscreants. Word quickly spreads, the scene drawing an influx of gawkers, a clamoring of new guests.

C'est ca.

Open expressions of affection are strictly discouraged. Ardent lovers find themselves spattered with fish guts. Upon discovery, grass-stained couples are forced to run a gauntlet, screaming as they're lashed with whips and green branches stripped from nearby trees. The group is notorious for prudishness, revolted by sensuality, except in its most extreme forms.

Thus their veneration of prostitutes and porn stars, who are urged to rut in full view of on-lookers, random orgies taking place in front of schools, government buildings, police stations, homes for the aged and infirm.

Other favorite targets for "actions": libraries, churches, synagogues and mosques. A horde of *artistes* descend on such places, driven by righteous fury. Library shelves are emptied of the so-called "classics", which are then burnt to prevent further contagion. Religion is delusionary, proscribed. Walls and windows of temples are defaced with obscene graffiti, sacred texts shredded, priests and practitioners ridiculed, assaulted, their clothes cut from their bodies, driven howling into the streets.

Mr. and Mrs. Something-Something, exchanging bland pleasantries over their second cup of morning coffee.

Without warning, without the slightest inkling, the ceiling peels back and the walls expand higher and higher, stretching up to pierce the overcast. The group has dumped a huge supply of lysergic acid into the reservoir, tripping out most of the city. Now see the world as it truly is, layers and camouflaging illusions stripped away, reality in its purest, most sublime state. Two million souls crying out in wonder and anguish, an eight-hour amusement ride, *sans* safety bars; penetrate the eyeballs, burrow into the soft matter within. Today's psychotic is tomorrow's visionary poet.

Bon voyage, madame et monsieur...

The group convenes at the Café Lautreamont to compare notes and receive a briefing regarding the latest actions. The room sulfurous with cigarette smoke, rife with gossip and innuendo.

And Monsieur B holds court, as always. Excommunication orders are drawn up for those who have deviated from the designated path. Back sliders. Art whores.

Cunts. The list is handed to B who confirms the roster. Some will readily admit the folly of their ways and apply for reinstatement but they will forever be regarded with suspicion. B barely bothers to pay lip service to consensus. He is high priest, absolute dictator, his will be done. Cold, analytical, humorless, brilliant.

C_____ reminds them of his upcoming art opening and B fixes him with that hard, grey stare. Lately C_____ has been straying into unapproved styles, nonrepresentation. This will not be tolerated, he is reminded.

B is suspicious of painters, feeling in his heart that the movement is primarily a literary one. Visual artists are unstable, not to be trusted. C_____ withers under that imperious gaze, dissolving like one of those melted clocks by—well, they ridicule him with the name "Avida Dollars" now. C_____ reaffirms his allegiance to the Cause and is relieved when they finally move on to other matters.

He will return to his studio and destroy the new paintings. The ones already turned to the wall. Mustn't take a chance someone will see them, report his heresy.

The recriminations are too terrible to consider.

A visiting foreign dignitary is given the full treatment. They wait until he disembarks from the plane, accepting greetings from the usual round of functionaries. Then someone steps from their midst and with some sort of Gallic cry, empties a bucket of pig bladders over his head. The photographers shout and jostle to get a picture of the gore-drenched diplomat.

His furious security detail grapple with the assailant but they, in turn, are pelted by members of the crowd. They retreat up the red carpet, shielding their charge against a rain of projectiles.

The imperialists depart to the cheers of many present.

That was for Africa and l'Indochine, you bastards!

J'ai peur qu'il ne veuille pas revenir en France de si tot.

Bah! Good riddance! Fascists! Militarists! Capitalist douchebags!

Choke on your blood money...

Their kind are not welcome here.

45

. . .

The launch of the new journal *Piss & Bile* is a huge success. Monsieur B's work takes up a good portion of the publication, poems and rants and a long introduction which explains, in great detail, what the magazine is not.

Apparently it is not *anything*. Imparting the slightest significance or relevance to it is completely missing the point. The various pieces, by sycophants and protégés, are worthless; writing for and about and by automatons. No philosophy, no ideology, no merit. "In conclusion," he writes, "this is an ichor-stained dagger, a sky threatening with clouds, a doorway leading nowhere. Fuck you and your precious belief systems and the banality they entail." Everyone congratulates him for his insightful commentary but when asked about future plans for the magazine, B merely sighs and shakes his head.

Once again, they just don't *get* it.

C_____ waits impatiently for their arrival. He has purchased, out of his own pocket, some very good wine and a variety of liqueurs. He even managed to scrounge up a couple of bottles of absinthe, which is harder to find than a virgin in Montparnasse. He's excluded anything from the show that could possibly offend his prickly mentor. It meant stripping the walls of all but a few pictures and even those he isn't sure of. Once B renders his verdict it is set in stone. People trickle in and out, hardly glancing at the framed wonders he has spent months executing.

It grows late. Finally, he spots Louis A and Philippe S, B's main errand boys. They eye the pictures critically and whisper amongst themselves. Sweat limns his forehead, collects in the waistband of his underwear. At last, Louis approaches. Monsieur B, it seems, will not be attending the opening. C_____ ventures to ask his opinion of the show. Louis purses his lips.

"It is difficult to say," he offers blandly. "That piece there, for instance. The tricolor. Is that meant to be a flag? Is it...*political?*" He practically spits the word.

"No, no." C_____ shakes his head vigorously. "That is not the intention."

But clearly the painting is suspect. It will have to go.

46

There are no sales, but that is inconsequential. He is not a *whore*. He illustrates erotic texts to make ends meet, one of the few activities that Monsieur B wholeheartedly endorses. After all, even the great Apollinaire authored numerous volumes of high quality smut.

Love is deception. Sex is exploitation. Revel in the carnal, the spilling of bodily fluids for sheer pleasure.

The prick is a sword. Use it.

The movement includes few women, no minorities. Pagan and African art are revered but as for admitting a black man or woman of any color to their intimate circle...no. It wouldn't be right. Only one or two musicians make the grade (Monsieur B boasts that he is quite tone deaf).

The Italians have made contributions, the Spanish are tolerated. The English are cunts, the Germans hopeless and the Americans, the poor Americans, are louts of the worst kind. To them, art is a *commodity*. The Japanese are the worst. One collector from Japan is nearly beaten to death with a dead fish for daring to discuss the relative monetary value of modern art in the presence of Monsieur B.

Attention! The poster proclaims: *The old republics, federations, city states, university trained elites, entrenched mediocrities, critics, philologists and politicians of every stripe are to be exterminated. Mob rule is hereby enjoined. No leaders, no followers, a mindless groundswell, primitivism unleashed. Romantic notions and closely guarded paradigms no longer hold sway. The law is nothing. You are free to express yourselves. Forget the alphabet, deny coherence. Rape at will, murder creates celebrity. Are you alive? Can your eyes see what has been done to you in the name of stupid conformity? Then pluck them out and be done with it! The eyes are liars, propagandists. Empty the windows of the soul and let the void seep in / out...*

And so on and so forth.

∘ ∘ ∘

One by one they have fallen by the wayside. For crimes against the movement, real and imagined. For daring to question Monsieur B. For refusing to toe the party line.

They are officially condemned, pronounced *persona non grata*, their readings and openings either boycotted or, even better, disrupted, their work torn from the walls, trampled underfoot.

"Who will be left?" The *enfant terrible* writes to Monsieur B from his Manhattan penthouse. "You are an unrepentant bulimic, purging yourself of all but your grossest secretions. Everything else is expelled from your faggoty lips, your puckered, cankerous arsehole…"

B reads the letter to the others without comment but the next day an assassin is dispatched to deliver B's rebuttal. Armed with what is said to be the same icepick that felled the mighty Trotsky. The holiest artifact in the arsenal, consecrated for a just and noble cause.

No one knows where Monsieur B found him. Allegedly it was near the amusement arcade by the river, a popular spot for homosexuals cruising for anonymous trysts. What was B doing there? No one dares ask.

The old man is filthy, his body giving off the foul odor of an unembalmed corpse. He converses in inaudible mumbles which, it seems, only Monsieur B can decipher.

"Here is the future of art!" B cries. "Observe…" He instructs the derelict to draw, on the spot, a rendering of Baudelaire's "diseased organ". The man scratches a few lines onto a pad, B barely waiting for him to finish before snatching it away and holding it aloft, brandishing the sketch for all to see.

The others are taken aback but when they discern the gleam in their leader's eyes they quickly burst out in a chorus of praise and approbation. Monsieur B beams at this newly discovered great master and the others press forward to embrace him, shake his stained hand, filling the air with "Bravo!" and "C'est magnifique!".

Meanwhile, B looks on, his face rapturous, a gloating expression of pride or, possibly, cunning.

It is too much.

C_____ flees the gathering, pushing his way outside, seeking escape, a sanctuary, some place where he can quiet the angry beehive buzzing in his head. Monsieur B has never mentioned his opening, his latest paintings, the leader's silence speaking volumes.

They will cast me out.

He does not remember how long or far he walks. The city seems foreign to him, bent Tanguy architectures, no recognizable landmarks, a stranger in this place, his wanderings without destination.

He finds himself on a dimly remembered avenue which, he finally realizes, is not far from the Proust Museum, a shrine for the group.

Now he sees him, his nemesis, his *bête noire*. Monsieur B is walking at a fast clip and gesticulating, followed by the usual entourage of hangers-on and adoring lackeys.

Where does the pistol come from? Is it his? C_____ vaguely recollects buying it, or one very much like it.

He places himself in their path, causing them to draw up in an uncertain huddle. C_____ speaks rapidly, a rambling, disjointed diatribe against everything Monsieur B represents. B's eyes take him in, his lips curling. An unforgivable affront. The letter of condemnation already being composed, a litany of C_____'s many sins delineated and codified.

The gun barks once, twice. The others retreat, take to their heels, making no attempt to shield their leader. B collapses, an idol whose feet have been cut from beneath him.

Later, there will be disagreement over his final words. Were they "Shit, I'm killed" or, even more appropriately, "After all, art is spectacle"?

49

C_____ is now in complete possession of his faculties. The full ramifications of his act are apparent, the body bleeding out before him.

"There is no movement!" He shouts after them. "Death to the demagogy of the irrational!"

Then he places the muzzle of the revolver under his chin and, *tout de suite*, bursts his brain, slipping his earthly shell and entering the all-encompassing realm of the Universal Genius.

The author acknowledges consulting the following texts in the preparation of this fictional work:

Surrealist Painters and Poets (An Anthology) edited by Mary Ann Caws (MIT Press; 2001)

Surreal Lives by Ruth Brandon (Grove Press; 1999)

Spies

"I'M SICK OF THIS," I say at last. "Let's *do* something...." Yes, but what? It's a hot, sticky morning, nothing going on. We're sitting around a wobbly picnic table, bored out of our minds, in need of distraction. Everyone older than eighteen hung over from last night's festivities, the rest of us left to fend for ourselves. And we don't mind one bit.

"Go exploring?" Travis suggests. He's ten and acts eight. He'll eat a ladybug on a dare but refuses to look at dirty pictures because it's a sin. Talk about screwed up.

"No," Taylor corrects him, "*spying*." One more example of why she's always been the leader of our little pack. The she wolf. Effortlessly drawing you into her plans and schemes. So smart and sure of herself. About to turn thirteen and "developing", as her mother put it. Growing up faster than the rest of us. I worship her. I can't help it. The others, Paul and Travis, are mere followers. They do whatever we say. Proper little minions.

We wander away from the campsite. Escaping the jealous, prying eyes of adults. Someone calls after us, the usual reminders to *be careful, don't go too far, watch out for cars*. We ignore them. Taylor out in front with me, as usual, right beside her. Paul and Travis hang further back so they can talk about childish things, stuff that me and Taylor can't be bothered with.

We slow down every time we come upon another campsite. Checking for kids our age, on the prowl for anything out of the ordinary.

Taylor is wearing her green two-piece bathing suit again. Despite her parents' demands that she *cover up*, at least when walking around in public. Her fierce independence in the face of their disapproval yet another source of wonder to me. I admire and envy her courage. She isn't the least bit intimidated by her mother and father (though they seem terrifyingly strict compared to my folks).

Without warning, she veers from the main road, taking a slanting path through the nearby woods. I fall in behind her, Paul and Travis trailing after us. I find myself staring at her bare shoulders and tanned, lightly freckled back. Inevitably, my treasonous eyes move down to the snug curve of her ass. My face heating up, body tingling. Good and bad feelings fighting for supremacy. She moves expertly through the reaching underbrush. My bare shins get scratched up and I stub my toe on a buried root. Suddenly overcome with an urge to start a forest fire…

Taylor pauses. I wait with the others in the speckled shade of the surrounding trees. Watching for her signal.

I am a few months shy of my twelfth birthday and nothing is the same any more. I'm madly in love with Taylor, but it is not a pure, sweet, innocent love. Lust is starting to confuse the issue. I know it is a doomed infatuation, a stupid crush (God, how I *hate* that word). Loving your cousin, after all, is wrong, impossible, *sick* (though for reasons I don't entirely understand).

I also know I am no longer a *child*, like Travis or Paul. I perceive things beyond their simple comprehension. My mother says I'm "sensitive" but it's more than that. I watch and listen, fade into the background. That's how I uncover stuff, family secrets and old feuds that would never be discussed if they knew a kid was around. My grandfather despises Uncle Fred for drinking so much. Aunt Bonnie and Uncle George like to flirt with each other. And pretty much everyone strongly disapproves of Aunt Amelia and her "partner" but no one is willing to confront them.

"Why do they call Jane her 'partner'?" I asked my mom as she made up the beds in our tent trailer our first night there. She glanced over her shoulder at me, taking her time replying.

"It's kind of complicated, Den." She kept fiddling with the top sheet. Once I realized I wasn't getting any more out of her, I returned my attention to my mug of cocoa and the *Simpsons* comic I was reading for the millionth time. Already itchy from at least a dozen mosquito bites and the smelly crap she insisted on dabbing on them didn't do any good.

Something is going on. Amelia and Jane are causing a lot of tension in our family and I need to know *why*. They seem to get along well, are very considerate to one another—why shouldn't they be friends? What's the big deal?

Taylor waves us on. The path she's chosen goes past the bathrooms. You can smell them from a mile away. We eventually join up with a narrow road and another line of campsites. Now we are among strangers and that is entirely to Taylor's satisfaction.

"We'll go slow here," she murmurs. "Take our time and look around." I turn and glare back at Paul and Travis, interrupting an animated discussion about some stupid video game. They both duck their heads sheepishly. As we proceed down the gravel track, Taylor whispers for us to keep our eyes open.

At one of the campsites an old guy sits on a fold-out chair. He's strumming a guitar and singing a song I recognize from church. We wave as we pass. Just some kids out for a stroll.

The next two spots are empty. And then we hear activity from inside a trailer just ahead, soft voices and laughter. Taylor raises a painted fingernail to her lips. Glances around, making sure the coast is clear. We creep closer until we're right next to the trailer. I look over and see Taylor grinning, her eyes bright and excited.

"—another hour it'll be too hot for this." A woman, giggling.

"Perfect timing. Then we can go for a swim."

"Well, c'mon then, big boy." A rustle. "Let's see if you're all talk and no action." The trailer creaks. "*Ah!* Watch my shoulders, they're still tender from yesterday." More rustling. "Oh. Oh, that's nice…"

"You smell like coconut."

"I hear it's an aphrodisiac." I don't know what that means. Now there's some bumping and shifting as they move around, small collisions above us.

"Ohhh, yes. That's…that's *wonderful*." The woman giggles again. The giggling type, like Aunt Bonnie. "We'll have to thank the Johners for taking Joey with them."

"We'll do the same for them sometime." They both laugh. "Although that probably won't be necessary."

"Can you imagine them doing it?" This time her chuckle sounds more like a growl. "The thought of fat Randy and poor Marla—"

Taylor's expression is weird. She's unaware of me or anything else except what's taking place in the camper. It's a yellow and white Jayco unit almost identical to the one my parents own.

I look back at Travis, who mouths "What are they doing?" I just smirk, although in actuality I have only a vague hunch. The voices are coming from what I know is the main bedroom compartment. The couple inside are only a foot or two away. The window open, a transparent screen separating us from them.

Now there are even stranger sounds and I feel my face getting redder and redder. This is *wrong*. I want to leave. But Taylor looks completely hypnotized. Like she's under a spell.

"Come on, baby," the woman urges. "Come on—"

Voices from up the road, people approaching. I touch Taylor's arm, alerting her to a potential threat. She jumps, like I've awakened her from a sound sleep. I tip my head toward the voices and her eyes widen. Backing up, using the trailer for cover, she beats a noiseless retreat, the rest of us following like baby ducks.

I can't forget the look on her face. How completely out of it she was. Travis and Paul are whispering back and forth, puzzling over what just happened. I maintain a mature and thoughtful silence. Taylor glances over at me and we exchange quick smiles. Recognizing that we've shared something special, something we'll never forget. It's like we've been initiated into a new and secret world.

Remembering the sounds they made. Imagining what they were doing.

"R" rated thoughts. Not suitable for children. Parental discretion definitely advised.

After lunch, Taylor asks if I want to join her for a walk. Happily, she doesn't include Paul and Travis in her invitation. At first I'm worried. Does she intend on going back to that trailer? But instead she heads in the opposite direction. Which is a relief, but I'm also disgusted with myself for being so chicken.

The day has gotten hotter but at least it's not as muggy. The sun is almost directly overhead, blazing down on us as we make our way toward the beach. Since it's the middle of the week, the campground is half-empty. We have the beach to ourselves, except for some teenagers playing a loud game of volleyball down by the water.

Taylor spreads out her towel, angling it to take advantage of the sun's rays. While I settle down beside her, she reclines, closing her eyes against the glare. She's so beautiful, I *have* to look at her. Posing like a movie star. After a few minutes, she glances at me and says, almost shyly: "I want to do my back, okay?"

By the time it dawns on me what she means, what she's about to do, she's already doing it. Reaching behind her and tugging the string securing her bathing suit. Arranging herself, lying on her stomach. "Let me know if you see anyone coming. I mean," she adds, "anyone we *know*."

I nod, mute as stone. Speechless with wonder. Inarticulate with love.

"This doesn't bother you, does it?" I shrug like it doesn't matter, making sure my eyes are otherwise occupied. Afraid to look. Afraid I won't be able to *stop* looking. My face feels hot, like I'm radioactive. I also have a pronounced boner. I hide my embarrassment by pretending to be interested in the volleyball game, which seems to be petering out, the two teams bad-mouthing each other, exchanging shoves. All in good fun.

"What did you think?" she asks and at first I'm not sure what she means. "Did it make you feel bad? Listening in like that?" Now I understand. Shake my head in response. "I found it *fascinating*." Fascinating. Yes, I think to myself, that's the perfect word for it. "They try to hide that stuff from us, pretend they don't do it, that they're so pure, so...so..."

"Yeah." I know exactly what she means.

"But we know. We're not stupid." She adjusts her position slightly, a risky maneuver, under the circumstances.

I tilt my head back, the sun beaming on my face.

"Your mom and dad do it, mine do. It's nothing to be ashamed of."

"I hear them sometimes," I surprise myself by saying it. One more secret between us.

"Sure you do." Raising up slightly, squinting at me. "They make enough noise at it." She snickers. "And it's not like *we* don't think about it too. It's only natural at our age."

I'm nodding, willing to admit it, if only to her. Sensing something building between us, a thrilling tension I haven't experienced before. The mid-summer sun heating our bare skin, drawing out delicate beads of sweat. Crooked rivulets trickle down her shoulders, the small of her back. I can't help it, as I watch their progress I want to lean over and lick them, *taste* them.

The teenagers collect their gear and head toward us. Taylor acknowledges their approach but doesn't bother covering up. The older kids eye us and one of them mumbles something that makes the others laugh. I hate them but they soon move on.

Some clouds have arrived and take turns blocking the sun. Taylor curses. She curses a lot around me. "No point in this." She reaches an arm across to hold her top in place, raises up until she's sitting with her back to me. "Can you..." She lifts her dark hair and I get on my knees, fumbling with the thin ties until I manage a loose, clumsy knot. She looks over her shoulder at me, so *gorgeous* that I forget to breathe. "You're my favorite cousin, Dennis." And there's this pause, an incredible, timeless moment when the universe seems filled with possibilities, a million bright futures looming before us.

So close I can feel her breath on my face.

"Guess we should be getting back," she says at last.

All at once I can hear the waves again and feel dry grit between my toes. I've got a slight headache and I'm thirsty. *The dream is over.* Everything back in sharp focus. The sudden return of harsh, unforgiving reality.

She shakes out the towel, wraps it around herself.

Even though the sun, I notice, chooses that moment to emerge from the clouds.

. . .

The last day, the adults take charge. They've been ignoring us up until now. Suddenly, there are planned activities: boring boat rides and group hikes. A big, communal supper at my grandparents' campsite, everyone pooling their food. There aren't many opportunities to get away.

Just after supper something happens. There are raised voices, tears, Aunt Amelia and Jane stalking off in a huff. They load their car in silence, ignoring my mother's efforts to make peace. Leave just as it's getting dark.

Taylor is slumped in a camp chair, pouting about something, showing no interest in events taking place around her. Travis and Paul are inside the camper, playing a board game, their high-pitched laughter a constant annoyance. When I ask permission to leave, my mother snaps at me. I flop into a chair opposite Taylor, trying to catch her gaze so we can exchange secret, knowing glances.

She ignores me.

Uncle Fred, whose company I normally enjoy, takes a seat beside me. "Hey, hey, Denny-boy." He's already half-plastered. "Howya doin', huh?" He punches my shoulder playfully, painfully. "What d'you say? Gonna get with the program, cheer for my Bruins this year?" I look across helplessly at Taylor. Decide to use the ol' wall of silence on him. Fred eventually takes the hint. Digs into a nearby cooler for another beer and goes off in search of better company. My grandfather glaring at him as he ambles by.

Abruptly, Taylor announces that she isn't feeling well. She's going back to their camper to lie down. I watch her leave, alert for any indication, the slightest hint she wants company. She gives no such sign and I sag back in the chair.

In the morning, we'll be busy packing up and I likely won't have a chance to see her. My parents will be short-tempered, anxious to be on their way. Then the farewell ritual, the usual crap, *nice seeing you, keep in touch, see you next year.*

Will Taylor make any effort to re-establish contact? Will she hug me…or will my cowardice today cost me even that? A casual nod will destroy me. What I crave is acknowledgment, something that confirms I'm special in her eyes. Not just some brat whose company she had to tolerate over four hot days in Greenwater Park.

I sleep badly that night, aware that in the morning my worst fears will likely materialize. I'm sick with anticipation. A dozen different scenes playing over and over in my head. Including one where I manage to get Taylor alone and have a chance to make things right. I tell her I love her and want her and don't care about what our family or anybody else in the world says.

When you think about it, it's the perfect outcome. And talk about brightening up the long drive home. I'd be totally psyched for not jamming out.

Her astonishment when I put my arms around her. Taylor's taller than me and has to sort of bend down. She keeps her eyes closed and I smell wood smoke in her hair. Her kisses taste like watermelon-flavored lip balm. Afterward, we swear a sacred oath of eternal fidelity to each other, promise to call or write. Holding hands as we drift back toward camp. Taking the long way and never mind if we're already late.

Among the Invisibles

FROM HIS FAVORITE HIDEAWAY, five storeys above the ground, Little Po is an inconspicuous witness to the chaos below.

There has been talk of trouble for weeks, soldiers and police setting up road blocks and check points, stopping and harassing people, making a nuisance of themselves. Intimidation is the norm with the ruling junta but this time, it seems, their tactics have only succeeded in making things worse.

Shouts and screams, the swift rattle of automatic weapons and *crak-crak-crak* of small arms fire. Smoke drifts over the neighborhood, a grey, evil-smelling pall. There are makeshift barricades and men roaming about with clubs and pop bottles filled with gasoline. The building shudders from a nearby explosion, a *crump* as a burning car bursts its seams, provoking whoops and cheers from the surrounding crowd.

Little Po is safe or, at least, safer than he would be down there, in the midst of the mob. Some women have joined in, adding their unmistakable shrieks to the din. Most of the men are intoxicated, swilling alcohol looted from a nearby store. They swagger about, brandishing crude weapons, their courage fortified by drink. The boy creeps back under an overhang created by ventilation ducts and piping. Finds his tattered blanket and slips into an uneasy sleep, sucking his thumb for comfort when the tumult disturbs his slumber. This sooty rooftop, shared with none save the occasional stray cat or roosting pigeon, is a refuge, shelter from a dangerous and hostile world.

He wakes to dull morning light, the stench of burning rubber.

His hunger is an undiminishing ache, a twisting, voracious worm in his guts. He spends most days in a surreal netherworld; sick, confused and disoriented. Bumping into buildings or colliding with passersby, clutching at them for support and being swatted and cursed for his trouble. He begs, he scrounges, he steals and *still* only manages to scrape by.

As he descends *via* the rickety fire escape, he is aware that slowly but surely he's losing the battle. Malnutrition is devouring his frail body and soon he will be reduced to nothing. When someone reaches such a state, people say that person has "joined the *invisibles*". One day, they're simply *gone*, evaporating into the air, leaving nothing behind, not even an ounce of bone dust to bury or mourn over.

The first person he spots when he ventures out is Old Fania. Her pet monkey chatters on her shoulder and she makes a warding gesture at him. He gives the witch a wide berth. The monkey eyes him sullenly but is constrained by a short leash of twine. The little beast has been known to inflict a painful and septic bite.

The streets and avenues have been transformed overnight. Rubble and debris are scattered carelessly, gutted buildings stripped of everything that can be carried or dragged away. He scours the ground for leftovers, something to eat or barter. But he's competing with other scavengers who fiercely guard the meager leavings, growling and threatening him if he approaches. He is smaller and weak and therefore must go without.

It is not that ordinary folk are unsympathetic or hard-hearted, it is merely that deprivation has become a way of life to the people in this part of the city. They have been herded together, marginalized, made to feel they must fend for themselves. Impoverished and increasingly desperate, they've lost any sense of shared or communal suffering. The riot last night followed days of demonstrations, spontaneous protests against the inhuman living conditions. There have been scores of deaths, nervous soldiers shooting into crowds, protesters beaten and dragged away by security forces.

And finally the world press has taken notice. Reporters flood in and, congruently, the economy goes into a tailspin as investment money dries up, foreign nationals leaving in droves. It is a familiar, sad story in this region of the world.

Little Po drinks from a puddle and forages from a dumpster behind a restaurant. He is covered in rat bites and festering sores that won't heal. He knows his situation is increasingly precarious but there is nothing to be done about it. As he clambers out of the stinking bin, the back door of the restaurant bangs open and an employee toting a five-gallon pail of slops spots him. They regard each other for a long moment and Little Po finally slinks away, what little food he has found clutched in his fist.

There are rumors that local businesses have hired squads of off-duty cops and given them the job of ridding the city of riff-raff. Some kids were gunned down as they sat on the steps of a church. A *church*. In the last two weeks, several dozen street urchins have been spirited off in dark vans, never to be seen again.

Later that morning, Little Po is walking through a park and spots Fish and the Silent One. Fish has fresh bruises on his face, rolled for pocket change. And the thing is, everyone knows Fish has absolutely nothing worth stealing. He tells the joke that he's so poor, someone once cut him open and stole his heart. And he'll show you the long, zippered scar to prove it. The Silent One glowers behind him, a menacing presence. His head is squashed, misshapen. He can't speak but his dangerous mien says *don't fuck with me, brother*.

Little Po falls in alongside and they head off to the mission together, stand in line for a bowl of watery soup. Supposedly there is a piece of chicken in there somewhere. Either donations are down or the priests have been dipping into the collection plate again. Little Po deftly palms an extra slice of bread, the maneuver escaping the sharp-eyed Brother's notice.

When they finish, they hang out in the graveyard for awhile. Fish produces three precious cigarettes but smoking only makes Little Po queasy so he puts his away until later. Then a cranky old caretaker shows up and chases them away.

Fish says he wants to stop by Ven's place, that he's heard something and Ven Ficus is the one to go to if you have information to sell. Depending on his mood, he'll either reward you generously or snap his fingers and have you turned in to a human pretzel. But Taft, Ven's imposing gatekeeper, says his bossman isn't in today and hints that it's in their best interest to fuck off. *Now.*

Fish is disappointed but vows to come back later. Taft goes back inside and they hear him say something to the other hoods. Mocking laughter follows the trio down the street.

As they walk, Fish has to keep stopping to retch. Every time he does, he groans. He says something feels broken inside. Little Po and the Silent One exchange grim looks. Who knows when the free clinic will re-open. The French doctors who ran it were declared *persona non grata* and given forty-eight hours to clear out. No one has replaced them. Word is the junta was embarrassed to have foreigners tending to the needs of the poor. This past winter Little Po caught a bug that made him cough until his ribs ached. He truly believed he was going to die. His lungs still feel tender, especially on cool days.

In the early afternoon he parts company with them, waving as he angles away.

Despite the soup he is still famished, light-headed. He thinks about the slice of bread in his pocket, the one he is saving. Little Po takes out the bread, raises it to his mouth, bites off a piece. This is the way it is. You are hungry and when you have food, you *eat*.

Later he will curse his greed. This, too, is the way of things.

But for Little Po, time has shrunk, contracted, the future no longer measured in years, months, weeks, but days, perhaps *hours*. His skin is transparent, his arms and legs thin, meatless. Pain, hunger and despair are constant companions. The world around him losing definition, leaking away at the edges.

Soon he will join the *invisibles*. It is almost certain. He knows this. Maybe even tonight, at his rooftop haven, under the high, eternal stars. He wonders what it will be like to be dead. His undernourished imagination has a hard time grasping the notion. During the sermons that are mandatory with the free meals they dispense, the priests speak of heaven and hell. In the afterlife, our sins are remembered and judged. The worthy richly rewarded, mortal sinners consigned to the all-consuming fire, where they burn forever and ever, a-*men*.

Little Po steers himself in the direction of his old neighborhood, making slow progress. Traffic rolls heedlessly by. The young soldier on the corner stares past him, through him. Suddenly, Little Po looks for his shadow and can't find it. Perhaps it is only the angle and intensity of the sun. He is dazed, weightless, all but dissipated. Barely visible even in broad daylight, passing among them but leaving no trace.

Strays

I DINT SEE NOTHIN', the kid kept saying to anyone who might be listening, only no one was.

A couple of times he tried to stop and explain but they just pushed him ahead of them, cussing and kicking him when he stumbled, meanwhile thanking their lucky stars it wasn't them squashed into those size sevens.

Tell at to the captin, Parker told him just prior to giving him a stiff-armed shove that almost toppled him. The kid started blubbering, wet, ratcheting sobs that were so pitiful they hit him just to make him quit.

It was still an hour before daybreak so most of the camp didn't take kindly to the commotion. They pitched and yawed in their bedrolls as the storm broke in their midst and soon the scuffles and moans really did wake the dead, deep dreamers who fumbled at wakefulness, clutching at its sharp edges. Somebody threatened to shoot them unless they shut the hell up.

They congressed before a battered trailer hitched to a half-ton poxy with rust. Parker banged on its side a few times, metallic thumps that echoed in the dawn's early light.

Move it or lose it, came from inside.

Captin, we got ourselfs a situation out here, Parker bellowed, think you'd better come have a looksee.

A threadbare curtain was pulled aside, revealing a sleep-stuck face, fierce, bloodshot eyes. Take care of it, Parker. That's what you was hired for, far as I can recollect.

Nossir. We need yer, Parker smirking like a big cat, expert advice.

A muttered oath from inside, then the door banged open and the captin was there, buck naked except for warpaint. The kid was jostled forward and tripped to the ground.

This young 'un here, Parker explained, had hisself a l'il shuteye while he was sposed to be mindin' the flock.

The captin rolled his eyes, petitioning the heavens for sanctuary from idjits. Dock him a week's wages, fer Chrissakes, and lemme get some—

Parker was shaking his head. Like I says, I caught him nappin' an' after I licked him good I did me a quick head count. Even the sleepyheads were listening now, wiping their eyes so they could hear better. An' we're three short, least by my reckonin'.

The captin swore and jumped out of the trailer, his pecker shriveling like a burnt grape. In two strides he reached the boy, fisting his hair, hauling him to his feet.

Ain't you jes' the one, he hissed, ain't you jes' the sorriest fucker I ever set eyes on. He punched the kid, a short, brutal blow that split his lips and unbucked his teeth. The boy sagged, bloody-mouthed and senseless—snarling, the captin threw him aside like a picked bone. How long they got on us?

This directed at Parker who was trying his damnedest to keep a silly-ass grin off his ugly face. Can't say fer sure. Two, mebbe three hours. He don't know hisself and right about now I don't figger we need bother askin' him agin.

Was they rustled or—

Naw, Parker demurred, the injun says there's only three sets o' tracks. They jes' got the lonelies, cap, and now the silly-ass grin wouldn't be denied, they's a pinin' fer the green, green grass o' home.

Well then, the captin scratched himself thoughtfully, that ain't so bad, is it?

Not as bad as it could be, Parker agreed easy enough, but there's jes' one other l'il thing: one of them strays is the bay.

The captin groaned and looked like he was fit to scalp the kid still bleeding onto the brittle ground in front of him. Which maybe he would have if he'd thought it was worth his while.

Right you lazy bastids, he roared, up and at 'em! Socks and jocks, boys, we got some ridin' to do.

The camp erupted in a flurry of activity, the men swearing and wisecracking as they saddled up, bowed legs scissoring modified dirt bikes and squat ATVs, wristing their throttles, waiting for the word. The captin got a lusty cheer when he declared a bonus for whichever one o' you no-account sonsabitches that catches up with those nags first.

The tracks be headed southeast, Parker screamed, and at the captin's signal they roared up the shallow side of the coulee, chewing up speargrass and flinging lethal divots of thistle.

The rest of the herd, spooked by the racket, started bawling and stampeding from one end of the corral to the other, banging against its sides, white-eyed and frothy-lipped. Not a prime bunch by any standards, scrawny, sway-backed mounts swollen with dropsy, afflicted by parasites and chronic mange. Once the search party was out of earshot, they bellied up the bars, clamoring for their first and only feeding of the day. But the men left behind paid them no heed. If the cowpokes returned and grub wasn't waiting for them there'd be hell to pay. Those dumb critters would have to wait their turn.

It was the captin who spotted the injun first. He was hunkered down in a field of wild rapeseed about a half mile from camp. He stood and waved to make sure they saw him and waited for them to slash their way through the wide, bright yellow to reach him.

What say you, injun, the captin asked, betraying a kind of grudging respect.

The injun took his time, like always. He liked to play the part. He dusted off his hands, sniffed the air while they raced their engines and picked grit out of their teeth. Easy signs, he said finally, won't take long. Then he was loping away, covering ground in long, easy strides that made it look like he was walking on air. Southeast, he called back to them, keep goin'.

I jes' hope they don't get theyselfs all cut up, the captin bitched, that bay alone is worth her weight in silver dollars.

With a wave, he sent them off again, skirting a narrow band of trees, the captin chaffing because of the time lost and fretting about dogs and cougars and anything else that might be wandering around these parts that's belly was empty and disposition poor.

But it sure enough was a glorious day to be alive and knowing it. Whorls of ground-hugging mist rising and dissipating, the lightening sky clear, the chill of the evening almost gone. The captin was bent over the handlebars, ass stuck up in the air, laughing like a madman and he knew without looking that the others felt the same.

Somehow the injun always managed to stay ahead of them, maybe because of the shortcuts he took, going places they couldn't, or maybe he knew secrets they weren't privy to. Maybe he was actually three injuns. Whenever they looked, there he was, gazelling through the tall grass, evaporating into the trees, a tireless runner, bronze ghost.

Less than an hour later they sighted the injun again, waving them on, shouting something they couldn't hear as they veered toward him, heeling the ground. Then the man nearest the captin was pointing and following his dirty finger the captin saw the strays.

They looked like they were on their last legs. The bay was practically dragging the others along but the chase was over and they knew it. Two of them gave up without further struggle, cramped and exhausted, gulping air. The injun stood over them, talking to them, trying to keep them settled. But the bay wasn't having any of it. She broke away again, limping across the field, legs buckling, lungs threatening to burst.

Yippee ki yi, the captin hollered, slipping his lariat off his handlebars and making to cut her off. The others whooped encouragement but hung back, knowing it was his show. They contented themselves by circling the other two, skidding dangerously close while the injun stood nearby, shaking his head and laughing.

The bay did her best, bobbing and weaving, but she was too done in and the captin too good. His first toss settled over her shoulders and he hung on with one arm as he steered the bike away, pulling her off her bloody feet and dragging her a ways to take some of the fight out of her. But she had enough left in her to *hate*, showing her teeth and growling at him and he thought again what a prize she was.

He dropped the bike on its side, collecting the rope in loops as he approached her, so full of himself he almost lost a chunk of his leg when she lunged at him, but he was just as quick and she only bit air.

Easy there, girl, he told her, chuckling, giving the rope a few vicious yanks just to remind her who was on the business end. Led us on a merry run, dint ya, he remarked, trying to keep it friendly.

You got no right, she started to say.

Yep, yep, I do, he answered back smartly. I gots the right and I gots the might. Slapping his leg, enjoying the joke on account of it being on her.

You gotta take us back, she panted, you got no right, she repeated and, again, all he did was laugh.

Reckon I won't—take you back that is. Then he pulled on the rope, tugging on it until she was standing. Git a move on now, helping her along with a boot to her bare backside.

They didn't give the strays much time to get their wind back. They were expected at the city stockyards by mid-week and maybe, just maybe, there was enough time left in the season for one more roundup. They drove the three ahead of them, whistling and rebel-yelling, even firing a few shots in the air until the captin made them quit. The bay led the way and, Lord, she looked proud, unbroken. A real thoroughbred, that one.

The corral was open and ready for them when they got back, the herd bunched together in one corner, mewling and squealing in fright.

Git! Git! Git! The strays were chased inside and the gate banged shut on their charges, all of them huddled and whipped except for the bay, who stalked around the pen, churlishly refusing to eat or drink, savaging the others when they tried to comfort her.

The cooks had biscuits cooling, bacon sizzling in the skillet and fresh, strong coffee that scalded their insides. Afterward, everyone was in such good spirits that Shorty felt compelled to favor them with a tune or two, the rest of them joining in on the bawdy parts, a few sneaking looks at the corral even though they knew it wasn't allowed to even *think* such things.

Well, a person can dream, can't he? These were strange times and maybe not even good times but at least some of the old urges remained, reminding you that you were still a man. And who knew? Maybe after a few more successful runs like this one they'd be able to afford mares of their own.

It was time to break camp. The roughnecks collapsed the corral, stowing the prefab sections on the flatbed faster than the injun could skin a rabbit.

The captin took point like usual with the injun, who didn't think much of noisy contraptions, trotting along beside him. The herd fell in behind, chaperoned by trailing riders who rousted stragglers, goosing them with prods if they got ornery.

The drive proceeded at a good, steady pace across a seemingly endless panorama of golden prairie, a burnished plain interrupted only by patches of scrubby chaparral and lonesome stands of poplar and spruce.

They were still some distance from the city but the men's spirits were as high as the sky was wide, and though the day grew increasingly hot and dusty, never was there heard a discouraging word.

Facing Mrs. Abercrombie

(for Amy Williams)

Look at her.

Sitting there, so high and mighty. Like the Queen of friggin' Sheba. Thinks she's got it all figured out and never mind any explanations or excuses.

"I'm sure you realize that the money we raise from our chocolate sales is of great benefit to the entire school," Mrs. Phyllis F. Abercrombie says. What does the *F* stand for, Deb wonders. Florence? Faye? But she also knows, it has been made perfectly clear to her, it isn't her place to ask.

She decides she isn't going to make it any easier for ol' fat ass Abercrombie. So she just sits there, staying mum, not offering any reaction. But Mrs. Abercrombie isn't fazed by the tactic, she just plows right ahead.

"Lucille was sent home with one container of chocolates. There are twenty boxes inside at three dollars each. That comes to sixty dollars."

Lucille. That just kills her. She must be the only person in the world who calls Lucy that. Joe, the big Kenny Rogers fan. *You picked a fine time to leave me, Lucille.* Only you were the one who did the leaving, weren't you, Joe?

Asshole.

"We ask our students to sell as many boxes as they can, returning the unsold portion." Deb knows this. They both know she knows it. Part of the torture. "The money is used to support and subsidize a wide variety of school activities and programs." Pausing but Deb keeps her lips tightly buttoned. "Everyone else brought back their money several weeks ago." Longer pause. "When we talked to Lucille she was...vague. We were hoping—" who's *we*? "—you might be able to come in and shed some light on this. That's why the note was sent home. Just to try to set the record straight."

Mrs. Abercrombie's desk is very neat and efficient looking. Everything in labeled file folders, no slips of paper showing or fluttering post-it notes required by a memory that apparently forgot *nothing*. A mug of pens and pencils within easy reach. Her chair is high-backed, like a throne. The Queen of Sheba, in the flesh.

"You must understand, we're not seeking to assign blame." *Oh, really?* "We asked you to come in because, well, we're not really sure of the best way to proceed. I guess what we're seeking is *clarification*. An *understanding*. We're not trying to turn anyone into a villain."

Deb almost snorts but manages to catch herself in time. She tries to meet Mrs. Abercrombie's gaze but finds nothing to cling to, no empathy, some of that understanding she was just talking about, so her eyes go back to exploring the desktop between them. Where are the cute keepsakes and family pictures? Mrs. Phyllis F. Abercrombie likes to keep her business and home life strictly segregated. There must be a *Mr.* Abercrombie. Did they have any kids? Deb has a hard time picturing it, imagining this woman purple-faced, features swollen and distorted from the effort of pushing a child out into the world.

"When our counsellor, Mrs. Price, met with her, Lucille insisted that she didn't know what happened to the sixty dollars. She was absolutely adamant that she sold the chocolates around her neighborhood, collected the money and put it away in a special envelope. But then she wouldn't say anything more and Mrs. Price didn't want to risk upsetting her further. Apparently she was quite…distraught."

Deb wishes she could smoke. No, what she *really* wishes is that she hadn't come here in the first place. Ignored the summons the way she brushed off the school secretary when she called last week.

Because it was plain right from the beginning that this Abercrombie bitch wasn't going to cut her any slack. Deb is pretty good at judging people, has a natural instinct for it. She can tell the woman isn't the least bit embarrassed or self-conscious about what she's doing. She wants that money and *nothing* is going to dissuade her. She is one hard seed as dear, old daddy would've said.

"Mrs. Perrault?"

"I spent it." There. The truth and the whole truth. Let her put *that* in her pipe and smoke it. And not apologetic about it, either. There's still a way out of this and she's surprised it hasn't occurred to her sooner. "The child tax credit was late last month and we needed money for groceries." Deb sits back, more satisfied and happy with herself than she's been in a long time. In charge again, holding all the cards and almost smirking about it. "That's the absolute, honest to God truth, Mrs. Abercrombie. It's not an easy thing to have to admit, but times are tough and a family needs to eat." She feels like a million dollars and this time has no trouble looking the principal right square in the eyes, not bashful or downcast, a woman to be reckoned with again.

"I see," Mrs. Abercrombie replies, but oddly enough she doesn't seem taken aback by Deb's heartfelt confession. If anything, the temperature in the room drops another few degrees. "But I'm afraid that doesn't quite explain...I have to be honest with you, Mrs. Perrault—"

"*Ms.* actually," Deb interrupts her, somewhat nettled that her moment of triumph hasn't been acknowledged. "My husband and I separated some time ago."

Mrs. Abercrombie purses her lips, her expression more annoyed than sympathetic. *What is wrong with this woman?* "Thank you for correcting me." Almost as if in retaliation, she reaches into a nearby file folder and pulls out a pink Hilroy notebook that looks vaguely familiar. "Lucille's home room teacher brought this to my attention. She has the class keep...I guess you could call it a journal, where they take a few minutes each day to write down their thoughts, what's on their minds or bothering them. It's very helpful and for some of our students quite therapeutic. I thought you might be interested in one particular entry."

Uh oh.

She finds the right page and pushes the notebook across to Deb, indicating with one polished fingernail a longish paragraph, Deb immediately recognizing her daughter's meandering scrawl:

Im so mad at my Mom rite now. She went to the bar

with her boyfreind and then the two of them went to
caseno and spend all that choclit money on boos and
slot masheens. How can a person ever do that? All she
ever thinks abowt is herselv and I am sick and tired of
it. I wish I could run a way some weres like the girl in
that book I am reading who gos to…

There was more, plenty more, and it doesn't get any better.

Shit.

"Our children aren't blind," Mrs. Abercrombie observes, retrieving the
notebook once she's satisfied Deb has seen enough. "They're not stupid either. They
have a well-developed sense of right and wrong and they—"

Deb finds herself on her feet but has no idea how she came to be standing. She
feels trapped in this little office smelling of paper and this woman's subtle, expensive
perfume. She wants *out* but first she has to do something to restore her pride and
recover vast tracts of lost ground. "You think it's so *easy*." Practically hissing it. "You
read that and tell yourself 'there's the answer, right there'. You bring me in here
today and all along you intended to pull this shit on me. Wave it in my face: 'here's
the evidence, guilty as charged'." Flustered and infuriated, but not tearful. Too
pissed off for that. "A nine year old writes that and you believe it without a second
thought. *Nine years old.* And it's supposed to be private, right? A journal is for private
stuff and instead you try and use it against me. Where's your—your decency, for
Christ's sake? What does she know? And while we're on the subject, what the Hell
do *you* know?"

She should have made Pete come in with her. Big Pete. They wouldn't mess
with *him*. Not with his temper. And come to think of it, he's to blame in a way, he
was the one who kept saying they had to get out and *do* something. Spoil themselves.
Have a good time instead of moping around the house.

And, God, she has to admit, it was fun, having a few drinks and dancing up a
storm, gambling, acting like a couple of high rollers. A person deserves that

73

sometimes. To let their hair down and cut loose. This Abercrombie bitch wouldn't know anything about that. Way too tight-assed.

"Certainly if there are special circumstances we're willing to—"

"You'll get your money, don't worry." Deb heads for the door, hearing her get up behind her. "I can see how important it is to you people. Funny, I thought this was supposed to be a *school*." She's thinking about the bottles and recycling on the back porch, that should bring in twenty or thirty bucks. She's been saving it to get her hair done but that can wait. Everything can wait. The chocolate money will be the only thing on her mind until she's finally able to pay it back. Every last goddamn cent.

The secretary jumps as she barges out of the office, practically steaming from the ears. "I guess it's asking too much to expect any sympathy from this place," she snaps, stalking away.

She's in the hallway, only heading the wrong way, so she has to turn around and stomp back in the other direction, past Mrs. Abercrombie, who doesn't appear even slightly ruffled, not a hair out of place. "Thank you for coming in today," she coos.

"Kiss my ass," Deb snarls, "and that goes for all of you. *Kiss my ass!*" Shoving through the front door and finally, thankfully, out of there, breathing real air again. Freedom, sweet freedom.

After about a block she starts to calm down, feel more like herself. Everything clearer now the pressure is gone. At least she'd said something, hadn't just sat there taking it.

Then she remembers there's another school not far from here. All right, it's Catholic but nowadays that isn't such a big deal. She could pull Lucy out of that other shit-hole and transfer her to—what's it called? St. Mary's or Margaret's or whatever. And that way she didn't have to worry about paying the money back. Nothing they could do about it either.

Lucy wouldn't be too happy about switching schools again but too bad for her. She shouldn't be writing stuff so people could read it. She knew better. You don't pull that kind of crap on someone who sacrifices and works hard and raises you against all the odds in the world. A person does their best to be a good parent and look where it gets you.

Lucy will have to learn. Life is hard sometimes. You make choices and then you have to live with the consequences. Deb knows all about that and she also knows it doesn't have anything to do with fairness or fate, it's just part of the price you pay for being alive.

And it adds up to a helluva lot more than sixty measly dollars, Lucy, my girl, and if you'd like to sit down and write that in your little, pink notebook for the whole world to see, you go right ahead. Your dear, old mom won't mind one damn bit.

Adult Children

EVEN WHEN I WAS a little kid, not much more than a toddler, I knew there was something *different* about my mother. She did things that set her apart from everyone else, acted and spoke in a manner that made people nervous, uncomfortable. But I wouldn't have said she was crazy, not back then. That would have been disloyal, disrespectful. She was my mom. She wasn't crazy or deluded or dangerous, no matter what others might think.

So what if she spouted off about Jews and space aliens and JFK and the power company (they were all connected somehow), wandered around naked most of the time, refusing to cover up for the meter guy or the Jehovah's Witnesses who once (and only once) dropped by for a chat? My friends wondered why I never invited them over. I made excuses. I don't know if I was sparing them or myself.

I tried to limit her public appearances, conveniently forgetting to inform her about parent-teacher meetings or upcoming school events. From an early age I acted as her unofficial agent in dealings with the outside world. Did grocery runs, paid our utility bills, cashed checks for her. It was better that way. For both of us.

My mother has never been shy about sharing her theories and once you get her going, well, she's pretty hard to stop, pinning you to the spot with her flesh-eating eyes while she expounds on some odd "fact" she's dredged up or invented.

Helen calls her a giant, sucking black hole: she absorbs everything and everyone around her, permitting nothing to escape, not even light. She distorts reality, ignores supposedly immutable laws of space and time. A walking singularity.

I pick up the phone and it's like she's *right there*, a physical presence in the room, already in mid-rant and, my God, her *voice*, like a high speed drill going right through my skull.

"—that *bitch* across the hall has been stealing my mail again. And I don't want to hear any more excuses. I'm calling the cops on her, see how she likes those apples."

Well, for one thing, Audrey—my completely nutty mother Audrey McWhirter, 53, self-styled social activist, spokesperson for lost causes and eco-terrorist—rarely gets mail that isn't addressed to "Occupant". Six months ago I arranged for everything to be re-directed to our place. She was doing things like signing up for credit cards and blowing her money on junk on the Shopping Channel. Hitting the booze quite hard back then too but I thought she'd been easing off of late.

And I'd met the neighbor in question, Florence Harding, and found her a charming woman. Very tolerant as well, putting up with the occasional threatening letter stuffed in her mailbox, not to mention one bizarre episode when my mother tailed her for *hours*, exhibiting classic stalking behavior. Why *she* hasn't called the cops on *Audrey* is beyond me.

I'd explained the situation to Florence (naturally) and was relieved when she immediately sympathized. Her own mother had had to be institutionalized because of senile dementia.

"I'm afraid it hasn't quite reached that point with Audrey," I said and I must have sounded wistful because Florence patted my arm consolingly.

"You mustn't give up hope," she said and we both smiled.

Poor Florence.

According to my mother, she's an alien, a serial killer, a high class hooker, a spy sent by the government, an assassin...and now, apparently, a notorious mail thief.

"My paper, even my fucking paper," Audrey splutters.

"Paper? Since when do you get a newspaper, mom?" More bloody money down the drain.

It turns out she's talking about a free neighborhood rag that lists garage sales, announces bar mitzvahs and covers the local community beat with its team of highly committed, muck-raking journalists. Their pictures on the editorial page, everyone looking fat, sick or wired.

I promise her I'll find out what happened to her priceless copy of the *Bulletin*. I promise I'll have the police run a background check on Florence. I'd promise her the Hope Diamond and the Queen's crown jewels if it meant a few days of peace and relative tranquility.

And then, just like that, she forgets Florence and starts acting coy with me, asking if I'm really, *really* busy and if I am, well, forget it, maybe some other time...

I sigh. Meanwhile, Helen wanders in for an apple from the ceramic bowl on the counter. She gives me a quizzical look. I mouth Audrey's name and make imploring gestures but she backs out of the kitchen, refusing to involve herself in my mother's latest misadventure.

Abandoning me in my hour of need.

Audrey gets lonely. Only Audrey isn't like the rest of us and can't just say, "Son, I really miss you, why don't you pop by and we'll haul out the old photo albums and shoot the bull for awhile." That kind of intimacy (and honesty) is beyond her.

For one thing, she *never* invites me to her place. Won't set foot over here either. A big believer in personal space. Not into touching or, God forbid, hugging. I can't for the life of me remember a kiss before bedtime, a word of praise, a smile of encouragement. A universe of one. It isn't her fault. You can't blame her for being sick.

"Say, mom, I've got an idea: why don't we meet somewhere for coffee."

She pretends to think it over. Hems and haws and finally decides it's okay. Only how about Tony's? It *has* to be Tony's. They know her there. Are used to her antics. Some places aren't so understanding: security guards firmly escorting her outside, not so subtle threats, non-imaginary bruises.

She once contacted a semi-famous lawyer, hoping he'd represent her (*pro bono*, of course). I had to call the guy's law office and explain. He still thought her rights were being violated, that no public venue should be allowed to bar her entry. I told him how she'd been arrested for stripping on a downtown street corner to protest global warming. I described the time it took three police officers to drag her out of a fountain at the Midtown Mall. Urinating in the water right in front of everyone, a symbolic statement about pollution caught on security cameras, horrified shoppers shielding their children's eyes...

The attorney countered by saying it was part of the price we pay for living in a free society.

I was polite but in retrospect I should have told him to shove it. How would he have felt if it was *his* mother who made the evening news, wrapped in a blanket, shooting everyone the finger, still raving as they wrestled her into the back of a police van?

I never got a chance to ask him that. He said he had a call to take on another line. He promised to keep in touch.

There's no one else, just her and me. Grandparents, distant cousins, relatives, forget it. I should be so lucky.

I don't even know who my biological father is or the circumstances that led to my conception. It's a taboo subject, guaranteed to set her off.

She did tell me at one point that there had been a marriage. There's no official certificate or paperwork, no ring, no evidence. Only my mother's vague recollection of a hasty, ill-planned ceremony, some two-bit justice of the peace, the records either lost or stolen.

Not a lie, exactly. The thing is...even *she* doesn't know any more. It's all mixed up in her mind, truth and fiction, reality and fantasy.

"I paid the price for my sins," she's remarked on more than one occasion, "and that was you." Not being cruel about it, just stating a fact.

Where had they met?

What was she like back then?

What was the attraction?

She's putting on weight again. Smelly, her hair downright scary. Acting hyper, talking fast with lots of big hand gestures. I make a note to call Doc Mortenson, inquire about her meds again. Has he seen her like this?

He'll say she's being uncooperative. Refusing to take proper care of herself. Audrey has lousy eating habits, a junk food junkie, chips and peanuts and Cheezies, with lots of gut-rotting pop to wash it down. Never mind that she's borderline diabetic, with a family history of heart disease. She only trusts packaged, mass-produced food. Harder to tamper with. Anonymous. *Safe.* Do you realize what they're spraying on fresh fruit and vegetables these days? The chemicals and insecticides? Etc., etc.

Audrey's up at the counter, watching as Tony's wife pours her coffee. Tony and Emily are really good about it. They even let her come into the back so she can see them preparing her food.

She doesn't like to be waited on—if she wants something, she waves her hand to get their attention. Otherwise she's to be left alone. A low maintenance customer. Sitting in the corner, talking to herself. Coffee, lots of cream, lots of sugar. Gruff but always conscientious about leaving a tip, whatever she can afford at that moment.

Audrey brings her coffee back to the table, sits down and then a familiar ritual, casually performed. Tipping her cup slightly, she allows the top millimeter or so to flow down the side and pool on the saucer. There are countless toxins in that surface layer, she'll tell you about them if you ask. They come from the cream, the crap they're feeding or injecting into cattle on those factory farms. Steroids, hormones, antibiotics, weird genes. Mutant milk.

I never bat an eye. Seen it a million times. As long as she keeps her clothes on, everything's hunky dory.

"How's Nancy?" she asks, suddenly quick and sharp, eyes flashing with self-awareness, malign intelligence.

"You mean Helen?"

"Whatever," she snaps, "you know who I mean."

"I went out with a Nancy back in high school. Nancy Gilchrist. Remember her? You liked her. She used to bake you brownies."

"I remember, you don't always have to remind me." Frustrated at being corrected. "Don't make a big deal out of it. Just a slip of the tongue."

"*Helen's* fine."

"Still no sign of kids, huh?"

Smile. *Smile.* "Not yet. Taking our time. You know, not rushing things. The way we look at it, we're both young so what's the hurry?"

"Huh," she grunts. "She doesn't want kids. They'd mess with her lifestyle too much. Her *career*."

I have to look away, take a couple of deep breaths. Audrey has met Helen a grand total of three times and *never* talks to her when she phones, just asks for me. So she has no way of knowing. Somehow picking it up on her radar. Don't ask me how.

"It's not like that, mom," I insist, trying to make light of it. "She'll change her mind. Once she starts hearing that ol' biological clock ticking…"

She doesn't believe it.

To be honest, neither do I.

Well, what about adoption?

Taking on someone else's problems and mistakes? Uh uh, no thanks.

Okay, how about—

I don't want to talk about this right now. Can't you see I'm not in the mood? Just get off my back will you, Herman?

Audrey slurps her poisoned coffee, smirking at my discomfort. Once again she's proven her power over me. She likes to say *Son, I've known you since before you were born.* I'm suddenly desperate to get out of there, away from her and she sees that too. Now I'm vulnerable. It turns out all she wants is some extra money. She's blown her social assistance check and now finds herself short.

Supposedly she's been borrowing off Ed, her building superintendent, and needs to pay him back.

Maybe true, maybe not.

Then she swiftly amends her story, telling me about a girl down the hall who's in trouble, dumped by her pothead boyfriend, who took off with the rent money. Now she's on the verge of being evicted so, in fact, the money is *really* intended for her—

Lies.

Fantasies.

Welcome to Audrey's World.

She settles for a hundred dollars. Part of the game. She's broke and scared, knows that without money you're nobody, you cease to exist. She would never put it that way. To Audrey that would be disconcertingly close to the truth.

She'll lose the money.

She'll give it away to the first bum she sees.

She'll buy a bottle of expensive champagne and stash it in the recesses of a closet, saving it for the end of the world.

Order five extra-large pizzas and leave four rotting on the kitchen counter.

She snatches the bills from me, examining them with obvious pleasure. "That's great, Herman. This'll come in handy. I'll put it to good use."

I give the money gladly. If it brings her some relief, preserves the illusion of independence a little while longer, so much the better. In the meantime, monitor her from afar. Call Mortenson every once in awhile, check on her progress.

Helen says I'm a dutiful son but I'm not so sure.

I do the bare minimum. I play my role. I listen and I do not condemn. I act not out of love but responsibility. Helen doesn't see the difference but, then again, she wouldn't.

Florence calls, sounding flustered, out of sorts. Trouble at Astoria Terrace. Audrey passed out in her apartment and some wieners boiled dry on the stove. The smoke got to her pretty good before the super used his master key to open the door and air the place out.

"Is she okay?"

"Well, she's pretty shook up, Herman. Still loaded but she knows she's done wrong. Can you...maybe it would be a good idea if you popped by and, um, kind of smoothed things over." She waits. "Are you still there?"

"Has she been asking for me?"

Florence is too honest to lie. "I know she'd appreciate you coming over and dealing with this. The super isn't too happy right now." Whispering the last part.

I picture the scene and, truth be known, don't want to get involved. Plus it's nearly ten o'clock. Helen's already in bed, reading. I'll have to go in and explain that Audrey's been at it again.

Good grief.

I say I'll be right over. Don't think too long or hard about it. Not giving myself time to come up with a plausible excuse. Go tell Helen. She doesn't seem surprised. Wants to know if maybe this isn't the last straw. We both know what she means. I say I don't know.

And I truly don't.

I can smell smoke as I approach the building. The front doors are propped open with cinderblocks and the smell gets worse the further down the hallway I go. The door to Audrey's apartment is ajar and I see Ed Gephardt stomping around with an ugly look on his face.

Fortunately Florence is there and greets me with obvious relief, taking my arm and steering me off to the side. Nodding toward the bedroom. "I think she's pretty embarrassed about all the fuss and trouble." She shakes her head. "Try to make her understand, these things happen. So she decided to tie one on, big deal."

With my money.

I can see where she's been blowing her modest monthly stipend. The walls are covered with posters of endangered species, Greenpeace symbols, teary-eyed seals. Glossy magazines scattered everywhere, dozens of issues of *Nature*, *National Geographic*, *Equinox*, *Discover*...

I step carefully through the mess, heading for the bedroom. Florence runs interference on Ed so Audrey and I can be alone for a while.

She's on the bed with a damp cloth draped over her eyes. She looks awful, her skin oily, face craggy, contracting in on itself like one of those time lapse films of a dying flower.

"Hey, kiddo," she calls weakly, the Voice diminished, robbed of its potency. "Heard you talking out there."

"Seems like you've gotten yourself into a spot of trouble." Unable to resist a dig: "That evil, conniving bitch Florence called and told me I'd better haul my butt over here and bail you out." Standing by the bed, very close to her. I could reach out and touch her.

"Stinks in here, don't it?" It's the only acknowledgment of her predicament she'll make. "Oughtta open some windows, air it out." Then, without missing a beat, she's dismissing me. "You should get home. Nancy'll be missing you."

I look back through the doorway. Ed has stationed himself outside and signals he wants a word with me. Florence comes up and stands next to him, her face one big question mark. By now Helen will be sleeping, oblivious to my absence, not giving one good goddamn if I'm there beside her or not.

"Tell 'em I forgot about those stupid wieners," my mother commands, pulling the cloth away, fierce now that she's cornered. "They're trying to make a big deal out of nothing. But I won't let 'em boot me out. No way. Tell Ed I'll sue their asses to kingdom come and I'm dead serious too. You tell 'em, Herman."

I promise I'll do what I can. She wants reassurance so I give it to her. I'll remember to thank Florence for her concern. Attempt to smooth things over with Ed, maybe slip him a few bucks to cover any smoke damage and inconvenience.

I also decide that I'm going to keep working on Helen about having a baby. Take a tougher stand, put my foot down, tell her there's never going to be a better time than now.

I honestly believe I'd make a terrific father. I want the chance to at least *try*. I know our children will be beautiful and happy and brilliant.

I can see them in my mind's eye, a boy and a girl, and they always seem to be laughing.

Harold Stensrud Watches the Olympics

HAROLD WONDERS WHAT *repêchage* means. At first he thinks they're saying *reportage* but that doesn't make any sense. It must have something to do with all this rowing stuff but other than that he hasn't the foggiest idea.

He watches with moderate interest as the long, needle-thin, state of the art sculls are propelled through the water at incredible speeds by well-synchronized rowers, four in each craft. Judging by the way the shoreline is flashing past in the long shots, the buggers have to be going at least thirty or forty clicks an hour. Or maybe they measure it in knots. Knots and leagues and fathoms—nautical enigmas to a confirmed landlubber like Harold.

Canada is doing quite well in the race and will likely finish in the top three. Which means, apparently, that they will advance to the next round. Make that *heat*. The next heat. When they actually get to go for the gold isn't clear.

Vera has fallen asleep in the recliner, her head canted to one side, a bowl of pretzels threatening to spill from her lap onto the rug. He thinks about it but decides not to disturb her. She is taking deep, regular breaths that he can hear from the sofa. Her nostrils are wind-filled caverns. He has always been partial to big-nosed women.

Like that Silken Laumann. Now that girl has a truly impressive proboscis. He's been secretly hoping that since they're showing rowing there might be some commentary from the lovely Miss Laumann. So far he has been disappointed.

There's a gal with true grit. Getting her leg mangled like that and going through rehab, busting her butt to get back into shape and somehow, through sheer courage and determination, snagging a bronze medal. On one leg, basically, a big bandage wrapped around the other one.

They should have given her a *special* medal for that, going above and beyond the call of duty and so forth. Shoot, if she'd been in the army they'd have given her a DSM at the very least. Maybe even the Victoria Cross.

Nope, no Silken. Now they've switched back to the main control center, Brian Williams with the latest update and some breaking news. Drugs again, by the sound of it. Harold takes the opportunity to use the john, grabbing a beer on the way back.

Yup, another doping scandal. Cocaine this time. Did they count that as a performance enhancing drug? Harold wonders what gets into people to make them go and do something like that. To themselves, to their country.

Then again, it seems to him that too much of the coverage is fixated on who is taking what. Which led to this eternal yakkety-yak instead of concentrating on the sports. And then when they finally get around to showing stuff, nine times out of ten it was junk like water polo or field hockey or crap like that.

Who wants to spend all day watching people half drown each other trying to get a stupid ball in a net? Not Harold.

He has to admit he likes the swimming though. Not the men, the women. The thighs and bums on those girls are something to behold. Not much in the chest department, probably gets in the way of their aerodynamics. You can't have everything.

Vera has hardly moved. Nothing less than a blast from an air horn is likely to provoke a reaction. Lucky woman. And she's always been like that, for as long as he's known her. Can fall asleep on a bed of nails while he flops around, trying to convince his brain to shut down. The beer helps some but he has to be careful Vera never catches on to how much he's been drinking lately to bring himself to the point where he can close his eyes at night. He buys a couple of twelve packs at a time, hides one in the basement or out in the garage, periodically topping up the box he keeps in plain view beside the fridge. Only two beer a night, that's my limit, yessirree.

Yeah, right.

87

And she'd out and out *kill* him if she caught him smoking again. So he has to watch it, do it outside or keep the windows open so the smell can dissipate by the time she comes home. One of these days she's bound to walk in on him—then what? What, exactly, would he say to her? Probably be better off having a massive heart attack right then and there, get it over with.

But, honestly, what does she expect? She still had her job and her circle of friends to keep herself occupied. Meanwhile, he's stuck at home, bored out of his skull. Sixty-six years old, retired, wore out and broken down, left to putter about looking for something to do to pass the time. During the day when he isn't watching the Olympics it's the bloody soaps. Meanwhile telling her that he'd gone out for a walk or changed the oil in the car or sharpened the lawnmower blade. Supposedly he's getting ready to paint the storm windows because it's just about time to replace the screens, fall already here, feeling it in his bones at night, two extra-strength Entrophen to dull the ache in his hips.

It's all bullshit, of course, he's dogging it and she likely knows it. But the thing is, she has no idea just how pitiful his life *really* is. That would come as a shock to her. Prick her illusions completely.

He's about to switch to another channel when Williams finally shuts up and announces that they're going down to the waterfront so they can   show—

Well, god*damn*. Beach volleyball. More to the point, *women's* beach volleyball. Now this is more like it.

He has no idea what countries are competing. Nor does he particularly care. Matter of fact, he turns the sound down so no sudden outburst of crowd noise will disturb Vera. Not that he has much to worry about on that count. Still.

One of the teams has a decidedly Scandinavian look to them; tall, blond and, my God, the *nose* on that one. Like a faucet. Harold shifts on the sofa to get more comfortable, peeking over at Vera again but she's out like a light.

Whoever thought of adding beach volleyball to the Olympics was some kind of genius. It's fast, it's exciting...not to mention the fact that the competitors wear the skimpiest outfits imaginable. Every time there's a stoppage in play, they have to reach back and tug at their bikini bottoms. Or brush talc-like sand off their tight, flat tummies.

It's even better than watching the Playboy channel.

It's a close game, thirteen to twelve for one side, which one he isn't sure. He can't figure out what the initials stand for, who represents what country. Doesn't matter. The slow motion replays make up for all that. He isn't too sure of the exact rules either. It's like table tennis, he deduces, you can't get a point unless it's your serve. Is that right?

The scoring is weird. The duo on the right ends up winning the match 17-15 but who ever heard of a game that ends at 17?

Afterwards they interviewed the victorious team but Harold doesn't have much interest in what's being said. He barely listens, staring raptly at the big-nosed blond, health and vitality radiating off both her and her stunning partner. The two of them looking like sisters. *Magnificent* shoulders.

They cut back to Brian Williams and that's that. Besides, it's nearly time for the late news and then off to bed. At least an hour of futile tossing and turning with Vera snoring away like a trooper beside him.

A few minutes into the news he drains the bottle and ponders another. Would that be over-doing it? His limbs feel heavy, ungainly, his thoughts definitely slowing. But is it enough?

The awful thing is that Harold remembers full well what it was like to be young and healthy. That's the worst part. He was known for working like a demon, lugging or toting anything put in front of him. A bull of a man. Powerful and indestructible.

Not any more. Now he's on muscle relaxants and these little green pills that, they tell him, will help with the dizzy spells. The blood not going where it's supposed to, his skin icy, Vera shying away from his chill touch.

There is nothing dignified about growing old, he has decided. There may be some cultures that treat their elders with respect, in recognition of their hard work and accumulated wisdom but he doesn't belong to one of them. He's a dumpy, ugly, old fart whose best days are behind him, consigned to the past. He can't even draw comfort from his memories, they only remind him of how far he's fallen.

Once upon a time, when he was a young, strapping stud, he had turned more than a few heads and planted his fair share of wild oats. He was an impressive figure of a man, tall and oak solid, his shoulders broad, back straight. At the church suppers and dances the girls used to fight to get next to him, and that is no exaggeration.

Another damn commercial. He thinks about going over and waking Vera but instead gets himself a beer. *Last one*. Because he senses that tonight is going to be another bad one.

He reminds himself to switch a couple of full bottles from the box downstairs. That way Vera won't catch wise. He's sure she checks sometimes. She's no dummy and no pushover either. It's important to maintain appearances, play the role of sober, dutiful husband right to the hilt.

Harold parks himself on the couch again, nursing his beer as he watches the rest of the news. People are dying like flies all over the place, starving or killing each other, the weather doing strange things and, meanwhile, tech stocks are soaring, those damn yuppies getting richer and richer...

Before he knows it, the beer is gone and so are the last vestiges of sobriety, a pleasant lassitude wrapping itself around him like a warm, fuzzy blanket. He fumbles with the remote, turns off the TV and in the quietness listens to Vera breathing. He rests his head on the back of the sofa, closing his eyes, intending to doze awhile before nudging her and heading upstairs.

"Enjoy yourself?" Vera asks, and it might be his imagination but from the way she says it he gets the feeling she's been wide awake over there for a considerable period of time.

Harold sighs, knowing that for the sake of sustaining those necessary illusions, it is the only possible reply he can make.

Femme Fatale

(for Caroline Ames)

"GOT A MINUTE?" CANDACE POULIN, hugging the doorway, wasp-waisted and *gorgeous* in a tailored, ivory coatdress that fit like a sock, tiny feet snugged inside killer Ann Marino pumps. And showing off her new teeth again; had to admit the caps looked good, clean and white and straight, like a freshly painted picket fence. At least ten grand worth of work courtesy her latest sugar daddy, a man not shy about throwing his money around (it compensated for his less than stellar performance in the sack).

Donna checked—Newsome was still on the phone, arguing with his mistress—then waved her inside. Her work station was small and cluttered, hemmed in by file cabinets, leafed with yellow Post-It notes that flapped like multicolored pennants every time the elevator opened. Poulin swept in, radiating importance and a subtle, intoxicating scent (she was partial to Alfred Sung).

"I think we have a problem." Poulin in scheming mode, clearly trying to drum up allies for a little corporate intrigue. "What do you know about a certain new receptionist? Have you *seen* this woman, Kurtenbach? Chronically perky and nauseatingly sweet—"

"I know who you mean," Donna confirmed. "Hair from the 1980s, nice figure—"

"*Nice?*" Her co-worker sniffed disdainfully, crossing her arms. "She's got an ass the size of a city bus. I'm not kidding, that ass of hers is a lethal weapon, especially in these narrow hallways."

Newsome's side of the conversation was clearly audible, even through the closed door: "Is that what you think? Is that what you *really* think? Well, let me explain something to you..." Then he lowered his voice and they couldn't hear the rest of it.

"What's going on in there?" Poulin inclined her head toward the inner office.

"Trouble in paradise." She frowned as Poulin propped her well-toned butt on the edge of her desk. She was facing a mountain of work and didn't appreciate the interruption. Easing her chair backward, trying to create some space. It bumped against the wall behind her, knocking the overflowing bulletin board off-kilter, a couple of *Cathy* cartoons beginning a slow-motion descent to the floor. "So, uh, what's the story with the new girl...what's her name again? Donahue or Monaghan—"

"Gallagher," Poulin corrected her, "only she wants everyone to call her *Beth*." They looked at each other, shuddered simultaneously.

Newsome shouted: "That is *not* what I said, goddamnit! Would you just listen to me for a minute—"

"We have a number of undisputed facts. One is, my God, her so-called wardrobe. Yesterday she was wearing an awful brown, shaggy cloth suit...thing. Did you see it? It looked like it was made out of *yak* fur. The poor thing has absolutely no sense of style." She leaned forward, pried off one of her shoes, wiggled her toes to get some feeling back. Donna sniffed surreptitiously but couldn't detect any foot odor. The woman was inhuman. "Two, she was hired under, shall we say, *unusual* circumstances. As in her name was added at the last minute at the request of one of the Directors and her entire interview lasted less than ten minutes. And yet Dietrich informs me she has trouble burping and picking her nose at the same time and is absolutely *hopeless* when it comes to computers."

"All very interesting."

Poulin slipped the elegant shoe back on, then reached down and scratched her sleek calf. Had someone of the male persuasion been present, she'd be fending him off with a Taser at this point. "There's more. Maybe it amounts to nothing. Or...maybe not." She got up, paced in what little space there was in front of the desk.

"Uh, have you talked to her? Gallagher, I mean."

"*God*, no." She appeared offended by the suggestion. "That would mean attempting to breach the toxic cloud of cheap perfume she surrounds herself with. I'm not kidding, she must spray it on with a garden hose."

"What about Dietrich, has he——"

"Dietrich, poor boy, is quite smitten with her. He even took it upon himself to ask her out. Claimed it was all in the line of duty." Rolling her eyes. "But, alas, Gallagher shot him down. Told him some crap about just getting out of a bad relationship and not feeling ready to start dating again. But when Dietrich told Fouts about it afterward, Fouts said 'That's bullshit' because Gallagher asked *him* if he knew of any decent singles bars she could check out."

"Another inconsistency?"

"Bingo. We'll talk more later." And she was off again, leaving a visible wake behind her. Donna couldn't help feeling sorry for Gallagher, wondering what the hell she'd done to get on Poulin's shit list.

"Do I have to *say* it? Do you have to *hear* it to believe me?" She turned to the stack of folders awaiting her attention, not even slightly interested in what Newsome was trying with all of his might not to say.

As soon as Donna entered the lunchroom, Poulin was waving to get her attention. But she was starving so she grabbed a tray and ordered soup and a salad first. The brain injury case behind the counter took *forever* with her order, so by the time she got to the table, the Queen Bee was fuming.

"Thanks for joining us," Poulin snapped, but Donna pretended she hadn't heard and set to work devouring the soup. Ted Fouts caught her eye and winked; not flirting, he'd been out of the closet (and his parents' lives) since he was sixteen. A tough nut, Fouts; you didn't want to get on his bad side. "Now that we're all here, we can put our heads together and decide on a plan of action as far as you know who is concerned. Now, if we look at the latest developments——"

"Look, Poulin, let's not, you know, go nuts on this," Freddie Dietrich interjected, ducking her withering stare. "Although I will admit there are, uh, certain factors that, you know, might bear investigating…"

Celia Dirksen, who hardly ever talked, said nothing. But that silence had *significance*.

"We agree that there are, to say the least, some questions as to this person's true status," Poulin piped up again, trying to regain the floor. "Some things don't add up, like how and *why* she was hired, which I think we need to delve into in a meaningful way."

"I just hope we're not getting ourselves into a snit over nothing," Fouts said. "Whatever we end up doing, I advise we proceed with caution."

"And I'll answer that by saying it's in our best interests to look into this further." Pouring on the charm. "After all, this is about protecting ourselves, watching our backs. We don't know who she might be. Is she legit or some kind of plant? We can't afford *not* to know." And then, as if it mattered, she put it to a vote. "Dietrich?"

Maybe if he hadn't been sitting right next to Poulin he might have put up more of an argument. "I guess…I have to agree. Let's check her out, find out if she's who she says she is." Poulin rewarded him with a friendly pat on the back and he practically humped her leg in abject gratitude.

"Dirksen?"

A nod, nothing more.

"Kurtenbach?"

"It all sounds pretty far-fetched to me. I say why beat around the bush, why not—"

Suddenly everyone was plastering on strained, constipated smiles and either turning their attention to their food or taking part in the contrived cross-chatter that had spontaneously erupted around the table.

Donna found herself engaged in a frivolous conversation with Poulin about the quality of the cream of asparagus soup. Meanwhile, Dietrich and Fouts were arguing about the *Monday Night Football* game and the links between sports and fascism.

Donna agreed that, yes, the soup *was* a tad bland, watching as Gallagher purchased a bag of dill pickle chips and a Fresca, taking a seat at a vacant table by the door. Occasionally glancing in their direction, not meeting anyone's eye, likely afraid of the answer she knew she'd find there.

Fouts was strenuously objecting to Dietrich's description of the Redskins' quarterback: "What do you mean, he throws like a *sissy*?" Dietrich, wisely, was trying to backtrack from the *faux pas*. Poulin took the opportunity to lean across and whisper:

"Be careful what you say when she's around."

"What?"

Poulin, impatient, gestured her closer. "Believe me, the walls have ears."

"But we don't know anything about her." Donna shifted in her seat and the next time Gallagher looked up, smiled at her warmly.

"What is she doing?" Fouts murmured.

"Getting some answers," Donna muttered back, collecting her tray and pushing back from the table.

But she had to admit, at that moment she wasn't really thinking things through, walking over to Gallagher's table and sliding into a chair opposite her, not a *clue* what was supposed to happen next. Knowing the rest of them were watching and wondering what she was up to, either admiring her for the display of sheer *chutzpah* or cringing in the face of her idiocy.

"Hi there."

"Hi...Donna, isn't it?" She nodded, wincing at the easy familiarity. "You're in Mr. Newsome's office. Sure. Hi."

"I noticed you sitting by yourself..."

"Yeah, I could hardly believe it when I saw you coming over here. I thought 'Right on', finally someone to talk to." She licked salt off her fingers, unaware of what she was doing. "And then I saw who it was and I thought, 'Right on, it's Donna'..." She paused. "I guess I was kind of surprised it was you."

Whatever that meant. She decided to let it pass. "Well, you know, we've run into each other a few times, said 'Hi' and all that—"

"Oh, sure," Gallagher said, "but that's just being polite." Donna stared at her. "It's not like, y'know, what we're doing right now, sitting down, face to face."

She didn't know how to answer that. "I think you'll find the longer you work here, the more you'll start to—"

Gallagher was only half-listening, watching her hands instead. "Sorry," she said, blushing. "An old habit. Looking for a ring."

"I'm a charter member of the First Wives Club. Married too young, paid for it later." Throwing it back at her. "You?"

Her face didn't noticeably change expression but Donna got a sense of *something*, a sudden undercurrent of tension, subliminal yet unmistakable.

"My husband is dead," Beth Gallagher said; toneless, succinct. Donna was mortified, not sure how to proceed. Fortunately, Gallagher noticed her discomfiture and attempted to ease the strain. "There was a…car accident. He didn't make it."

Donna wanted to run away, hide in her office and eat the chocolate bar she kept stashed in her bottom drawer for just such emergencies. "I'm sorry," she said, "it must have been really hard on you and—and—" (hating herself for it) "—were there—did you have any children?"

There was a long pause. "Children? Um, no," Gallagher finally allowed. "No kids. Didn't work out."

Rather an odd way of putting it but at least she'd found out what she needed to know. Mission accomplished. Now all she had to do was make an excuse, slip away and avoid meaningful contact with the woman for the rest of her natural life. But, again, she surprised herself. "Sounds like you've been through the proverbial wringer, Gallagher."

"Please, call me Beth."

Donna looked up from the last of her salad. "Around here we have kind of an office custom or culture or whatever. We always call each other by our last names. Even when we socialize. It…suits the atmosphere somehow."

Gallagher giggled. "I suppose. I find it completely *weird*."

Donna shrugged, not entirely disagreeing. "Well, it is and it isn't. But the point is that if you really want to fit in, you have to kind of go with the flow. Unless you're just a temp—"

"Oh, no, this is permanent. There's, like, a six-month probationary period but as far as I'm concerned, I'm here to stay."

"That's good. Glad to hear it, *Gallagher*." They smiled at one another.

"That's right. So you'd better get used to having me around, *Kurtenbach*."

The two of them laughing, momentarily oblivious of everyone else.

Poulin, twenty minutes later, lurking at the door, feigning nonchalance but eyeing her with new respect and calculation.

"Don't pretend you don't see me, Kurtenbach. But before we discuss your uncharacteristic display of initiative...*tell me everything she said*."

Giving her a thumbnail sketch: Elizabeth Gallagher, widow, early 30s. Husband dead in tragic car wreck, details somewhat sketchy. No mysteries, no conspiracies, just one more sad story in the naked city. Bad luck. Somebody had to have it. Donna finished her account, waited for Poulin's reaction, but just then Newsome wandered out and the two of them had to ad lib something work-related to cover their butts. Poulin scurried off, no doubt on the look-out for Dietrich and Fouts, many more whispered conversations to follow.

The worst thing about Poulin was that she really *was* capable of killing with a single, well-aimed word. It was entirely within her power. She could destroy your reputation, wreck your job prospects, poison people against you. She was plugged into *everything* and responsible for half the leaks and gossip going around the office. She oozed competence and gave the impression of being indispensible. Ryerson, her boss, swore by Poulin and claimed he'd be lost without her. Each Christmas he rewarded her with a fat bonus—she vehemently denied sleeping with him but admitted he once drunkenly slipped her the tongue under the mistletoe and spent the next *year* apologizing for it. Terrified she was going to quit on him and then turn around and sue for sexual harassment.

Donna looked up at Newsome, smiling, expectant: "You needed something, sir?"

"I want you to send some flowers."

"Yes, sir. Usual address?"

"Yes, yes. And you needn't act so smug about it, Kurtenbach."

"Wouldn't think of it, sir. Daisies again?"

"Make it those calla lilies she likes."

Ooo, he must have really pissed her off this time. Newsome wordlessly handed her his credit card and walked, sag-shouldered, back to his office while she made the call.

Dietrich said he would have a word with a guy he knew in *Personnel*. Fouts said he'd check with an acquaintance who had an on again/off again thing going with someone who interviewed her. Poulin wanted to break into Gallagher's computer over lunch hour. Dirksen never said a word.

Donna cleared her throat and informed them that she'd made a date with Gallagher to see the new Jane Campion film. They stared at her and Poulin's gaze would've soured milk.

"I don't see why you had to go *that* far," she snapped, eyes narrowing to epicanthic slits.

"She's lonely, wants to talk," Donna answered, refusing to be cowed. "This is a chance for her to get out. Maybe she'll let something slip," pulling out all the stops, "—drop her guard, tell me if she really *is* some kind of spy. You never know."

Poulin was suspicious. She questioned the need to fraternize with the enemy and wondered if Donna wasn't falling under Gallagher's spell, like someone else she knew. Dietrich hung his head, still doing penance for what amounted to a thought crime.

Donna solemnly promised to pass along every scrap of relevant information. As she left, she couldn't help wondering what Poulin would be saying about her the moment she was out of the room. Poulin was dangerous and unscrupulous, her enmity *lethal*.

And now I've made her doubt my loyalty, Donna thought.

Strange how little it seemed to bother her...

They hated the film, with its unrelentingly bleak conclusion that neither of them completely understood.

"I just found it so godawful *depressing*," Donna remarked as they stood in the foyer. "It's hard to understand how that poor woman could go on living like that, year after year."

Gallagher hadn't said much since the movie ended. At one point during the film, the central character was subjected to a savage on-screen beating and she'd hastily excused herself to use the washroom.

But she was the one who proposed they go for a drink somewhere and pleaded with Donna to say 'Yes' as they shivered on the sidewalk outside the theater.

Donna was surprised and touched by the invitation. And it just so happened there was a pseudo-English pub just down the block—

"I hope they're ready for a couple of hot, rockin' chicks like us," Gallagher said, but it was the *way* she said it, in this perfect dead-pan...

Donna burst out laughing and an instant later the two of them were clutching at each other, breathless and practically insensible.

Then they were ducking into the pub, where they discovered a good-looking bartender on duty, polishing wine glasses in time to Sheryl Crow's new CD. They seated themselves at an empty table. Donna went up and ordered a couple of tall— "as in *towering*, darling"—margaritas and told the bartender to start a tab.

* * *

She looked young for thirty-two. Great skin, virtually unlined. She wasn't terribly bright but she was an awfully *nice* person and Donna found herself liking Gallagher, *Beth*, more and more.

She was well-proportioned but had to work hard to keep in shape. That earned another valuable piece of intelligence.

"I swim three or four times a week down at the Aquatic Centre. God, Donna, I swear it's made a new woman out of me. I've always loved swimming so getting up early in the morning and doing laps for an hour is a real treat. Not like exercise at all."

They laughed and switched topics a few more times before finally coming back to the movie.

"I sort of disagree with you on one thing," Gallagher admitted shyly. She was nearly done her drink and loosening up. "You thought the show was too depressing. To me, the problem was it was too *real*." Donna was paying close attention, mental notebook open and waiting. "That woman, her life was hell, she spent most of her days in isolation and fear...but she— she didn't give up. That's the main thing. So, you see, when you look at it that way, it's a story of *hope*."

Donna wasn't sure and said so. They sat for awhile, sipping their cocktails and talking it over. Gallagher insisted on buying the next round and Donna listened with amusement as she flirted with the young bartender, hardly acting like a grieving widow.

Christ, she was starting to sound like Poulin.

"My God, he's cute," Gallagher whispered when she came back. "Did you see his *arms*? A bit on the short side maybe, but I could put up with that."

"Beth, I'm surprised at you..." And then wishing she hadn't said anything because it happened *again*: that same impression of emotions surging and churning just below the surface.

Donna pretended not to notice, changing the subject, chattering on about the first thing that came into her head.

Gallagher quickly recovered her composure and appeared grateful for her companion's tact. The rest of the evening went well, lots of laughter and good discussions, the atmosphere relaxed, the rapport excellent. Two old friends enjoying a night out on the town. Getting reacquainted, catching up on the latest news...

Her report to Poulin was brief and to the point. She also stated her opinion that Gallagher's story was consistent and plausible, no loose ends. Poulin went away dissatisfied, unable to ply her with questions because of an unusually large workload. Fretting needlessly about losing that lucrative Christmas bonus.

"You wanna go across the street for some Chinese, Donna?"

"Sure, Beth, sounds good." Both of them having reached a tacit agreement to declare a temporary truce in their battle of the bulge. She hoped Poulin and the others appreciated the sacrifices she was making to gain Beth's trust, the lengths she was willing to go to in order to achieve that goal.

It took every ounce of her willpower and her body truly hated her for dragging it out of bed at 5:30 so she could get ready for her first morning swim since childhood.

She yawned all the way to the Aquatic Center. And, oh, wouldn't you know it, there was Beth Gallagher's car, now wasn't *that* a coincidence?

An aquacize class was in progress over in the shallow end; she checked but didn't see Beth. She approached the edge of the pool, took a deep breath and dove in. It was *cold* but the shock served its purpose, her blood speeding through her veins, her body experiencing a jolting wake-up call, the whole world suddenly bursting to life as she broke surface—

—*and there was Beth*, treading water near the tiled wall, staring, clearly not happy to see her, giving off none of her usual good vibes.

Confused, Donna literally swam in circles until she wore herself out from the effort. Afterward, chilled to the bone, she paddled to the side and climbed out.

She took a long, hot shower, hot enough to raise steam, and gradually could feel warmth spreading beneath her prickling skin. It was awhile before the shaking stopped. She toweled off, retrieved her clothes from the locker, finally taking notice of the time. If she didn't hurry, she was going to be late for work. She looked around. Beth still hadn't emerged from the pool—

Beth came in, walked past her without a word. There was no chance to speak or explain. Donna heard the water come on, tried to concentrate on getting her shoes on the right feet.

She felt embarrassed and ashamed. Not entirely sure why she'd decided to come swimming, what she had hoped to accomplish. She didn't know *what*, exactly, she had done wrong. She had to say something to Beth, let her know there was no harm intended—

Beth stood naked in the blunt spray, facing the wall, the water spiraling down her long torso…and across a ruinous topography that stretched from her shoulders to her buttocks, an expanse of flesh violently striped and gouged. She was still backing away as Beth turned toward her and opened her eyes…

She never told Poulin or the others about any of it.

Dietrich reported that Gallagher's employment file was wafer thin. Just a cover sheet with her home address, phone number and a one-page resume that listed a few classes at a community college and absolute zilch in terms of previous job experience.

It definitely didn't look good.

One morning Dietrich pulled Donna aside and told her that Poulin was all but convinced the receptionist was some sort of company stooge, and that they had better be on their toes. Dietrich wanted to know what *she* thought.

I think we're talking about a person in the process of healing, she wanted to tell him, I think she's trying to rebuild herself from the ground up. "Beth is doing her best to get over some pretty terrible things," she confided, "I think we should cut her some slack."

At first she thought she had gotten through to him. "I see," he nodded, his expression solemn and thoughtful. Then: "Um…who's Beth?"

Ted Fouts fell into step beside her as she hustled off to get more paper for the stupid copier. "Haven't seen much of you lately, kiddo." Donna hemmed and hawed but didn't deny it. The truth was she hadn't seen much of *anybody* lately and hadn't any desire to.

Beth was basically ignoring her; not being mean about it, just not seeking her out for lunch or making any attempt to interact with her except in a work-related capacity. She appeared skittish in Donna's presence; shy, watchful, wounded, distant.

"Are you making any progress with our office snoop?" Fouts inquired, his manner suddenly more business-like, operating in his official capacity as personal messenger of the Queen.

He was a big man, over six feet tall and rock solid thanks to weight training and racquetball but that didn't matter. She put out her hand, stopping him in the middle of the hallway. "It just so happens, Fouts, that Beth is a *wonderful* person, a real credit to her species, unlike some of the specimens around here. I wish you people would get off the poor woman's case. And I know you're going to run and tell everyone what I just said so just…fuck off, Fouts. You hear me? *Get lost.*" He gaped at her, sidling away, ready to bolt if she tried to lunge at him.

"Hey, take it easy, Kurtenbach. *Jesus…*" Scurrying off to report the encounter to the rest of the posse.

The excommunication order went out almost immediately but Donna was beyond caring, hardly noticing the snubs in the corridors and staff lunch room, the occasional piece of obscene inter-office e-mail…

But after one particularly shitty day, Donna couldn't wait to get out of there

103

and raced for the elevator, not realizing until it was too late that it was already occupied by none other than Beth Gallagher.

They tried not to look at each other the whole way down and then Donna couldn't hold back any longer.

"So…seen any depressing movies lately?"

Beth stared at her. Then she was reaching out, dragging Donna to her, crying all over her designer blazer and calling her 'Donna' and it sounded nice, it sounded right, Beth and Donna, sure, why not?

A little grass seemed appropriate for the occasion. Beth didn't appear shocked or surprised when she held up the joint; on the contrary, she literally dove for the CD stacks. "I'll find us something to listen to."

And she did, Joni Mitchell's *Blue*. Intimate, confessional. The good, the bad and the ugly of love, loneliness and desire according to the skinny chick from Saskatchewan.

It was *wonderful*. They sat on her big cushions and soaked it in. The weed was first rate (the last vestiges of Ken, the asshole architect). She poured them each a glass of red wine. Greek. Very dry.

They toasted each other and she looked at Beth and Beth looked back at her and this time it was different, no sensation of crushing forces, soul tremors, only a need to share, confide…unburden. Beth took a sip and put down her drink. One last pause to think things over and then:

"I'm Beth Gallagher. That's my maiden name. But…" Her voice was barely audible over the music. "You might know me better by my married name."

She studied Beth's pale, round face. "I thought you looked familiar but I can't quite—"

"I…used to be Elizabeth Graham." And, again, the name rang a bell but it wasn't clicking, the right image or sound bite wouldn't come to mind. "My husband was Randall Earl Graham and I…" —taking a breath—"…killed him just over three years ago."

She remembered.

Elizabeth Graham. Oh, my God, you poor woman—

And was instantly, reflexively reaching for Beth's hand, angry with herself for not figuring it out sooner. Because now that she knew, she found it easy to see past the dye job, the weight loss...and discover, underneath, a frightened, dumpy woman, shepherded by her lawyers, menaced by news cameras, forced to reveal her terrible life for all to see and hear, showing the scars so they would *believe.*

She came over and sat with them as if nothing had happened, munching a chicken finger while they sized her up.

"Well, what do you know," Fouts observed, "the return of the prodigal daughter."

Candace Poulin, looking sharp in a chenille cardigan and textured, velor leggings, wasn't having any of it. "Do you have something to say to us, Kurtenbach?"

"Only that our worst fears have been justified," she replied and Fouts sucked in his breath, even Dirksen showing interest. "Ms. Beth Gallagher is just as common and boring and insignificant as she appears."

Dietrich laughed but a furious look from Poulin silenced him like a slap.

"So what you're saying is—"

"What I'm *saying*, Fouts," not sparing anyone her ire, "is that she's a widow, no kids, no life, dead-end job, trying to make a go of it and that's pretty much *it.* No big mystery, nothing to concern any of us."

She could tell most of them believed her and were willing to let bygones be bygones. But Poulin had made it personal. Poulin was going to put up a fight.

"Look, maybe somebody needs to remind you people that Gallagher just basically materialized on our doorstep one day, no experience, no *anything.* And suddenly she's hired, like *that.* So don't tell me there isn't something going on here."

"Does that make her the *enemy,* some kind of master criminal?" Donna shook her head, exasperated. "What exactly do you have against the woman, Poulin? What has she ever done to *you?*" Poulin tried to look genuinely aggrieved and outraged by the charges but had to settle for pissed off. The rest of them glanced at each other but no one rushed to her defense so she spent the remainder of the break sulking and, no doubt, plotting her revenge.

Later that day, as Donna was preparing to head home, Fouts leaned in the door. "So have you heard about your friend?" She shook her head and he gave her the bad news.

She wasn't surprised that Beth had resigned and felt an immediate responsibility; if it hadn't been for her clumsy investigations and stupid curiosity—

But moments after Fouts left, Beth stopped by to tell her the news herself. She asked Donna to join her for a few drinks, an offer her guilt-stricken co-worker quickly accepted. Soon they were on their way to a nearby bar.

Noticing her glum expression, Beth did her best to cheer her up. After all, this was—or had been—her first real job. It just hadn't worked out as well as she'd hoped. The police back in Phoenix helped arrange the move and even put in a good word with the firm's bigwigs.

"Sounds like they were really sympathetic. That's kind of rare, isn't it?"

Beth shrugged. "I never had any trouble with the cops or the prosecutors. The night the police came and I showed them Randy and what he'd done to *me*, this young cop—Marty Rydell, I still remember his name—all he said was, 'Ma'am, why'd you wait so long?'"

It was as close as she ever came to talking about the crime for which she was (in)famous. Maybe she was tired of telling the story over and over again. Besides, the whole affair had been splattered across the front pages of tabloids and magazines from coast to coast, her face and name appropriated for causes ranging from feminism to capital punishment. But she turned her back on all of it, dropped out of sight to avoid the public's hungry scrutiny, their insatiable need for the gruesome details, all the news sordid enough to print.

"I want you to know that I'm not leaving because of anything that happened between you and me. You've been a good friend, Donna, my only friend really."

"I feel the same way. It's going to be hard when you—"

"I know. But I think it's for the better. To tell you the truth," Beth looked sheepish, "I don't really like working there that much. Nobody goes out of their way to be friendly or smile at you. That's the reason I decided to leave. It just wasn't any *fun*." Donna nodded, seeing her colleagues though Beth Gallagher's eyes and disliking them intensely (herself most of all). "My friends in high places found me a job in a law office downtown. Old firm, very quiet and laid back. Plenty of government connections, or so I'm told."

She couldn't help it, blurting it out: "I'm going to miss you, Beth. I wish you could stay and we could hang out and—and argue over movies—" Astonished to find herself weeping, Beth consoling her, using a kleenex to dab at the runaway tears.

"Well, it's not like you can't visit," she joked.

When she had sufficiently recovered, Donna held up her glass, offering a heartfelt toast. "To another new beginning," she proposed and Beth smiled gratefully.

"I'll drink to that."

The following Monday Beth was gone, a new girl at her desk, cool and efficient and heartless. Poulin took an immediate liking to her and Vera Blomquist was granted swift admittance to their group. Blomquist didn't care for blacks or "orientals", thought that people on welfare should be made to pick up garbage and had never really suffered in her entire life.

I know someone, Donna Kurtenbach wanted to tell them, *who puts all of you to shame. Imagine a woman who loves kids more than anything in the world, yet secretly has two abortions to save her unborn children from her monster of a husband.*

Sometimes she thought about calling Beth to find out how she was doing. She wondered if her new employers knew who she was, her incredible story.

Not that she would willingly play the role of victim or martyr. She'd already had that opportunity and said "thanks, but no thanks".

"It's my life, Donna," Beth once told her without the slightest trace of rancor or self-pity, "what am I gonna do, ask God for a refund?"

The way she could face the world with that kind of attitude, putting one foot ahead of the other and persevering, no matter what.

A woman who had endured an unimaginably miserable existence for nearly a decade, absorbing terrible punishment, surviving despite her husband's best efforts. He tried to break her, destroy her a million different ways but never understood, likely right up to the very end, that he was dealing with someone *stronger* than he was, a resolved and bitter adversary who literally fought to the death.

And killed, according to her own sworn testimony, with a mind completely devoid of pity, conditioned to feel nothing at all.

Printed Matter

for Mark Ziesing

General Delivery
Sawich Island, B.C.
V8K 1A4
CANADA

June 15, 1996

Stanley Schaefer, Proprieter
c/o Gryphon Books
P.O. Box 774
Arkham, CA
96088

Dear Mr. Schaefer:

Just received your catalogue this afternoon, delivered by Long John Dunham, the fiestiest (sp?) 74-year-old grizzled islander type you're ever likely to meet. Every week or so John makes the run across to Sawich to collect his and Aggie's mail and he's usually pretty good about asking for mine while he's at it. Normally there's not much, but sometimes there's a magazine or "Publisher's Sweepstakes" or what have you. (It don't matter to me—I read <u>everything</u>!)

I must say that, at least at first glance, I am deeply impressed with Gryphon Books. This has got to be the most eclectic selection of books I have ever come across!

I am greatly anticipating paging through your catalogue at my leisure and I think you can expect an order from me very soon.

Looking forward to doing business with you!

Sincerely,
Russell Q. Hewitt,
(Bibliophile Xtraordinaire)

P.S. Where the heck <u>is</u> Arkham? I have a Rand-McNally road atlas and it doesn't show up anywhere in California. Did you go to Miskatonic U? (Ha Ha) I guess you probably get a lot of cracks like that. Hope you don't take offence. In appreciation,

RQH

General Delivery
Sawich Island, BC
V8K 1A4
CANADA

June 23, 1996

Stanley Schaefer, Proprieter
c/o Gryphon Books
P.O. Box 774
Arkham, CA
96088

Dear Mr. Schaefer:

I finally had a chance to sit down and make it all
the way through your excellent and most stimulating
catalogue. My brain is still realing from the sheer
wealth and diversity of titles you are bold enough to
offer. My compliments to you, sir!
Where else could a guy get a copy of DEVIANT, that
unparalleled examination of the sick mind of Ed Gein,
complete with never-before-seen photos...and (could this
be true?) PSYCHOPATHIA SEXUALIS, the seminal (ha) text
on weirdness and depravity...and (talk about
indispensable!) WRITTEN IN BLOOD, a book with lotsa
purty pictures by and of people drawing with their own
excreted bodily fluids (encore! encore!). And toss in
SKINNED ALIVE (TRUE TALES OF TAXIDERMY), Mirbeau's
exquisite THE TORTURE GARDEN (an old militia buddy of
mine absconded my copy) and, for fiction, I'll take that
Jeter-penned sequel to BLADE RUNNER, which looks
suitably trashy.
I see you prefer payment in U.S. currency so I'll
get John to buy a money order at the post office. The $$
will arrive along with one great, big shit load of
thanks for making this homeboy's <u>decade</u>.
Finally I have met someone who understands my warped
mind!
Keep up the good work!

Sincerely,

Russell Q. Hewitt

P.S. Do you happen to have a copy of THE TURNER DIARIES
in stock?

General Delivery
Sawich Island, BC
V8K 1A4

July 29, 1996

Stanley Schaefer, Proprieter
c/o Gryphon Books
P.O. Box 774
Arkham, CA
96088

Dear Stanley:

Thanks for the incredibly funky card and I hope you
don't mind if I call you "Stanley" which, I think, is a
very dignified name—are you British, by any chance?

You addressed me as "Russell" and that's okay but
most of the time I guess I'm just plain, old Russ.
That's me, your basic shy, withdrawn type with an
affinity for good guns and bad women and an otherwise
above average I.Q. who's got a lot (too much) of time on
his hands to bury his nose in any book that strikes his
fancy whenever he damn well pleases (and a firm
intention of keeping it that way!).

I do go on, don't I?

Sawich Island is just where the mail goes. I live on
this skinny, little fingernail of rock further down the
way, far enough from Sawich to maintain my solitary
existance. Around here, folks like to keep to themselves
and we kind of discourage auslanders (sp?) from
cluttering up our space with their vacuous, annoying
bullshit.

Still, at certain times of the year it's really
crazy around here. The stupid bloody tourists are
everywhere, like ticks. Do you have tourists in Arkham?
What are some of the local sights? Just wondering...

I'll close off for now and merely add that I hope
this is the beginning of a beautiful friendship,
pardner!

Sincerely,
Russell Q. Hewitt

P.S. Do you have much stuff by Giger? And I really like
that guy J.K. Potter. I actually have nightmares about
my fingers coming to life on their own. Waking up and
they're already clawing at my throat. You know what I
mean?

RQH

General Delivery
Sawich Island, BC
V8K 1A4
CANADA

August 10, 1996

Stanley Schaefer, Proprieter
c/o Gryphon Books
P.O. Box 774
Arkham, CA
96088

Dear Stanley:

Call this a supplementary order. Call this a "holy
shit Russ Hewitt can't believe how much good shit he
left in the Gryphon Books catalogue after his first,
paltry order" spasm attack!
Enclose another hefty sum and an itemized listing of
my purchases and their retail prices (don't worry, I
won't forget to add on the postage):

DID SIX MILLION REALLY DIE? $8.00
TALES FROM THE CLIT (Cherie Matrix)   12.00
THE CUNT COLORING BOOK (T. Corinne)   10.00
NASA, NAZIS & JFK (Kenn Thomas)   18.95
HITLER & STALIN: PARALLEL LIVES   22.00
"SPANK ME, FUCK ME" (AN S & M READER)   16.00
BLUE-EYED CHRIST (Revisionist Look At the Bible) 12.99

Just looking at that roster of titles is enough to
set a confirmed book-lover like myself to drooling. Hope
these are all in stock and will be keeping one very
anxious eye out for the mail over the next little while,
believe you me!
By the way, I had a buddy of mine do an Internet
search for Arkham and he came up with lots of hits, of
course, but nothing for Arkham, California. Are you
anywhere near Mount Shasta? Gordie said that's where
your zip code figures you to be. Am I getting warm?
All the best to you,

Sincerely,
Russell Q. Hewitt

P.S. Yes, bears really do shit in the woods!!! The
other day I was out walking and came upon this big old
mangey sow doing her business and (fortunately) paying
me no mind. Grunting like a trooper. The smell was
incredible (almost hallucinegenic clarity). Beautiful
moment, man. Nature in its most raw.

General Delivery
Sawich Island, BC
V8K 1A4
CANADA

August 25, 1996

Stanley Schaefer
c/o Gryphon Books
P.O. Box 774
Arkham, CA
96088

Dear Stanley:

I received your truly warped card about a week ago, updating the status of my orders. Glad to hear something's on its way.

Nope, this place is nowhere near Prince Rupert—so you're _wayyy_ off there. We're much more discreet and out of the way. You'd need one of those U.S. spy satellites to find us. The ones that can register a bald eagle farting from 18,000 miles up (ha ha!).

As I already said, I really dug the card you sent. Very foreboding and Lovecraftian, dude. Didn't see the name of the artist but whoever it was sure gave me a chill. There's this sense that there's something lurking just off to the side, something _almost_ about to leap into the open and reveal itself in all its inhuman glory. The best Lovecraft is like that. Of course, when he actually tries to describe what his boogeymen look like, he can't write worth a crap. He has to make up the words. Or, better yet, leave it unsaid. <u>Unspeakable</u>.

Forgot to ask last time: do you have any books on Gilles de Rais?

Also medical and/or anatomy texts, car crash injuries, dissection, etc.

The weather here has been really lousy lately. How's it been down your way? Where the heck _is_ "down your way", anyway (ha ha)?

Be well, my friend.

Your chum,
(and devoted patron),

Russell Q. Hewitt

General Delivery
Sawich Island, BC
V8K 1A4
CANADA

September 8, 1996

Stanley Schaefer
c/o Gryphon Books
P.O. Box 774
Arkham, CA
96088

Dear Stanley:

I nearly had a heart attack when I came around front today and saw a box sitting out there all lonesome and wet at the end of the dock. We've been getting pissed on with this steady drizzle here for the past week and I thought that whatever it was would be soaked right through.

But I have to commend the packing job you did. You used a good quality box and lots of tape and, as a result, everything was pretty much watertight. I don't know why John or Aggie didn't bother throwing some plastic over it or lugging it up to the porch. (?!!!)

I guess they thought I was home but, as luck would have it, I've been sleeping in the great outdoors for the past three or four days. Grabbed my backpack and sleeping bag and decided to rough it for awhile, just to clear my head. Beans for breakfast, beans for dinner and acute gastritus to keep the cold nights lively. Do you ever have to get away from things, Stanley? Or are you basically a peaceful, laidback person? It's hard to tell from your cards and short notes.

You're obviously a person who believes that people should read whatever they darn well want and that it's your job to satisfy just about every taste there is. Can there be a higher calling than that?

...and, thanks to you, right now I'm sitting here, all warm and dry for the first time in bloody days, and I've got a fire going, CBC Radio (on my cheap Radio Shack shortwave) playing something by Bach and, oh yeah, meanwhile I'm looking at a book with a photograph of a man suspended from his nipples and shreiking in either agony or exultation. Like that Russian comic used to say: "What a country!"

Sincerely,

Russ Hewitt

General Delivery
Sawich Island, BC
V8K 1A4
CANADA (eh?)

November 14, 1996

Stanley Schaefer
c/o Gryphon Books
P.O. Box 774
Arkham, CA
96088

Dear Stanley:

   Your so-called "Christmas Catalogue" is an
abomination against everything that is decent and pure
in the world. I LOVE IT! You'll be lucky if They (the
Vatican, the feminists, the political correctness
thought police, the liberals, etc.) don't burn you at
the stake!
   You've got the latest issue of GRIMMSTONE, with
autopsy photos of JFK and Lassie (ouch! I'll take one,
please!). You've got THRILL KILLS, a novel that purports
to be an unwholesome collaboration between Charlie
Manson and Karla Homolka (how did they manage it?)—I'll
grab 2 copies of that puppy, one for Aggie, who could
likely use a good jolt. And let us not forget an <u>awesome</u>
collection of poetry by the much-maligned Ed Kemper
(wasn't he the evil genius who came up with that great
line—I'm paraphrasing—about how when he sees a great-
looking chick part of him wants to ask her out and
another part wonders what her head would look like on a
stick? Now <u>that's</u> poetry, my friend!)
   Another money order will soon be on its way (thanks,
Postman John!) and may I say that, with the Christmas
season coming up, I hope Kris Kringle looks kindly on
whacked out, weirdo booksellers this year. All the best,
buddy.

Sincerely,

Russ Hewitt

General Delivery
Sawich Island, BC
V8K 1A4
CANADA

December 10, 1996

Dear Stanley:

    Just a quick card to say "thanks" for being you and
for running the world's greatest fucking bookstore in a
small town somewhere in California that apparently
doesn't exist any more than this ficticious (sp?) island
of mine does.
    Let's raise our glasses to enigmas, shall we?
    Happy holidays and take care, big guy!

Yours very sincerely,

Russ Hewitt

General Delivery
Sawich Island, BC
V8K 1A4

December 29, 1996

Stanley Schaefer
c/o Gryphon Books
P.O. Box 774
Arkham, CA
96088

Dear Stanley:

    A real bugger of a storm blowing outside—seems like
the weather here has been lousy for the past month. It's
been especially atrocious for the last twenty-four hours
or so. I've been completely housebound, listening to the
wind howling and feeling the cold seaping right through
the cracks in the walls. Keeping the fire going has
become an all-day, all-night proposition.
    And meanwhile, my mind is racing a mile a minute,
thinking about my livelihood, totally obsessing about my
traps and snares, wondering if something worthwhile will
stumble into them. Especially on a night like this, with
a murderous, driving, blinding sleet. I'm not sure what

your feelings are about this but I figure I might as well own up to it right now:

I live off the land, off of whatever she gives me. When she's feeling bountiful, I celebrate, and when she's being stingey (sp?) and spiteful, like right now, I make do. I never take more than I need and I use every scrap. I was composting long before the media got on the bandwagon about it, believe you me!

I find I can make do on very little. Except books. My brain has _got_ to have a steady supply of words just to give it something to work on. I can't _stand_ not having a book on the go. I'm a very smart person with way above-average I.Q. Being alone and isolated is sometimes good but sometimes it can also be a pretty mind-altering experience.

For instance, (and not to freak you completely out), I find that my senses are _unreal_. My sense of smell, my eyesight, absolutely 20/20. After awhile out here in the bush, you develop your instincts and you _know_ when something's coming, moving through the trees—but what you _don't_ know is whether it's friend or foe. That's the adreneline rush, man.

No order this time. Just wanted to tell you I was thinking about you as its Christmas (or thereabouts) and all that. You've made an important contribution to my life and I believe we should acknowledge such things when we have the time and opportunity.

Got your Christmas card, you sick bugger. Was that really Kurt Cobain's face (what was left of it)? You'd better hope Courtney doesn't get ahold of you. Helluva jolt when I opened that sumbitch up. It's a pleasure to have the acquaintance of a fellow _sicko_.

Talk to you again next year, buddy.

Sincerely,
On a dark & stormy night, somewhere off
the west coast of Canada,

Russ

```
                                    General Delivery
                                    Sawich Island, BC
                                         V8K 1A4
                                         CANADA

                                    January 28, 1997
```

Stanley Schaefer
c/o Gryphon Books
P.O. Box 774
Arkham, CA
96088

Dear Stanley:

I was on the verge of writing you a short note, wondering if you maybe hadn't received my pre-Christmas order, when I heard the tell-tail "putt-putt" of John Dunham's pitiful one-horse motorboat. I'm exaggerating but you'd laugh if you ever saw the thing. Aggie absolutely forbids him to take it out of sight of shore and even <u>that</u> might be pushing his luck.

I went outside to meet him and found myself so shocked by the way he looked, I almost dropped your box when he went to hand it up to me. His appearance was so awful I could hardly bear to look at him. Like I may have told you, John is no spring chicken but he's still a man to be reckoned with. Well, at least he <u>used</u> to be. Almost overnight he's changed into this shaky old man with grey skin and puffy eyes and the smell of death all over him. He's slipping away <u>and he knows it</u>.

When he talked, I had to bend down close to hear him. He told me he was feeling pretty much shot and that he and Aggie were shutting up their cottage and moving down to Nanaimo to be near their kids. He asked if I wanted to buy his boat. "For collecting the mail." He kept reaching up and patting my arm with his cold, boney fingers. We were both crying. Because we both know that John <u>belongs</u> here. He's like me. He'll never be happy anywhere else.

God, I wish I could do something for the poor guy.

Stanley, words from the wise: <u>always make sure that no matter where you are, you're always in a place where you belong</u>.

So sayeth this Soothsayer.
Thintherely

Ruth

January 29, 1997

Dear Stanley:

I just finished tossing a depressing note I wrote you yesterday into the cleansing fire of my wood stove. Nobody needs that kind of shit, right?

It's been a pretty heavy time around here and maybe I'll tell you about it sometime...but not right now (it would just bum us both out).

Instead let me just say how much I appreciated the latest package of books. Thanks for the note too—it just kills me that you are just as interested in where I live as I am in your purported location in real time and space.

As for your card, with its brief and puzzling salutation, it is truly repellent and horrific. I'm only glad my dear, departed mother (devoured from within by cancer eight blissful years ago) isn't alive today to see a world that produces something so graphic and irredeemably fucking evil. "The Death Room of Mary Ann Nichols". Hmmm. Wasn't she one of Jack the Ripper's victims? Have to say, you have to admire the artful savagery of this poor woman's killer. Speaking on a purely clinical basis, of course!

I'm wondering: do you ever get any complaints about your cards? I have pretty extreme tastes but even I have to admit, they sometimes set off my "ick-o-meter" big time. Is that the intention? To shock for the sake of shocking? Not that I'm finding fault with your motivations, just kind of wondering where you're coming from.

Pee Ess. You give me some kind of idea where Arkham is and I'll point out (roughly) the location of my personal Avalon which, oh, yes indeed, is a very real place, paradise on earth, touched by very few human hands, where the old gods still wander freely and the sky is always crying.

Due to the impending move of John and Aggie, there might be some problems with the mail for the next while so I'll hold off on orders for now. Whereever I am, I'm pretty remote and things like a steady supply of asswipe and regular mail are luxuries, not to be taken for granted.

And whereever you are, I send my best wishes, for 1997...and beyond.

Sincerely,
Russ Hewitt

General Delivery
Sawich Island, BC
V8K 1A4
CANADA

March 3, 1997

Stanley Schaefer
c/o Gryphon Books
P.O. Box 774
Arkham, CA 96088

Dear Stanley:

Well, through wind or rain or across storm-tossed straits...
I thought to Hell with it, today's the day, so I took John's little pissant boat (he ended up giving it to me) and made directly for Sawich. The crossing was a bit breezy but I made it, thanks to favourable winds, in just over a couple of hours. After which, I picked up the mail—including some girlie mags and, hooo baby! the latest box from Gryphon Books. Then I bought two bags of Cheezies, a couple of doughnuts, waved to the assembled well-wishers (three loitering sea birds and the spreading corpse of something that might have once been a seal), hopped aboard my tiny boat and toodled off back home again.
Brrrr, it was <u>cold</u>. But, brrrr, it was worth it. Because I am now in possession of some terrific books that promise to rock my world.
Thankyouthankyouthankyouthankyou! Even if I die of triple pneumonia, it'll have been worth it. Stanley, without you, life would have no meaning. Take care and keep in touch—

Sincerely (gratefully),
Russ

General Delivery
Sawich Island, BC
V8K 1A4
CANADA

March 20, 1997

Stanley:

Still have the other letter I wrote to you over on the table—I can see it from here—but (obviously) haven't

120

yet gotten around to making another trip to semi-civilization.

I've been feeling kind of poorly off and on for awhile, weak and light-headed. It may be that I ate some bad meat. Not to gross you out but you should never take shortcuts with your preparation. You can't afford to get lazy with the curing and preserving and what have you. Do you have any/know of any good books on dressing venison and wild game? I'll bet that would be of interest to some of your readers. Also: anything on intestinal parisites—how about RE/Search's BODILY FLUIDS issue?

I'm curious: do you get many orders for THE KAMA SUTRA FOR QUADRIPLEGICS (pg. 9)? Offering something like that really helps restore my faith in humanity because we're only going to keep growing and developping as a species if we have access to all sorts of alternative lifestyles. It's not my particular cup of tea but, hey, different strokes for different folks, as far as I'm concerned!

Whatever happened to Amok Press and Loompanics? They used to have really _extreme_ catalogues too. Sorry, I'm babbling but basically the only thing I can do right now (besides retch and twitch with cold sweats) is sit here with this old portable Brother typewriter, pecking away and free associating (at your expense) to beat Hell.

No card in with the last catalogue. Hope I didn't bum you out or anything. I can have that effect on people. That's why I live out here in the middle of nowhere, where I can't get on too many people's cases.

Hey, do you know the difference between a good book and a good woman? A good book knows when to _shut the fuck up_. On that note (always leave 'em laughing),

Your friend (I hope),

Russ Hewitt

P.S. I guess I want to clarify re: your "far-out" postcards. I totally and utterly defend your constitutional right to free speech and all that, dig? But...answer me this: _Are there any limits_? For instance (and I'm not accusing), aren't you responsible for the books you flog? Can stuff like THE ANARCHIST COOKBOOK or THE JOY OF NON-CONSENSUAL SEX actually do serious _harm_? I don't know but I'm always open to debate. How about it? Any thoughts? Or do you plead the Fifth?

General Delivery
Sawich Island, BC
V8K 1A4
CANADA

April 4, 1997

Stanley Schaefer
c/o Gryphon Books
P.O. Box 774
Arkham, CA
96088

Dear Stanley:

There are now two unmailed letters to you on the table by the door but the good news is there's a guy coming by in a little while to chat about a business proposition and I'm sure he won't mind mailing some stuff for me. Especially if I make it worth his while.

You'd love this guy, Stanley. His name is Terry the Hippie and he is known locally for two reasons: the first is his well-known fondness for interdimensional travel. In the parlance (sp?), he is crazy for dem 'shrooms. The deal is that I let him hunt around on my little island for anything that might alter his consciousness and in return he'll do things like bring me smokes and liquor (trying to quit both) and make the occasional mail run for me.

I'm giving him a note for the good folks at Canada Post at Sawich so they'll let him collect my mail. But I don't think they'll give him much of a hassle about it. You see, the second thing Terry is known for is that he has this thing against washing himself. As a direct result, he has the worst body odour imaginable. No one can withstand his physical proximity for more than 30 seconds at a time, I kid you not. Sometimes you'd swear the guy is actually decomposing, it gets so bad. But, hey, you know what? Whereever Terry goes, he always gets immediate and great service. You have to hand it to him for that.

Glad to be finally getting these letters off to you. Will keep you informed of future developments.

Sincerely,

Russ

P.S.   I promised Terry a good book on mushroom cultivation—can you comply?

General Delivery
Sawich Island, BC
V8K 1A4
CANADA

May 27, 1997

Stanley Schaefer
c/o Gryphon Books
P.O. Box 774
Arkham, CA
96088

Dear Stanley:

   Thanks to Terry the Hippie, I now get mail and
newspaper delivery directly to my door at least once a
week. My hirsuit (sp?) new postman isn't nearly as
friendly and out-going as John or Aggie were (and he
smells a whole helluva lot worse) but just this morning
he brought me a huge swack of magazines and goodies so I
guess I can't complain...
   ...including, the latest Gryphon Books catalogue,
with that distinctive (unsettling) logo on the envelope.
Tonight, I've been skimming through that baby as well as
a couple of back issues of SOLDIER OF FORTUNE while
making good progress on the pint of Irish whiskey Terry
was decent enough to bring me (yet another weakness of
mine).
   In all honesty, what I <u>don't</u> like about the current
arrangement is that I never know exactly when Terry is
coming by. He is irregular in his thought patterns, the
direct result of certain fungal excesses we need not
delve into here. <u>He also never fucking stops talking</u>!!!
All of which could lead to major problems down the road
but I'm trying not to get too far ahead of myself.
   All I really need is the bugger's <u>boat</u> (it'd be a
big improvement on John's old beater). I'm thinking I
should convince him to sell it to me. The weather's been
pretty nice lately and with his tub I could make it to
Sawich in an hour, maybe less. I guess it wouldn't hurt
to at least ask. The worst he can do is say "no". But I
have a feeling I'll be able to bring him around to my
point of view. I'll just use my (in)famous powers of
persuasion on him.

Sincerely,

Russ

P.S. Okay, it's now a couple of hours later and I just
picked up your envelope, the big white one the catalogue

came in...and out slides your latest card which I guess
I somehow missed. Lucky me.

    Man, I honestly don't know what to say to you. If
this is real then it's _too_ real, if you get my meaning.
I can do autopsy photos and car wreck scenes and from my
own life I can tell you about shit that would absolutely
make your hair stand on end. Or maybe not. After looking
at this card it makes me realize that you must be a
pretty jaded, borderline individual. Again, I have to
ask you, Stanley—is there such a thing as going _too far_?

    I guess at this point I'd have to say: YES.

    I'll check out the catalogue later but right now I
can't get my mind off this bloody card.

    For tonight, at least (to paraphrase the Bard), I
fear you have murdered sleep.

Russ

                                    General Delivery
                                    Sawich Island, BC
                                         V8K 1A4
                                         CANADA

                                    August 11, 1997

Dear Stanley:

    Got your card. I _guess_ it's an improvement over the
last one. Sort of.

    And, yeah, you're right, it's been awhile since my
last order but there have been many things weighing on
my mind.

    I have been keeping myself very busy. It's tourist
season (still), and the islands around here have been
swarming with eco-nuts and campers. I have been working
pretty steadily, to the extent that I have had to build
another smokehouse, this one a lot bigger and set
further back in the trees. It seems like I never stop,
from dawn to dusk. All work and no play…

    …and not much more to say. Hope business is booming.
Have a great summer, okay?

Sincerely,
Russell Q. Hewitt

P.S. Returning the book on mushroom cultivation for
credit. Terry the Hippie is now officially "missing in
action" (long story) but at least he left me his boat.

Been too busy for reading (or anything else) so no order
this time. Sorry. All the best anyway. Take care.

RQH

                                        General Delivery
                                     Sawich Island, BC
                                             V8K 1A4
                                              CANADA

                                     September 15, 1997

Stanley Schaefer, Proprieter
c/o Gryphon Books
P.O. Box 774
Arkham, CA
96088

Mr. Schaefer:

    Your latest card was blank inside, not even signed.
No words necessary, huh?
    Stanley, I've seen some pretty fucking sick shit in
my life but this card pretty much takes the cake. I'll
be dead honest with you and tell you that it's gotten to
the point where I no longer look forward to receiving
any kind of correspondence from your establishment.
    I think it would be better for both of us concerned
if we stopped communicating with each other. I can tell
by this card (and others of the same ilk) the type of
person I'm dealing with now and I'm no longer amused.
Just pissed off and extremely disappointed and wierded
out.
    Please consider our business and personal
relationship at an end.
    Adios and farewell.

Sincerely,
(and for the last time),

Russell Q. Hewitt

P.S. My buddy Gordie sent me a news clipping he
downloaded off the net that mentions Arkham. I guess
there's been a lot of forest fires in your area. Now at
least I know where it is so I can make sure never to
come within a 100 miles of the place!

General Delivery
Sawich Island, BC
V8K 1A4
CANADA

November 17, 1997

Stanley Schaefer
c/o Gryphon Books
P.O. Box 774
Arkham, CA
96088

Dear Stanley:

I picked up your envelope with the rest of my mail
today. At first I wasn't going to open it, but then I
got curious and so...
What can I say?
<u>You win</u>.
It doesn't matter <u>how</u> you found me or how you
managed to poke around out here without me catching wind
of you. It's clear that I have completely underestimated
you. There is no limit to your capabilities and I am
left with a real and lasting appreciation of your
special talents. My compliments to you, sir!
I guess at this point the only thing I can do is
throw myself at your mercy.
With a few clicks of your devious shutter, you have
uncovered the skeletons in my closet (or, in this case,
my smokehouse) and taken away all the safety and
security I've worked so long and hard to maintain. When
I look at those pictures, it's like suddenly I'm viewing
it all from another, totally different perspective.
Because now I actually <u>see</u> what I've done and have
an inkling of what I represent in the eyes of the rest
of the world. And I can't help it, I am left wondering
what type of mind could do such things and be so
methodical, knowing all along that it isn't <u>right</u>, that
I'm committing acts of desecration and sacrelege
(sp?)...and yet doing it anyway, humming and even
<u>smiling</u> to myself as I go about my cruel and despicable
work.
Do you know what I mean?
But I guess what it comes down to, the single most
important thing right now is that you have discovered my
dirty little secret and have made your awesome knowledge
known to me. And in return I must learn to accept this
new reality and do my best to adapt and come to terms
with it. Let me state for the record (as it were) that I
don't think there will be any further misunderstandings,
at least on my end. I am enclosing an itemized (and
fairly lengthy) list of books I would like to purchase

from you. I'll add a money order for the full amount owing.

Please let me know if this sum is sufficient for your present requirements. If not, I am sure we can come to a more satisfactory arrangement.

I am, of course, entirely reliant on your discretion and goodwill and wish to acknowledge as much at this time.

I shall look forward with great anticipation to your next communication and humbly await any further instructions you might have.

Sincerely and respectfully,
Russell Quentin Hewitt

The Daddy Monster

An Urban Legend

THERE WAS ONCE A *cruel and despicable ogre who decided, one sunny Wednesday, that he was going to devour his children and use their bones to create smart but functional end tables. When the ogre's wife got home after a hard day of work—the ogre, by his very nature, was virtually unemployable—she would no doubt be pleased by the new furniture but would likely express concern at the absence of her two beloved children. If confronted, the crafty ogre intended to be vague and evasive and, should all else fail, would offer to massage her hideously calloused feet and file her eyeeteeth and put fresh poultices on her eleven hundred and sixty-seven warts, goiters and bunions...*

I hate my kids.

It was a hard thing to own up to. Not something he'd let slip in mixed company. Like in front of Pam, for instance.

I hate my kids. Lester Kincaid, "The Official Voice of the Great Northwest!" (he wondered how long before the billboards and ads on city buses came down), the self-proclaimed "conscience of the airwaves", *hated* his children.

Well, maybe *hate* was too strong a word.

What he really hated was being cooped up with the little motherfuckers all the live long day and never having so much as one single, adult, intelligible conversation with *anybody,* except maybe the postman or a friendly clerk at the grocery store.

So...this was what life was like for your plain, average, stay-at-home dad. *Hey, didn't I do a show on that a couple of years ago? Yeah, "Daddy Dearest". The asshole I interviewed made full-time fatherhood sound like frigging nirvana compared to this constantly-wiping-pee-off-the-toilet-seat-and-forming-an-intimate-bond-with-your-washing-machine shit.*

It was going on two months since the day he had, let's face it, pissed his entire career down the drain and time (once again) to ask himself: *what am I doing?* What was with this "Life With Father" shtick? As far as Les could tell, it amounted to nothing more than an endless cycle of meaningless, brain-draining fucking *chores*.

If he had known what was in store for him, what would transpire immediately following the, ah, alleged incident at the station, would he have done what he did?

No. Not a fucking chance. Being stuck with two pre-school age children was worse than doing time. Frankly, he could do with a few weeks of solitary confinement right about now.

It wasn't that they were particularly *bad* kids, Les reflected dourly, sipping his morning java, it was just that they did such incredibly fucking dumb things *for no apparent reason*. Like the other day, when Dougie came along and dunked his fingers into Les's coffee cup, burning himself and then having the gall to snivel about it for hours afterward.

No fucking kidding, you stupid brat. It's not like you're a baby anymore, fer Chrissake. By now you should know: if it steams, you scream.

Audrey was sneakier, devising carefully hatched plots meant to unnerve and infuriate him while, simultaneously, demonstrating her independence. Like getting a chair and climbing up to retrieve a cereal box or bag of cookies from the cupboard. Never mind that she had to stand on top of a stove element to do it. Or she would lock herself in the john for an hour and *sit* in there, humming away, the same tuneless melody, over and over again. It sounded weird and primitive and spooky as hell. When he pounded on the door and told her to knock it off and get out of there, she'd reply, quite serenely: "Excuse me, this washroom is occupied."

Dougie worshipped the ground Audrey walked on. Dougie would follow Audrey off the edge of the world and never look back. His absolute and unconditional devotion to his older sister was frightening. He was her butler, lapdog and personal doormat, slave to her every whim. He would pester and pester Les on her behalf until Les finally exploded at him: "*Would you get away from me? Scram, and I mean it!*"

But he wasn't dissuaded long, he'd keep at it until Les finally gave in to shut the kid up. And off Dougie would trot with a fruit rollup or a graham cracker for her, happy to be of service, pissing himself with joy should Her Majesty happen to share a tiny piece of the bounty with him as a reward for a job well done.

Pam, of course, thought Les was kidding when he told her the two of them were in cahoots together. She laughed and laughed while he kept his head down, pretending to focus on his food, trying not to show how furious he was. "It's like they take turns," he insisted, as she attempted to stifle her giggles, "they make sure I never get a break, never have a minute to myself."

"Thanks," she said, dabbing at her eyes with the bottom of her shirt. "I needed that after staring at a computer screen most of the day. Have I mentioned that Friday is the deadline for that drama unit? Have I mentioned that I haven't even started it yet?"

"I tell you our children are conspiring to drive me nuts and you're giving me shop talk?"

"Hon…" She wrapped her arms around him, pulling him close and whispering in his ear: "Welcome to the wonderful world of parenthood."

"God, how did I let myself get talked into this?"

But, again, she thought he was joking.

Pam was the kind of person who believed every cloud had a silver lining and every dog had its day. The eternal optimist. Lose your job? Assault your boss and be accused of sexually harassing a colleague, getting yourself permanently blacklisted in the bargain? That's okay, we'll pull the kids out of daycare and you can stay at home and bond with them and everyone will live happily ever after.

And for a couple of weeks or so, it was fun. He avoided and shunned the radio, only mildly curious to know who was sitting in for him or if any of his regulars were calling in to find out what had happened to Les, what the official line would be. A local columnist hinted that he'd demanded a big pay hike and the station had balked. Les refused comment, referring inquiring minds to the firm of Forsythe, Wade & Osgoode. Determined to keep to the high road.

At least for now.

There was a park about two blocks from the duplex and he took Audrey and Dougie there almost every day, turning them loose and allowing them to devolve to their primate roots on the swings, slides and climbing apparatus. Meanwhile, he'd unfold his newspaper and sit on an ugly, slippery, uncomfortable bench composed (according to an accompanying plaque) of recycled plastic bottles and disposable diapers. An amazing scientific advance that was supposed to make him feel proud to be a member of the human race or something.

If these bozos spent half as much time and money brow-beating conservation into the great unwashed they wouldn't have bend their brains trying to figure out 101 uses for toxic baby shit.

The preceding editorial brought to you by Les Kincaid, voted by listeners as "Favourite On-Air Personality" (Les dubbed it "The Golden Fop Award") count 'em, *three* years in a row. That was no mean feat in the cut-throat world of radio, buster. It meant winning the folks over, one show at a time. Hours of prepwork and subscriptions to twenty different magazines, including the ones he got on-line. He was hip, he was informed, he was smart...and yet here he was, getting his forehead sunburned in an ugly, ersatz urban park, watching Dougie bring another handful of polluted sand up to his mouth despite being warned off three different times already.

"*Dougie, goddamnit*—"

"Shouldn't swear," Audrey mumbled and for some reason Les was convinced the remark was meant to be insolent, maybe because he detected a hint of Pam in her tone.

"You shut your mouth." Surprised at the menace in his voice.

"Shouldn't say 'shut up'," Dougie shot back and that was enough for Les. He closed his newspaper and stood, scowling at them.

"C'mon," he gestured impatiently, "let's go. We're leaving."

Dougie whined all the way home and Audrey sulked which meant they didn't get the treat he promised them. Instead it was nap time for both of them, do not pass "Go" or collect *fuck all*. At that turn of events, Dougie threw what appeared to be a *grand mal* seizure and when Les picked him up, screamed blue murder and waved his small fists in Les's face. He could feel himself losing it and Audrey looked anxious as she led the way to their bedroom. Les dropped Dougie onto his bed and he immediately began to flail about, kicking off his covers and hollering, no tears, just making a bloody racket, lashing out with his boney foot and connecting solidly with Les's thigh—

Les slapped him.

It wasn't that hard but it was on the *face*. It happened so quickly that at first no one was sure how to react. Dougie broke into a puzzled grin...his face abruptly changing, transformed by shock, outrage and disbelief. Then he was howling like a scalded monkey and there was no way of calming him, of taking back what he'd done.

Les tried the firm approach first: "You know you had that coming to you..." When that didn't work, he went for conciliatory: "Daddy's really sorry he had to do that." Once that failed, Les wallowed in abjectness, the reddening cheek making it easier. "—sorry, Dougie, daddy's sorry, okay? *Okay?*"

In the end it was Audrey who settled him down. She started humming, that same odd, creepy tune again. Almost at once, Dougie went slack in Les's arms. Not submitting, *listening*. The song had a certain hypnotic quality and Les was certain he'd heard it before. He asked Audrey about it once and she'd merely shrugged. Was it a hymn, a nursery rhyme, perhaps an old folk tune? And where had she picked it up?

He never told Pam about what happened. The bruise was explained away as another mishap of childhood, of no great concern. Dougie claimed he couldn't remember how he'd gotten it and Audrey point blank refused to answer. Pam had her suspicions and told Les to keep his eye on Audrey. She was worried about the girl. She was so quiet and withdrawn lately...

* * *

It didn't take Stephen bloody Hawking to figure out that his career as a broadcaster, at least in "the Great Northwest", was, to put it bluntly, *kaput*.

There was no way of out and out *proving* that Duane was going around slam-dunking his reputation but Les knew the vindictive prick wasn't the type to let a love tap or two go by without exacting some kind of revenge. Duane had the power, Duane had the connections and, thanks to Les, he sure as hell had more than enough incentive. Not to mention the added complication that the rumblings about Duane and Suzanne Plante had, woe unto Les, turned out to have more than a kernel of truth to them. Any way you looked at it, he was fucked.

The absolute pisser of it was that he had really *loved* his job. The phone-in show, in particular, had been a great source of fun. Taking the emotional temperature of listeners, finding out what was going on in the minds of the immoral majority. Yakking it up with the yokels or just generally riffing, trying to see what buttons he could push on any given day. Gun control, abortion, nuclear power, tree huggers; he had very firmly held opinions on anything and everything under the sun and who cared if they sometimes flat out contradicted one another?

On the air, he was the ringmaster of the world's greatest flea circus. It was all in the suckers' minds, there really wasn't anything to see or touch, only the *voice*...and even that was put on: deepened, a slight mid-western drawl added as a homey touch. Careful not to let the three aimless semesters he'd spent at Trinity show. One too many references to Goethe and he'd end up on public radio, interviewing Ralph Nader and the latest indie folk-fusion sensation, pinching himself to stay awake.

The best part about doing radio was being responsible for filling in the silence, all that dead air, with basically anything that came into his head: half-remembered facts and cooked statistics, a kind of stream-of-consciousness, post-modernist diatribe, part editorial, part rant, guaranteed to offend somebody or else you've been listening to *wayyyy* too much Howard Stern.

133

The night following what came to be known as Black Thursday, Pam told him that he was too good for radio, too smart and talented, and maybe that was true. But that didn't stop him from missing it, some days more than others (stripping the sheets off Dougie's bed after another "accident" or cleaning the bathroom or doing the umpteenth load of laundry).

Just to be able to hear nutty Mrs. Andreychuk from Pressler ("out on Number 16, east of Clarke's Falls") go on about the banks and "international cabals" again or chew the fat with Floyd Evans, who believed global warming was a convoluted scam involving the United Nations, the I.M.F. and the Freemasons.

Shit, when it came right down to it he'd announce fucking *hog futures* if it meant he never had to have another upclose and personal encounter with Dougie's septic butt.

"Daddy, can Awd-wee haf jooz?"

Les stared at the kid. The kitchen looked like Hiroshima. They'd only finished lunch a few minutes ago.

"*Goddamnit!*'" His son flinched. "I told you to stay out of Daddy's way, didn't I? *Didn't I?*" He was yelling and at the same time fetching a plastic glass and banging it on the counter, slopping in a few ounces of cranapple juice. Some sticky coldness splashed on his wrist. "*Fuck!* Here, take this." Thrusting the cup at Dougie and pushing him toward the door. "Now, g'wan. Get! Get! And don't come back, I mean it."

But he always did.

Dear sir or madam:

Thank you for your inquiry regarding possible employment at this station. At the present time, however...

Les's biggest problem, and he was the first to admit it, was that he was too selfish to be either a good husband or doting parent. He jealously protected his personal space, even from Pam. He always insisted, for instance, that they keep separate bank accounts and split the bills evenly between them.

Maybe she was right when she said he had "intimacy issues". There were times when, for no reason he could fathom, his emotions simply shut down on him and he didn't feel anything for anybody. He'd even go so far as sleep on the couch rather than share a bed—and close, human contact—with his wife. The next night or a few nights later, whenever the mood passed, he'd slip back into bed with her, acting like nothing had happened. When she tried to question him, find out if it was anything *she* had done, he deflected her queries and would become genuinely angry if she persisted.

"Leave me alone!"

Confrontations with Pam were rare. She was so *Pam*; as positive as he was negative. Refusing to believe anything that didn't fit in with her rosy worldview. Utterly convinced that despite all the evidence to the contrary, everything was right with the cosmos.

With Pam, *nothing* was impossible. She was able to talk him into having kids and that was saying something. She made it seem like it was the next, most logical step in their relationship. They had shared everything else (well, except those aforementioned bank accounts and it still drove him crazy when she used his bike...).

At first, whenever she brought up the baby thing he would protest that she was hitting him with it totally out of the blue, he needed time to think it over. That tactic worked for awhile but then the pressure got to be pretty much constant and in the end he figured, why not? Financially, they were up to it. He was making decent money at the station and the commercials he did on the side, shilling for a furniture store and a local Ford dealership, paid a tidy stipend. Pam was in the process of finishing her Master's, impressing the pants off her faculty advisor and dazzling her Dean.

There didn't seem to be any black clouds on the horizon, nothing but clear sailing ahead. He was, without question, a bona fide celebrity, a man of stature. That was what he missed most: the way people acted when they realized they were talking to the one and only Lester Kincaid *himself*...and you'd better be on your toes 'cause ol' Les was always looking to put one over on you, even when you were only calling in to report a lost kitten.

Yeah, he was smart, all right, but he still somehow ended up experiencing the gory splendor of childbirth not once but *twice* (hey, he'd sat through "Waterworld" a second time too, come to think of it).

He missed two days of work when Pam had Audrey. When he got back, he found his coffin-sized cubicle at the station overflowing with cards and baby toys sent by faithful listeners.

Dougie's birth was tougher and Pam suffered bad back labor for more than twenty hours until it got to be too much, too intense, and she told them to go ahead with the epidural. Which, it turned out, was the right decision because it seemed to ease the pressure and got things moving again. Two hours later, Douglas Pierce Kincaid was officially welcomed into the world, to the manifest relief of everyone involved.

Les managed to squeeze in a shower and still made it to work by 12:30, in time to eviscerate (*via* long distance) a loony Senator who thought paper money and credit should be abolished, the economy converted to the barter system of ages past...while accepting a steady stream of phone calls congratulating him on the recent addition to the Kincaid family.

To Pam, he'd claimed it was a case of the show must go on. She wasn't fooled. Wrung dry after the long, drawn out delivery, she waved him away with a resigned smile.

"You get going," she told him, "you'll go crazy if you have to sit around here with nothing to do."

On the way out, he stopped to see Dougie (he was "Dougie" right from the first). The new-born was wide awake and appeared startled and unnerved by the light and constant noise and commotion around him, a blur of threatening shapes.

Of course, someone recognized him and before Les knew it he had nurses and residents and even a few patients clustering around him, holding out anything they could lay their hands on for him to sign. Dougie, in his glass cage, was soon forgotten—though at one point he started crying and Les remarked, with mock pride: "Sounds like a chip off the ol' block".

The ensuing outburst of laughter only making Dougie bawl harder...

After those first few weeks, reality began to rear its ugly head. He was bored and crankier by the day. Within a month of taking over as primary caregiver to his children, Les had pretty much come to the conclusion that he would rather call *bingos* than spend another hour walled up alive with the fruits of his loins.

He never had a moment of peace.

Dougie, especially, was constantly trying to crawl up into his lap for a "snuggle" or else he wanted Les to read him a story or fix a frigging toy or get a frigging banana for frigging *Aud-wee*—

"Leave me alone!" Les shouted, those three words repeated with increasing frequency as the days and then weeks went by and no one responded to the resumés he sent out (or bothered to return his calls, for that matter). "*Get the hell away from me!*" or even "*Fuck off, both of you!*" also popped out on occasion, at least when Pam wasn't around. The kids were young and didn't understand. He tried to make them see that daddy was in a bad way, daddy had been a big man once, with a tall shadow, and now he was a non-entity, just another *prole*. And it was eating his guts out.

"Daddy, Aud wee wananotha quacka."

"Douglas, for the last time, *go away!*"

On the other hand, *Pam's* career seemed to be thriving. Les wasn't too sure what she did in her downtown office but it involved curriculum development and "student-centered learning", whatever that meant. Her bosses loved her, the performance evaluations were glowing, there were regular raises and promotions...it was safe to say she was very, very good at her job.

Truth to be told, before the station cashiered his sorry ass she'd been pulling down nearly as much as him and didn't mind needling Les about it every once in awhile either.

They had a fair amount of savings and investments so if they minded their Ps and Qs they could live comfortably on one salary (but good-bye separate bank accounts).

Taking the kids out of daycare saved over a grand a month, which helped *a lot*. Unfortunately that particular move also precipitated a major crisis. As soon as he found out he wouldn't be going to Faye's anymore, Dougie became distraught. Even when Pam told him he would get to stay at home with Daddy from now on—"won't that be fun?" —he wasn't cheered.

As Pam held him, he eyed Les over her shoulder, assessing him critically. Judging by the number of tears shed for the dear, departed, hideously expensive Faye Tyler, Les didn't measure up well in comparison.

"Arnie Delschneider called me into his office today. I guess everyone was really knocked out by my idea for the theme modules. He told me it's all very hush-hush at this point but it looks like at least three different schools have said they'd be willing to pilot the—"

"—great, great—*Dougie, get out of there!*"

"How have the kids been today?"

"*Dougie! Dougie, goddamnit, I told you*—hang on a sec—"

"That's okay, I've got to run."

"Okay. I'll see you at 5:00."

"Might be a bit later. I've got some catching up to do."

"*Grrrrrr...*"

"Honey, what can I tell you? The pay's great but the hours are lousy."

"I'd pity you if I didn't envy you so much."

She clucked sympathetically. "I'll try to get out of here as quick as I can. Meanwhile, do your best not to kill the wee ones today."

"Sometimes it's very, very hard."

"I know. Hang in there. Gotta run. Bye, love."

Les stared at the empty phone. Hung up. Turned around and Dougie was back in the garbage again, holding up a droopy, black banana peel, waving it around like a dead bird. "Oooooo, *yuk*!"

Les slapped his hand.

Smack!

Dougie shrieked, the skin on his fingers still sensitive from the coffee burns.

The whole thing started, honest to God, over *brassieres*.

Suzanne Plante, his new "co-producer" (compliments dimwit Duane), was a real go-getter, not to mention your prototypical boot-licking corporate lackey with shit for brains and the instincts of someone with a thoroughly undistinguished background in sales and promotion. Nevertheless, the word around the station was that the Powers That Be had big plans for Suzanne. According to office scuttlebutt, she and Duane were doing the dirty hula on the sly, which made her a force to be reckoned with.

Les could never quite put a finger on exactly why he loathed Duane Shipman as much as he did. Likely it had something to do with the station manager's proto-reptilian nature, pea-sized brain and almost pathological mendacity. The man was slime, plain and simple.

Duane, like Suzanne, was a company man to the bitter end and a live wire like Les Kincaid was bound to offend such limited sensibilities. Les was (in)famous for his occasionally outlandish remarks and wasn't averse to tweaking sponsors or complaining about the (as Les saw it) somewhat miserly disposition of the station's administrators. He had a running on-air joke about having to pay for his own coffee. It was supposed to be in good fun but people like Suzanne and Duane hadn't gotten as far as they had because of their terrific sense of humor. They were drones, efficient and single-minded, bred for obedience, thick as a pair of mud-baked bricks.

Which was why Les knew Suzanne wasn't kidding when she proposed devoting an entire phone-in show to *bras*.

"*Huh*. Sorry, not on my watch, doll."

"What do you mean?" Suzanne bristled. Les intimidated most people but Suzanne's curare-tipped glare could kill at twenty paces. And since she was the flavor of the month and apparently fucking the main man—

"It's just that…" Les finding himself (uncharacteristically) on the defensive, "something like that, the *delicacy* it requires. I mean, the minute I even start *thinking* about women's, ah, you know, I get the giggles. Must be a Freudian thing."

"That's *your* problem. According to my research, thousands of women suffer back pain and severe posture problems each year because of inadequate or poorly fitting bras. What's so funny? Why are you sitting there smiling like an idiot?"

"You said the word 'bra'. See? I can't help myself. It makes me laugh. It's totally silly, I know." Les shrugged, trying to make light of it.

"I'd say that's putting it mildly."

He took a deep breath. "What I'm saying, Suzanne, is that it's probably better for someone else to do the piece. *Candace*. Candace is the one you want. Do it as a segment for the supper hour news. Shit, make it a *feature*, eight or ten minutes. Go for it."

"But with Candace. Because she's a woman."

"Yeah. Sure. Absolutely." Les was sweating, trying with every ounce of his willpower not to stare at her almost *infinitesimally* tiny breasts. She was the most flat-chested woman he had ever met. Like a plank. On the other hand, she was blessed with a well-nigh perfect set of buns. The Lord giveth and the Lord taketh away. "Candace would bring a lot more to it than I could."

She frowned and crossed her arms. "Maybe we could still do it as a phone-in but with Candace as guest host. I know she's been dying for a shot."

Ho ho, has she indeed? Les thought. *Sweet, innocent Candace, who used to bring me my coffee. Stabbing me in the back.* "Well, we can *think* about it but I'm not sure I really—I just don't see this, uh, breast thing—" (*grinning stupidly*) "—playing well right after lunch, you know, with people still digesting their food."

She brushed aside his reservations with an impatient gesture. "The point is, the subject is relevant *and* important. I've been reading a book called *Lift and Separate* and it really opened my eyes. Shoot, I've got it here somewhere. I called the writer and I think she'd be a perfect guest for the show. She's bright, she's articulate—"

"Great," Les muttered, "a tit expert."

"*What?*" He had seriously blown it, he saw that right away. "*What did you just say?*"

"It was a bad joke. The point I was trying to make—"

She was trembling with rage, vibrating in her high-backed chair. "Get out of my office. *Now.* Go. And I suggest you do some serious thinking about your general attitude toward women."

"If you'd let me explain—"

But she just pointed, not giving him a chance. Word of what happened spread around the station and soon the story took on a life of its own, until the fateful (fatal?) exchange went something like this:

Suzanne:

I want to do a show about brassieres.

I think many of our listeners would be interested and—

Les:

(*Leering at her breasts*)

What the hell would *you* know about bras, haw haw haw…

To add fuel to the fire, some evil-minded motherfucker (he suspected Ted, the goofy sports guy) left a frilly, purple bra on Suzanne's desk. Naturally, suspicion quickly fell on *guess who?* and before you could say "Alfie Dreyfus", Les received a curt summons and found himself face-to-face with an irate Duane Shipman.

"Jesus *Christ*, Les!" The station manager erupted, twirling the incriminating undergarment on his finger like an erotic lariat, "this is too fucking much, okay? You've gone too far this time, can't you see that?"

141

"Could I say something? First of all, I am not responsible for the prank in question, nor do I have any knowledge—"

"Oh, *bullshit*," Suzanne barked. "You are one sick bastard, you know that, Kincaid? You're sick and you're disgusting and your ass is *suspended*. Tell him, Duane."

Suddenly Les had to sit down. "Yeah, Duane," he echoed weakly, "tell me."

So Duane told him. Two weeks off the air, eager beaver Candace filling in in his absence, trying the big chair on for size. An apology to Suzanne in front of the entire staff *and* mandatory enrollment in a "gender sensitization" workshop. Les had a feeling that last part was Suzanne's contribution. She knew how he felt about "group therapy, feel good seminars, self-help gurus and weirdos of the subconscious" (to quote from one of his on-air tirades).

After laying down the law, Duane leaned back in his chair, clasped his hands behind his head, glanced over at Suzanne—

And *winked*.

That did it.

Les had been getting madder and madder as their mini-Inquisition number played out to its preordained conclusion. The suspension came as a genuine shock and the fact that the people upstairs were apparently backing Duane in this power play, while expecting Lester J. Kincaid to bend over and take it up the you-know-what—

He was primed to blow, all right.

When he saw Duane drop his eyelid in Suzanne's direction, well, it was like something way back in the cobwebbed recesses of Les's ancient hindbrain reared up and *roared*.

Lunging across the desk, he grabbed the front of his boss's shirt, twisting it in his fist and jerking him forward, directly into the path of a looping right hook that connected somewhere near his left ear. Duane *yelped* in pain/surprise/panic and ducked below the level of the desk, nearly pulling Les over on top of him as the irate radio host rained mainly ineffectual blows on his neck and shoulders.

Suzanne flung herself on Les, trying to pry him off her lover, but when Les growled low in his throat and bared his coffee-stained teeth, she backed away in a hurry.

"Goddamnit, Les," Duane moaned from underneath the desk, "it wasn't supposed to be like this."

"Fuck you, Duane," Les spat, panting from the exertion. He climbed off the desk and Suzanne retreated, keeping a safe distance between them.

"Okay, whatever," came the reply. "By the way, uh, obviously your services will no longer, uh, be required."

Les had to laugh. "Yeah, I figured." Bonnie and one of the other receptionists were at the door. They peered inside, their expressions timid, fearful. Not eager to involve themselves.

"Please escort Mr. Kincaid from the building," the desk ordered imperiously. "His employment is terminated and he is permanently barred from the premises."

But neither of them moved to obey him and after a minute or two Les left of his own volition, taking with him nothing but his jacket.

He walked out with his head held high, marching down the front steps to the sidewalk, following it around to the parking lot behind the station...and then just standing there, while they crowded at the windows, watching him, everyone wondering what he was going to do next.

It bugged Les the way the kids *ran* to Pam when she came home from work, like she was liberating them from Attila the Hun or Freddy Krueger.

True, he was much harder on them than she was, fussy about the way things were done and uptight when something unforeseen screwed up his daily routine. It was unfair to expect kids their age to meet his standards of meticulousness *all* the time but he still couldn't help flaring about stuff like—like how many times he had caught Dougie in the frigging garbage. No matter how often Les told him, the kid just wouldn't learn. He had some kind of trash fetish. Threats and spankings did absolutely no good. Likely nothing short of killing him would.

Audrey was different (in more ways than one). But at least you could reason with Audrey. She was old enough to understand the way the world worked and much more adept at reading his moods. She was sharp too, often displaying wisdom far beyond her years. One day they were out walking and she spotted a dead moth being carried off by a platoon of ants. "Oh, well," she remarked, "that's life." And once Dougie came to him, crying, claiming that Audrey had whacked him and when confronted, she immediately 'fessed up. "I told him not to touch my nanny (*blanket*)," she explained, "I told him if he did, I would hit him."

Truth and consequences.

He admired her strength of mind, that familiar streak of self-righteousness.

He had to admit, she came by it honestly.

"I don't know. It's hard to put it into words or a—a context. I'm not feeling fulfilled and there's this sense that half my brain has gone to sleep on me. I feel like I'm only partly here. I want to have some kind of existence outside the kids. There's more to me than Mr. Mom. I used to have a career...I used to have a *life*."

"I understand. You're right. You're a vital and dynamic man and you need that extra energy channeled into something."

"*I'm going out of my fucking mind.* I mean it's *Dad, Dad, Dad* day in and day out, until I'm actively pondering infanticide. This isn't funny, Pam, goddamnit."

"I'm sorry. You've had a rough day with the kids. They must both be going through a really bad phase right now. It sounds like they're being extra demanding. Hang in there. They're growing up so darned fast. Audrey's just about ready for kindergarten and—"

"No, you don't understand..."

"Things will look up, you'll see. Your name might be mud for awhile but sooner or later somebody's gonna call. They can't keep you off the air forever, darlin'. There'd be rioting in the streets." She rubbed his shoulders, digging her thumbs into the taut sinew and muscle. "Consider this a much-needed vacation."

"Yeah, but..." He couldn't finish, couldn't explain.

"You're a star, sweetheart, and don't ever forget it." Kissing his bald spot.

"Thanks," Les sighed. "You're a great lady, you know that? My number one fan."

"Darlin', like the man with the big lips says: 'Wild horses couldn't drag me away…'"

"—sorry, Mr. Kincaid, but there are simply no tables available. The entire dining room has been booked for a wedding banquet."

"Look, maybe you didn't hear me. This is *Les Kincaid*. Les Kincaid. Doesn't that name ring any bells? C'mon, man, this is our anniversary we're talking about. I'd consider it a personal favor and, hey, I'm more than willing to make it worth your while, if you get my meaning."

"Perhaps if you had phoned earlier in the week—"

"Hey, pal, do you know who you're talking to?"

"Yes, certainly, you already said."

"*And?*"

"And if you'd only gotten in touch earlier in the week we might have been able to…"

"Dougie, *goddamnit*—" It was the absolute last and final straw. The stupid brat stood up to his ankles in an incriminating debris field of eggshells, tea bags and coffee grounds.

The slap was high, catching Dougie on the side of his head with enough force to knock him back into the mess he'd made. Dougie moaned, drawing up into a ball, trying to make himself as small as possible. "*Why won't you learn?*" Les bellowed. "*Why do you have to be so fucking stupid? Why? Why? WHY?*"

"—sorry, daddy, sorry…" Dougie whimpered, Les looming over him, his anger making him appear ten feet tall in Dougie's eyes, with razor sharp teeth and hands made of stone.

"What's wrong with you?" Les yelled, kicking at the trash around Dougie's legs, resisting the urge to clout him again for good measure. The boy cowered, blubbering, almost incoherent:

"…Aud-wee…Aud-wee said I could…she tol' me …"

Maybe it was true and maybe not.

At that moment, it didn't matter.

She was in their room, sitting on the side of her bed.

Les watched her from the doorway. Her head was bowed and a fringe of straight, dark hair hid her face. He went over to the child's desk in the corner, picked up a pair of plastic scissors that were lying on top of some mutilated sheets of construction paper. Not thinking of anything, his head empty and airless; a vacuum, a *void*.

He approached the bed, snagged some of her fine hair between his fingers and *hacked* away at it, starting on her bangs and working his way around. The scissors were dull, pulling and ripping her hair, and she started crying, a rarity for her—*"no, daddy, no, please…"*—but if he heard, he gave no indication.

"She did the worst of it herself," he informed a horrified Pam that night, lying with an ease that should have bothered him. "I tried to fix it but gave up. Better to just let it grow out."

"It looks—good heavens, sweetie, what would make you *do* such a thing?"

But Audrey only shook her head, crying soundlessly, so Pam hugged her, surrounding her with comforting arms. Dougie, meanwhile, bounced around the room, hollering "Gimme haircut too, Daddy!" until Les finally told him to shut up. Pam gave him a funny look but said nothing. Her arms tightening about her daughter, instinctively seeking to protect her from further indignity.

"Shhhhh, baby, shhhhh…"

"Hello and welcome to 'The Afternoon Show'. I'm your host, Candace Wilcox and today, among other things, we'll be looking at the growing problem of sexual harassment in the workplace—"

. . .

The station rejected mediation and offered an insultingly meager severance package, considering the numbers he'd racked up for them over the years. They obviously thought they were in a strong bargaining position. After all, *so far* Duane hadn't laid any charges but there were two very hostile witnesses who could testify to the attack and to misogynistic and insensitive comments, insubordination, and so on. Their lawyers more or less threatened to ruin his good name and fuck his mother unless he accepted their generous terms and got the hell out of Dodge.

Phil Wade, Les's attorney, wasn't hopeful about winning any sort of wrongful dismissal suit. "You'd be getting into a pissing contest with a skunk the size of the *Hindenberg*. Take the money, Les, accept a few months of purgatory, a year at the most, then announce your big comeback. But...you might want to consider a move at some point, just in case I'm wrong and people around here have longer memories than I think."

So he took their offer. He admitted no blame or impropriety and in his only public statement spoke of a difference in philosophies, an amiable parting of the ways. The old-timers weren't fooled for a minute.

"Poor Les. Never saw which way the pendulum was swinging. Got it right in the balls."

They decided, although Les needed some persuading, that Pam would accept a special contract job designing an on-line mentoring program. It added up to an extra four thousand dollars that they could use to pay the house and car insurance and top up their RRSPs.

It also meant Pam staying after work and going in on weekends for awhile, leaving him stuck with the kids for even *longer* periods of time.

Meanwhile, he was running out of things to do with them. Neither was much interested in TV or DVDs (besides a few favorites), and while he could get Dougie screwing around with playdough or fingerpainting, Audrey couldn't be bothered with such childish things. Usually he left her to her own devices, which meant she spent most of the day in her room, "reading" picture books or listening to the ones she had on tape and CD. It kept her out of sight and (usually) out of trouble...well, except for when she did things like use a black permanent marker to "polish" her shoes or the time she washed her toys in the sink and flooded the bathroom.

And whereas he would've given poor Dougie a swat for committing far less serious infractions, with Audrey it was harder to punish—

Gimme haircut too, Daddy

—something about the way she looked at him now, without fear, without feeling, without *anything*.

"—and then I heard about the P.D. job here through an old buddy of mine and, well, what can I say? I got lucky."

"That's great, Tony. If anyone deserves it, it's you. God knows, you've paid your dues."

"Thanks, Les. Coming from you, that means a lot."

"No jiving, that's the honest truth. Glad you landed on your feet. I'm, ah, hoping to do the same. As you've no doubt heard, I am presently seeking employment and willing to explore any reasonable offers. So, y'know, make sure to spread the word."

"Will do, Les. Yeah, I heard you got canned. What did you do, grab somebody's ass or something?"

"There was more to it than that." Distracted by Dougie coming down the hall, peeking around the corner. Waving him away.

"So what happened? The boss walk in on you or—"

"No, you've got it all wrong, man. Believe it or not, I'm completely innocent."

"Ho ho. Sure you are."

"No kidding, Tony. I'm being railroaded and that's no bullshit. It's something cooked up by that asshole Duane and—hang on a sec." Dougie was still hovering about, trying to get his attention. "Would you piss off? I'm on the *phone*."

"—have any plans?"

"Plans? I'm looking for a job, man."

"Sure, but what I'm saying is maybe now might be a good time to get certain things in perspective. Do some self-reflection. Use this opportunity and, y'know, take a good, hard look at yourself, your life, the way you approach things. Make some changes and—and get with the program."

"I'm a professional, Tony, what more do they want? I show up and do my job every day, five days a week, forty-eight weeks of the year, year in and year out— *Dougie, would you get lost?*"

"—mean you have a license to be an asshole. I guess what I'm saying is, there's a message here maybe you're not seeing and it's telling you to straighten up, be more of a team player. That's what they're looking for these days and we both know it."

"You don't say. Jesus, Tony, what happened to you? The moment you become program director you start spouting the party line."

"It's called growing up, Les. Give it a try some time."

"Hey, Tony: fuck you."

"Right back at ya, Les. Don't call me, I'll call you."

"Don't bother."

"I won't."

Hardly putting down the phone before: "Daddy, can Aud-wee haf a—"

The next thing Les knew, he had Dougie by the arm and he was *charging* down the hallway, moving so fast Dougie's toes were barely touching the floor. All Les was thinking at that moment was how sick and tired he was of having kids and what he wouldn't give to be shed of them, both of them—

"—*ow, daddy, you're hurting*—"

There was only so much you could do with children their age, only so many trips to the park and the library you could take before the novelty wore off. Everything revolved around them, *their* wants and needs. When was the last time he and Pam had gone to see a movie or had an evening to themselves or had really great sex?

Bam!

Booting open the door with the "Pooh Bear" growth chart on it and slinging Dougie into the room ahead of him.

Audrey was playing with cutouts and listening to her favorite Robert Munsch CD. She didn't look up at the commotion, merely paused, giving the impression of waiting expectantly. "*Don't you assholes understand? I want to be left alone.*" She still hadn't reacted so he grabbed her shoulder and gave her a shake. The cutouts slid off her lap and fluttered to the floor.

Les thought he was going to out and out *kill* her when he realized what she'd done. She had taken some of their best pictures and snipped the figures out. The Kincaid family were scattered on the carpet, most of them landing face up, smiling Pam in her Ecuadorian sweater and Dougie, captured in mid-squirm—

—*fucking pictures were part of a set, almost two hundred bucks and the little bitch*—

Then he saw it, a bit separate from the others, saw what she had done to him or, rather, his likeness, with scissors and colored markers and *hate*. Les swayed, feeling light-headed, nauseous, suddenly wanting nothing more than to flee from the presence of this thing, this *creature*. Audrey made no move to retrieve or conceal the cut-outs. She ignored Les, turning her attention to Dougie, who was holding his arm and moaning, carrying on like the bloody bone was sticking out through the skin. Audrey started humming and that served two purposes: it comforted Dougie and drove her father from the room.

Les took one last look from the doorway. Audrey was rocking back and forth on the bed, humming or keening or whatever the hell you called it. Dougie was at her feet, poking at the cut-outs, favoring his sore arm. As he walked down the hallway, Les could hear his son ask, more out of curiosity than concern: "Who hurted daddy, Aud-wee? Who hurted his picha? See? See?"

...while the ogre was preparing his massive oven for the horrific feast, his children crept

up behind him and tucked his apron strings inside, so that they brushed against the red-hot coals.

The ogre's clothes caught fire and he rolled around and around on the floor, trying to extinguish the flames. In desperation, he begged his children to come to his aid, but they waited until the ogre's arms and legs had burned off and his eyeballs were boiled in their sockets before they finally relented, emptying their bladders onto what remained of him.

The ogre spent the rest of his days blind and immobile, tormented by his ghastly injuries. He was totally reliant on his family, who cared for him and saw to his every need. At night, his devoted daughter would often go in and sing to him, a haunting ditty he seemed to recognize. She said it was a melody from another time, another place, a distant and dimly remembered past when he had lived and laughed and known something other than pain.

One day, she'd teach the strange song to her daughters. Crooning to them until they knew it by heart, adamant that it would preserve them from harm.

Death Threats

I ACTUALLY BELIEVED I was dying. Terminally ill. My life dangling by a thin, tenuous thread.

I had all the classic symptoms: dizziness, blurred vision, headaches; heart palpitations, shortness of breath. Loss of libido, lack of appetite, insomnia...

I remember trying to tell you about it. Not to alarm you or anything, just mentioning in passing that I wasn't feeling so great. But it was after we'd turned in so maybe the timing wasn't right. Yes, that explains it. Because you were tired and noncommittal. Not exactly forthcoming with the reassurances I was seeking. Falling asleep within a few seconds, as usual. Leaving me to thrash things out, wakeful and fretting long into the night.

And it wasn't about turning forty or the latest stuff with my dad or Barb's chemotherapy, Uncle Arnold's dementia. Those may have been contributing factors but there had to be more to it than that. I'm sure of it.

I developed mortal dreads. It got really, really bad. To the extent that I couldn't leave the apartment. The tenants would call and I'd say I had the flu. Sometimes I'd sit in our big armchair all day and shake. I had visions—very real and sickeningly graphic—tumors growing inside me, feasting on my organs, gnawing at my brain stem.

I am cursed with an especially vivid imagination.

The worst of it lasted two or three weeks before, gradually, the pall lifted and some light shone through.

You never suspected, never even had an inkling of how awful it was.

To be nearly paralyzed by fear, unmanned by anxieties with no rational source. Lying in sweat-soaked pajamas night after night, turning everything over in my mind, an endless series of gruesome scenarios, trying to anticipate what might be coming, expecting the very, very worst...

. . .

Tess walked in as I was weighing myself. We have a digital scale, accurate as an atomic clock. Bright green numerals, easy to read. I was still mulling over what they signified when she made her surprise entrance.

Normally the bathroom is a "no go" zone when I'm in there. Call it a guy thing, or maybe it's a manifestation of childhood fears of inadequacy or merely a petulant display of emotional immaturity on my part. When I'm in the john, I'm in there on private business and she usually knows to wait her turn.

But she was hustling that morning and, to be fair, gave a couple of taps before barging in. Looking for the mate of her favorite earring, which, it turned out, she never found. A pearl teardrop doohickey she picked up in Italy. Wouldn't tell me what it cost.

It wasn't on the counter by the window so she reversed direction, preoccupied and annoyed, finally noticing me, perched on the scale like a giant, sway-backed crane.

"You're losing weight," she observed. Reaching out and pinching a flap of skin by my navel. "Lookin' good." She had to stand on tiptoes to peck my cheek. Then she was gone.

"Down four pounds in the past week," I called after her.

"Good for you." Still worrying about her bloody earring.

And there I was, y'know, *dying*.

The internet. Designed and constructed for the socially impaired and chronically self-obsessed: trivia buffs, perverts, fan boys, completists and hypochondriacs.

It took me only moments to discover I was seven pounds under the optimum weight for males my size. Then I started poking around, looking up various conditions and afflictions and found out far more than I needed to know about heart disease, cancer, diabetes, M.S., Cystic Fibrosis, ALS and leprosy (hey, why not?).

I blew an entire Saturday morning surfing from site to site, reading reams of stuff on chronic, wasting illnesses…and for the rest of that weekend I was *useless*. I couldn't get over how many different ways there were to die and how few of them were pleasant and dignified.

I also learned that cloudy urine might signify renal dysfunction and my dizzy spells could be caused by a walnut-sized tumor on my cerebral cortex. The tingling in my fingers and toes, how cold my extremities got, indicated poor circulation, and the constant cramping in my legs might be relieved by taking extra doses of potassium and drinking more water.

I came to the conclusion that the most merciful end for me would probably be a massive heart attack. It would hurt like bejesus but hopefully I'd lose consciousness right away. No prolonged, painful death for yours truly, I wouldn't be able to handle that.

—flashing to the face of Coach Busby, yelling at me as old Mike, our trainer, tried to straighten my ring finger after a collision with a monstrous center from a rival school. But I couldn't stop bawling and even after they taped me up, I wouldn't go back in. Sat on the end of the bench, cradling my hand, crying like a baby. What a dope.

"Big bastard like you," Busby snapped at me the next day in his office, "acting like a sissy in front of the team. You should be a man among boys," he said, his tone more resigned than angry. "You always play like you're afraid of getting hurt."

I was benched, Travis Brossard taking over at point guard. Coach Busby stuck with the story that my finger was to blame for the demotion. A small act of kindness on his part.

But my teammates were there, witnesses to my disgrace, and I could see from their faces that none of them were fooled.

Somehow I'd forgotten the Seattle conference. More likely I'd blocked it out.

But there was no denying it now: her bags were on the bed and I could hear hangers rattling in the closet. My legs gave out and I sat on the edge of the mattress, feeling shaky. I didn't want to be left alone. Not in the state I was in. I'd be too

154

freaked out. The emptiness of the apartment. Suppose something *really* went haywire in the building, something I couldn't handle? And if I went out, the streets would be filled with faces and none if them would be welcoming or familiar.

I'm a creature of habit. Last year the owners decided to repaint the exterior of our building. They hired a local outfit to scrape and sand it down and redid the whole thing in this drab blue, so neutral it's almost grey. Every time I go outside, it *still* gives me a jolt.

And this past winter Tess changed the towels in the bathroom, replacing the dark, navy ones with a nice, marine green set. I hated them on sight and had to pretend it was all right, no problem, change whatever you want, nail the furniture to the goddamn ceiling for all I care. Feigned nonchalance: I'm getting good at it.

But, meanwhile, packing for Seattle, departure time looming...

Making small talk. What sessions she'd be attending and the name of the keynote speaker. All of it acknowledged, noted and quickly forgotten.

On to more important things. Apropos nothing: "So, um, if I was, y'know, an invalid, like braindead or that locked in syndrome, comatose but not technically—"

"I'd smother you." Barely giving it any thought, holding up a cream blouse, checking if it went with her favorite skirt.

Later, as she vacillated between two different pairs of walking shoes: "And—and if I found out I had only three months left to live—"

"Empty our savings, cash in our RRSPs and go on a round-the-world trip," she filled in without pause. "Paris, Madrid, Rome, the whole shebang." Settling on the Merrill sneakers, they were better for her arches.

She caught a cab to the airport. Said there was no point me tagging along. Kind of a brusque "good-bye" at the front door. Warning me to behave myself, managing to miss my mouth with an errant kiss.

I waved from the entranceway, telling myself to be brave, she'd be back in nine days, no need to keep standing there, she was *gone* and nothing was going to change that simple, irrefutable fact...

* * *

I made out my will. Tore up the old one and started fresh.

Except I couldn't think of anything to say. Total blank. Finally had to resort to taping the previous version back together and recopying it. Except for the poem at the end. I switched to something by William Butler Yeats. From a book I found in a thrift store, fifty cents and heavily highlighted by its previous owner.

Dr. Varney wasn't convinced anything was wrong but booked me for a full round of tests anyway. Blood work, urine…I even had to provide a stool sample.

But my intestinal fortitude was further tested when he announced his intention to perform a digital rectal examination. "You're, what, nearly forty. It's probably time." Looking at me, unable to hide his amusement at my obvious discomfort. "And we want to eliminate all possibilities, don't we?"

No argument there. "Fine," I agreed, and the next thing I knew I was making an appointment to undergo the most invasive medical procedure imaginable. That was one red-bordered square on the calendar I wouldn't be looking forward to.

Varney tried to put me at ease. "Nothing to worry about," offering me a rare, crooked smile, "you're still a pup."

"What about the weight loss?"

"Keep it up," heading for the door, "I should lose some myself."

I received a much more sympathetic hearing from Edith Carmody. I explained the situation in detail as I banged away ineffectually beneath her sink. There was a leak somewhere but do you think I could find it? I paused and just then a drop of water splashed onto my cheek. Where the bloody hell did *that* come from?

I cursed but ol' Edith didn't seem to mind. She was eighty-five, deaf as a tree and blind in one eye. Thanks to a stroke she hadn't spoken in a decade but despite her infirmities still somehow managed on her own. A community aid worker came by once or twice a week and her grandchildren sometimes visited, but otherwise she fended for herself. "Sorry, ma'am." I crawled out from under the sink, wiped my hands on an old t-shirt I kept in my toolkit. "This one's beyond me."

She didn't respond, hardly seemed to be breathing. It had taken her ten minutes to walk the few steps from her living room to the kitchen. But she made it. Inching along with the aid of her walker. Operating more out of instinct than conscious intent. As light and insubstantial as a flapping sheet. If I was getting on the thin side, she was positively *spectral*.

"Looks like we're gonna have to call in Ernst, Mrs. C." In truth, I was hopeless at plumbing and even worse when it came to wiring or anything to do with the building's ancient heating and air circulation system. I think my ineptitude was an open secret among tenants. They didn't seem to hold it against me; at least I knew enough to bring in an expert rather than jury-rig something that was bound to go south at the first opportunity.

She gave me a slow wink. Not my imagination, her left eyelid definitely dipped in ironic acknowledgement. So someone was still in there after all. Someone all too aware of what a useless caretaker I was. Not to be trusted with anything more challenging than a sticky door or more sophisticated than a plunger.

I'd fibbed—well, maybe it was more than that—when we first moved in, claiming I'd worked for my journeyman father, learning basic plumbing and wiring at his feet. Not quite true. Okay, not at all true. Before he got sick, my father worked for thirty years in the city greenhouse and didn't know one end of a hammer from another. But at that point I'd been out of work for eight months and Tess was just getting started at the bank so reduced rent sounded too good to resist.

Most of the time I winged it and when I was stumped and couldn't stall any longer, I brought in someone like Ernst. The owners, some management company out of Calgary, occasionally groused about the bills I submitted, but considering the age of the building and the amount of deterioration, all in all I think I ran a pretty tight ship. So far the place hadn't fallen down on my watch and we'd dodged major renos and that definitely worked in my favor.

"I'll see if he can make it by tomorrow. This has been dragging on too long." *Time*? What did time mean to someone her age? What was a day, a week, to her? Like the blink of an eye…

It would be great to see Ernst again. Ernst Rathgeber. As in "Ernst Rathgeber & Son". Only there is no "Son", not anymore, just Ernst, his four "majors", two bypasses and the pacemaker that keeps him on his feet and gainfully employed.

If anyone could help me come to terms with my fears and anxieties, the terror of living day to day in the valley of the shadow of death, it was Ernst. He'd been there, man. On the brink of crossing over. Stared into the Abyss. And it hadn't fazed him, not one bit.

"I vas dead two, mebbe tree minutes. Zey told me later. Zey gave me last rights, ja? Und no vone expected I should live. But here I am." A pack of Export A cigarettes crammed in his shirt pocket, an eager young apprentice along for the scut work. Lugging and toting, paying his dues while learning at the feet of a master. "Zis old building," he clucked his tongue. "One day, *ker-poof*! Vy do ve bother, eh? Bash it down, start again vit ze new. No? You don't sink? Okay, 'til zen ve try to make it vork."

"Don't you have any sense of nostalgia?" I liked to kid him and he enjoyed being kidded. His assistant was unpacking his tools in front of the sink. Laying everything out like in an operating theater.

"Everything old must make vay for ze new. Zat is nature und you cannot fool vit nature. Ve die und somesing better succeeds us. Survival of ze fittest. More power to it, I say."

"I'm not sure I like the sound of that," I confessed. "According to your standards, I'm already obsolete."

He jabbed a thumb at Edith Carmody, who, having completed an epic journey of just over two meters, was slumped in a kitchen chair, snoring, her chin on her collapsed chest. "You vould rather be like zat vone? Caught between two vorlds?" Shaking his head in disgust. "Better to eat a bullet, *ja*?" He turned his attention to the recalcitrant sink, grimacing at what he expected to find. "*Ach*. Und zis plumbing. It is even older zen *she* is…"

· · ·

Tess called from Seattle. A rush job, between sessions and sounding like she couldn't wait to get back at it. I said maybe ten words. She ignored them, even the last three, the most important ones, left hanging there, like a song missing its final notes.

I love you.

Her silence speaking volumes, an excruciating interval that accentuated the distance between us, two thousand miles and growing by the second.

A clean bill of health from Doc Varney and he was the only one who seemed pleased by the results. A single sheet of paper contained all the relevant information. Is that possible?

"Nothing anomalous, everything well within norms..."

I kept staring at him. He was expecting me to say something. Waiting for me to break into a grin and grip his hand in abject gratitude. Instead I just sat there, looking at him. Finally he leaned back in his ergonomic chair, his expression vexed. "I must say, this isn't the reaction I expected—*what's that?*" I must have formed the syllables. "What did you say?"

"You're wrong," I told him. "There's something you've missed."

Now clearly perturbed by my attitude, he snapped the folder shut and stood, signaling the conference was over. All but ushering me out.

I started the car, then reached over and turned it off.

Sat there awhile and gradually that horrible weight or sense of oppression that had been hovering over me for weeks sort of...well, it wasn't *gone* but it seemed to dissipate, at least a little. From a dangerous, threatening sky to a heavy overcast. But definitely an improvement.

No more bad spells, not even a month later when I found Edith Carmody on her living room floor. I didn't lose it and was even able to close her eyes for her. Maybe it was because she was so old and on some level I'd been expecting it. It also might have had something to do with the airless calm I felt in her presence that day. I didn't see any sign of pain or struggle, her passing swift and seemingly unforced, made without fuss or regret.

The Future

AND THEN IT WAS SUNDAY night, nearly nine o'clock. *Shit, how did it get to be so late?* No putting it off any longer. Conrad marked his place halfway through *The Golden Apples of the Sun,* setting it aside with regret.

Time to get with the program. First, haul his sad sack ass out of bed and find his school binder under that two-foot pile of clothes and miscellaneous debris over in the corner. The binder in question was in rough shape, papers sticking out every which way, torn loose from the metal rings, unattached handouts going back to the beginning of the semester. Conrad dropped the mess on his desk and switched on a gooseneck lamp, adjusting the light so it was facing away from him. His eyes definitely feeling the effects of a couple hours of steady reading. Man, that Bradbury guy could write!

He took his time getting set up. Went through his notes until he located the assignment (though he'd known where it was all along). Flipped to the back, liberating three or four sheets of blank loose leaf. Then a brief but spirited search for a pen, finally locating a Bic, the kind you could shoot into a block of wood and it would still write perfectly afterward. The commercials were *great*.

Tested it out with a few errant lines and squiggles: medium point blue, just the way he liked it.

Then, without hesitation, commencing work on the assignment.

Wrote: *The Shape of the Future*

Then his name: *Conrad Dahl*

Just like that. Well, okay, he came up with the title last week. But it was still damn good. It led you right into it and he bent forward in the chair, pen poised over the page, waiting for inspiration to strike.

Unfortunately, what popped into mind, completely unbidden, was the lovely face of Bonnie Gottselig. Not an unwelcome sight, by any means, but did it have to be right *now*? Conrad could picture her clearly, the shallow cleft in her chin, the scar beside her eye from where a swing seat hit her back in grade five. And that "V" of skin at the base of her throat when she left the top button undone. He found that particular portion of her anatomy absolutely mesmerizing. To the extent that the other day she caught him staring at her and, get this, slipped him a wink. *The sly little fox...*

Oops, almost forgot the date. Miss Bigelow was really strict about that. She'd dock you marks. If she wasn't so lustfully good-looking, he'd almost hate her.

May 4th, 1975

Would future historians attach special significance to that day? It hardly seemed likely. As far as he was concerned, it was just as dull and pointless as all the rest. But isn't each *second* important and unique in its own right? An interesting philosophical counter-argument, one that posed certain—

That line of thought snipped off by an abrupt change of scene: walking in and surprising Miss Bigelow as she was getting dressed (for some reason) in her classroom. Turning toward him, her shirt unbuttoned, the white cups of her bra exposed. And not exactly in a huge hurry to cover herself...

Okay, okay, stick to the assignment. Grasping his boner impatiently, shifting it to a more comfortable angle.

Suddenly, the opening came to him and Conrad scribbled:

Within fifteen years the Soviet Union will land the first man on Mars. A war will break out a short time afterward but our side will win because of a secret base on the Moon, which provides us with important strategic advantages. The Russians will be forced to surrender—

He hunted around for his thesaurus, looked up "surrender", then scratched that out and replaced it with "capitulate". *Much* better. He found himself noticing that more lately. The way certain words went together, how it sounded when they combined. Bradbury was good at that, providing enough description so that you saw a scene vividly, like it was happening right in front of you.

The other day Miss Huard, his math teacher, confessed to feeling *logy*. *Bowdlerize* and *inchoate* and *sanguine*; he collected funky-sounding words and phrases like some people collected stamps.

Ten years after the war, most of the world is united under one government, except Japan and China, who form a dangerous new alliance in the Far East...

For the past few months the news had been filled with images of the Americans getting the *hell* out of Saigon, barely escaping ahead of the Commies. There were helicopters taking off, mobs stampeding to get on board. Vietnam was just this tiny country but they were basically kicking made-in-America ass. They had to be pretty tough people to slap around the US of A like that. *Nobody* seemed to like Yankees in that part of the world.

His dad said you could never really trust a *chink*, they were clever, resourceful and totally ruthless. One of his bosses, Mr. Cho, was a prime example. When things went right, who took the credit? And when everything went south, guess who dodged the fallout? Smart, those people. You had to hand it to them.

Conrad's father, Alan Dahl, was currently facing some kind of disciplinary action because of Cho. There had been a major league screw-up at work and his father was made into the scapegoat. Conrad asked but no one seemed willing or able to explain what was going on. Like it was some kind of state secret or something.

By the year 2000 most serious diseases will be—

Destroyed? No, *eradicated!* Much better.

—and people will be living longer lives. There will be an end to world hunger thanks to scientific advances in agriculture and medicine...

He faltered. In truth, he knew little about science and cared less. Science and math, the banes of his existence. Endless combinations of numbers and equations to memorize and spew out on demand. Any vocation requiring the use of a machine more advanced than a pocket calculator was not for him.

So dump the science crapola.

People will not only be living longer lives, they can also replace vital organs with transplants so that their bodies never wear out.

Ah, he thought, but that means—

With people living extended lives, the population skyrockets to astronomical levels, which leads to a demand for colonies, the human species venturing deeper and deeper into the solar system...

Now Conrad was on firmer ground and could let his imagination run wild. Scratching away, he envisioned an ambitious, space-faring civilization. Enormous vessels, half a mile long, constructed in orbital drydocks, capable of reaching the Oort Cloud in a matter of weeks. And a massive, double-wheeled space station, hovering above the blue splendor of Mother Earth, rotating to give inhabitants the impression of gravity. Ten thousand people lived on the *Clarke*, the facility serving as a way station for liners and ore transporters and all manner of vehicles that flitted about human space.

The first years of the 21st century will be a time of great wealth and a desire for adventure. Space will become an important if not essential tourist destination for travelers wishing to experience the wonder and beauty of exotic, unknown places.

He re-read the paragraph he had just written, nodding in satisfaction. He was about to continue when he heard the front door opening. That would be his father, finally making it home.

Let the strangeness begin...

"When does a marriage stop being a marriage?" Peg once cracked. But she could afford to make jokes. She wasn't around to watch their weird act unfold, night after night. He could hear his father hanging up his coat in the closet, cursing when a hanger clattered to the floor. Conrad snuck over and cracked open his door. His father was moving around in the kitchen. Sheila, Conrad's mother, was in the living room, likely curled up with a book and her third (or fourth) glass of wine. His parents rarely spoke these days, their exchanges short and to the point. Business-like.

It was obvious something had happened between them, something that poisoned the air, causing a deep and permanent rift. Whatever it was, neither side seemed willing to acknowledge it or call it by name. Better, maybe, to ignore the problem, pretend it didn't exist…or hope it would go away on its own.

These days his father was prickly, easily wounded. Withdrawn, barely participating in family life. For her part, Sheila basically ignored him, left his food out and did his laundry, that was about it. Her attitude was dismissive, almost contemptuous. And for the past month or so he'd been demoted to sleeping on the couch. They thought Conrad was unaware of that development but they were kidding themselves.

A chair scraped on linoleum. A fragile silence, the air in the house unnaturally still. Alan Dahl had had another long, hard day at work. Doing penance for whatever they thought he'd done. Probably stopped off for a few belts of courage on the way home.

The fridge cut out with a *clunk*. It needed a new compressor.

There was movement from the living room as Sheila stirred herself, padding past the kitchen on her way to the bathroom. Not pausing to greet her husband or acknowledge his existence. Closing the door behind her. Moments later the shower curtain rattled and the water came on. She did love her baths.

No sound from the kitchen. *Nothing*.

It was downright creepy. Conrad started back toward the desk, switching directions so he could grab his transistor radio off the nightstand. Piece of shit *Realistic*; the earphone cut in and out and it only picked up AM. He caught the tail end of a news update and then a bombshell:

"*The flags are flying at half-mast in Stoogeville tonight, folks. Moe Howard from the Three Stooges has passed away from lung cancer. That's right, Moe Howard, dead at seventy-seven. Truly the end of an era. Those guys were great, weren't they? Hey, I got a Stones super-set coming up, right after—*"

He had an extension in his room, used it to call Neil. "Holy shit, man, did you hear? Moe's dead. From the Three Stooges?"

"No way." *Crunch, crunch*.

"You eating something?"

"Yeah. Your mama." *Crunch, crunch*.

"You've been listening to too many Richard Pryor albums, man."

"Yeah? Hey, you catch Boom-Boom on Friday?" Neil's nickname for Miss Bigelow. *Crunch, crunch.* "That blouse she was wearing. Those buttons must of been sewed on with fuckin' fishing line. To hold those babies in." *Crunch, crunch, crunch.*

Conrad made a face. Sad, but true: his best friend was the worst sex deviant in grade seven. Neil's knowledge of female anatomy was mind-boggling. He knew the lingo and could tell you in great detail what went where. Sometimes he stole his father's old *Hustlers.* They showed *everything*, even stuff you didn't want to see.

Now Neil was going on about the new girl, Naomi what's her name. Apparently she looked amazingly hot in gym shorts.

"Hey, man, you finish that English assignment yet?"

"Which one?" *Crunch, crunch, crunch.*

"The essay about life in the future."

"Oh, yeah." *Crunch, crunch.* "I mostly copied from a *Newsweek.* One we had lying around."

Conrad gritted his teeth. "Gotta go, man."

"Me too." *Crunch, crunch, crunch.* "'The Six Million Dollar Man' is on."

"You are the idiot offspring of an ugly, fat chick." Slamming the receiver down.

Let him crunch on *that.*

He turned up the radio and managed to catch the last half of "Space Oddity". Perfect mood music.

Except then he remembered, holy shit, it was "Space Oddity" that was playing when Bonnie came up to him and asked him to dance. Good grief. Neil and Tom kept egging him on but he made up some dopey excuse, completely chickening out on the greatest moment of his life. And the thing was, he knew at the time he was going to regret it *and went ahead and did it anyway.* Which, to his mind, was the ultimate sign of stupidity. Yet one more compelling reason why he was doomed to remain a virgin to his dying day.

By the year 2020 (he continued doggedly), *mankind will reach the outer limits of our solar system. Thanks to advances in computers, we can send robot ships to the nearest stars. Soon we come into contact with different species other than our own and are asked to join a federation of free planets...*

Holy crap, Conrad thought, this is taking place in *my* lifetime. I'll be, what, sixty years old. And by then people will live to a hundred and twenty, maybe longer, so when you look at it like that—

He heard his father in the hallway outside the bathroom door.

tap tap tap

Conrad never caught what she said but it must have been stabbing sharp because Big Al practically *scuttled* away, retreating to the living room with his tail between his legs. Where, out of sheer spite, he switched on the TV and upped the volume. Which meant once her bath was done, Sheila would stomp off to the bedroom with her book...and so much for another thrilling evening at the Dahl residence.

All at once, he missed Peggie. She could be a giant pain, especially around her period, but at least she was someone who knew about the strange dynamics in this house and what living here was like. He thought about calling her but dreaded having to deal with Rafe. Rafe zoned out or Rafe the bullying asshole or Rafe conveniently forgetting to mention he'd phoned and left a message. Living with Rafe, presumably, preferable to sticking it out here at home but, for the life of him, Conrad couldn't see *how*.

Having Peg around had given their folks someone to focus their insanity on and once she took her act elsewhere things *really* fell apart. Everyone shooting off in separate directions. His parents could barely stand being in the same room together and as long as Conrad maintained a low profile, they seemed content to leave him be. But there was a constant, inescapable feeling that with all that anger and disappointment in the air, something had to give, the inevitable blow-up could only be postponed so long. It was like watching a slow-burning fuse. But each day continued on into the next and gradually a pattern of, well, *nothingness* developed. Every so often Peg would pop in and introduce some random chaos into their closed, little universe, but those visits petered out as the months went by.

Where was I? Oh, yeah, 2020…

Twenty-twenty, which was, uh, forty-five years away. By then he'd be well-established, with a career and wife and, let's face it, it probably wouldn't be Bonnie Gottselig.

Or…maybe it would. Stranger things happened.

And *maybe* he'd come home one bright summer day in 2020 and find Bonnie crying. Standing in their spotless, fully automated kitchen with tears streaming down her face.

"Darling, what's wrong?" Taking her in his arms. One hand resting on her soft, inviting butt.

"I feel so *silly*. Afraid you'll think me a foolish, ungrateful woman…."

But eventually he got it out of her. What it came down to was that she was *bored*. Stuck in a state of the art, semi-sentient house, with nothing to do, nothing to occupy her mind. Tyler and Wendy gone—Tyler in line for chief pilot of Pan Am's new moon shuttle and their daughter finishing up her Ph.D on Titan—which left Bonnie feeling somewhat adrift. As they necked passionately on the couch, he rubbed and cupped her ample breasts and soon she was putty in his hands. Afterward, he told her that he'd come to an important decision: namely, that his fancy, high-paying job wasn't going to get in the way of their happiness. There was more to life than money and all the toys that went with it.

Because it turned out they were both of the same mind, needing a change of scenery, fresh challenges to add excitement to their mundane existence. They weren't exactly young any more but thanks to the miracles of modern science it wasn't too late to pull up stakes and start over somewhere else, some place not nearly as safe and hospitable.

There were freezer ships leaving every week. All you had to do was sign the necessary forms, climb into a box…and the next thing you knew, you were waking up on some far-flung world, an unfamiliar, alien sun shining overhead.

And Bonnie would be right there beside him, not a day older. Still beautiful and vigorous, eager to begin their new life, undaunted by what might lie ahead.

I wonder what year this is. It was almost impossible to tell. Because of the time dilation and distances involved. Did it matter? From this point on, there could be no regrets, no turning back.

He took Bonnie's hand. Neither of them showing the slightest sign of fear or apprehension, even as that first night approached, darkness racing at breakneck speed toward them.

"We're home," he told her. It sounded so good, he said it again.

Home.

Bedeviled

Oppression.

That was the word.

This sense of something hanging over him, not a razor-edged sword, more like a heavy, dark curtain, poised to descend. The feeling never completely went away. It lingered, waiting. With the patience of a hungry cat. And there was no doubt in Andrew's mind that the source of his malaise, his *condition,* was external. It wasn't just his imagination, his mind playing tricks on him. The evidence indicated otherwise. *The whole building felt wrong.* Like he didn't belong there any more. Every time he left his apartment, he was navigating alien terrain.

He didn't blame the recent influx of new tenants, though the corridors and stairwells were ripe with sour, exotic aromas and constantly echoed with excited, chattering voices. There were families, kids, people coming and going day and night. Whenever he encountered anyone, Andrew always had difficulty meeting their eyes. He got the impression his neighbors thought him queer and talked about him behind his back.

Part of the problem was that he had no friends, no one he could relate to. Someone who would understand what he was experiencing. The only person who came to mind was Paul Dupree, his caseworker. It was a long shot but he decided he had to at least *try.* At their next appointment, Andrew alluded to the sad and tragic turns life can take, with no advance warning. Almost (*ahem!*) like we're victims of larger forces. For instance:

The story dominating the news that morning concerned the owner of a local car dealership who, during a weekend barbeque, killed his entire family before turning his weapon on himself. Friends, employees and neighbors expressed shock. No one saw it coming. They seemed to get along wonderfully, the kids honor roll students, his wife well-known for her volunteer and philanthropic work. A model family.

Paul hadn't heard the story and didn't seem particularly impressed. There was a thick stack of folders on his desk and some kind of Trojan virus playing hell with the hard drive of his computer. He wasn't in the most receptive mood.

"I'm sure they'll find out the guy owed money or his wife was cheating on him. *Something* set him off."

Andrew persisted. "But what if it didn't? What if there isn't any logical reason why this guy walked out of his house and fucking *slaughtered* his loved ones? That's even scarier, don't you think?"

"Not sure I get you, Andrew. What happened was a tragedy, no doubt about it, but I don't think there's any big mystery behind it." He paused. "Unless you know something I don't..."

But Andrew figured he'd pushed his luck far enough. "I just think it's odd. Sometimes things happen that, y'know, defy understanding. And I'm noticing them more and more lately."

"People don't need a reason to behave badly, Andrew. The toughest crimes to solve are those that have no motive whatsoever. Just random acts." He leaned back, stared at a point above Andrew's head. "Shit happens."

Deep thoughts, coming from Paul.

Well, after all, his background was social work, not philosophy. At least he wasn't a shrink. Andrew had dealt with his fair share of those and didn't care for them as a breed. He'd take their pills and listen to their bullshit, but would *never* buy into the voodoo science they preached. Reducing people to symptoms and categories, tossing out diagnoses based on a few minutes of interaction and observation. This one normal, this one not. The psych ward for you, the executive boardroom for you...

Pill pushers. Witch doctors.

After that, it was back to routine, Paul asking the standard questions, Andrew giving his standard replies. Part of the game they played, the roles they automatically assumed. Social services paid the rent, picked up the tab for basic groceries and his monthly bus pass. That was the extent of their largesse. And no one seemed to know how much longer the situation would continue. Years, maybe. Or it was just as conceivable he could get cut off next week.

Andrew had no family to speak of, no one to see to his care. Which made him a ward of the state; a "leech", the old man would've said. *Takin' hand-outs while your back is still fit and your heart strong. Shame on ye!* His Irish brogue thickening when he was drunk or in full chastisement mode.

But the old man had to cope with his own dark spells, depressive interludes that often left him virtually catatonic. He used booze to sedate himself against the worst attacks and ended up pretty much drinking himself to death. Andrew dreaded a similar fate. Alone, in some basement room. No one finding you for days. *Anything* was better than that.

The pills deadened, the pills flattened, but, alas, they didn't *cure*. They shaved the rough edges off, that was about it. Except the pills weren't helping much lately, doing little to combat that bad feeling, an intimation or premonition of approaching calamity. Something out of his control. A bullet already in flight.

Today I saw:

-a black cat in a window—its cool, unnerving regard.

-someone cursed me from a passing vehicle/stupid, undirected fury

-a pool of blood in the street, bright red, going black and scabby around the edges

-a lunatic in ragged, filthy coveralls. Roaring: "It's the end of the world, you fuckers!"

My daily horoscope: "Beware of wolves masquerading as sheep. Know where to put your trust."

Entering his apartment block after the unrewarding *tête-a-tête* with Paul, the first person Andrew encountered was the building's resident manager-caretaker, Sammy Haha.

Sammy must have been up late again because he looked like hell. His dark, straight hair greasy and unkempt, circles under his eyes.

"Two a.m. gig at the casino," Sammy confirmed, without any prompting. "Mostly a buncha fuckin' Shriners. Are those the fuckahs with the hats? The beanies?" Sammy scowled. "I heard one of them call me a Jap. Like 'the little Jap's pretty funny, huh?'. Fuckin' racist crackah motherfuckah." Sammy took great pains to emphasize his Korean heritage, the historical and cultural traits that distinguished his mother country from its larger, more powerful Asian neighbors. But his pride in his ethnicity didn't prevent him from legally changing his original name, "Myeong", to his present moniker, which he thought more fitting for a naturalized citizen and comic genius.

He frequently tried out new material on tenants and, Andrew suspected, gave preferential treatment to those who showed the most enthusiasm for his act. If you laughed, you got that drip under your sink fixed, pronto. If not...

Andrew always made sure to smile, even if he found a joke too heavy-handed or the punch line telegraphed well in advance of its actual delivery. Sammy's "humor" centered around how hard-working Koreans are and, conversely, how lazy and selfish North Americans stack up in comparison. Sometimes his audiences were receptive but apparently the Shriners had been less than enthralled.

"I told them the one about my Korean mother, how tough she is, like Chairman Mao in drag...fuckahs just sat there."

Andrew sympathized, waiting for his moment. "Yeah, that's, uh, typical, isn't it? Listen, Sammy, d'you happen to know what this is?" He took the little object from his pocket. He tried to be careful but it must have snagged on the lining. One of the small arms was askew, hanging by a sliver of wood. Sammy took it from him, gave it a cursory inspection.

"Some kid make it," he shrugged. "Maybe that Pilar on the third floor."

"I found it outside my door," Andrew explained. "There was another by the washing machine when I went down to do my laundry." Sammy's reaction was underwhelming; mild curiosity, if that. "Kind of a weird, don't you think? That stuff wrapped it, holding the sticks together? That's not thread, it's human hair. See?"

Sammy saw. But Sammy was tired and too focused on his show biz career. Useless. He would have to pursue his investigations on his own.

As a matter of fact, he *had* confronted Pilar as she was going outside with a friend and she denied responsibility. She asked if she could play with the figures but Andrew refused. He knew they were important clues, key to what was going on.

Cream of celery soup, a few crackers and two slices of cheese for lunch. He didn't have much of an appetite these days. The stress and anxiety affecting his mood, playing havoc with his guts. He was having trouble sleeping too. Waking frequently during the night, perplexed and tormented by crazy dreams...

Andrew picked up the fetish—for he was certain that's what it was—subjecting it to another close examination. So simple in design and execution. Four small sticks or twigs, positioned and secured with human hair. Dark brown, almost black. Wiry. Brittle. He'd unwound one strand and found it to be fairly long. So...likely from a woman. Was that telling? Persuasive or suggestive? He wasn't sure.

He needed facts, further information. And since no one else seemed inclined to lend assistance, it was up to him to take the initiative.

Andrew checked again, making sure he had his pass. Totally obsessive about it. But he kept imagining getting on the bus, reaching into his pocket and finding nothing there. The stares of passengers, the contempt of the driver. So...best to make sure.

The trip downtown went without a hitch and he disembarked within a block of the main library. He chose that one, rather than any of the branches, because he figured there would be more information there, especially on such a specialized subject.

He hadn't been in the new building and as soon as he walked inside knew he was in trouble. Once you passed by the checkout area, it opened up, spreading out in all directions. The middle section was hollow, revealing two more floors stacked above them. He got that bug-under-a-microscope feeling. He *hated* that. Like he was insignificantly small, the world swelling and expanding to monstrous proportions around him.

Andrew was sweating like a pig and, worse, his insides were bilious, churning. He needed to find a bathroom, quickly. There was an old guy, a commissionaire, parked at a little table. He closed his search-a-word book, gazing at Andrew with a quizzical smile...

He barely had time to lock the stall and peel down his jeans. The cramps hit hard and he moaned involuntarily as his bowels cut loose, fouling the air around him. Other patrons came in to use the facilities, including a father with his young son. No one stayed long. Andrew was mortified.

The library, its size and scale, was too much for him. All the people, activity. When he emerged from the washroom, he felt disoriented. His clothes plastered to his body and he probably had terrible b.o. too. Christ, what a mess.

There was no way he'd be able to navigate his way around on his own. He could spend the entire day here and never come across what he was looking for. The free computers were all occupied but there was no one in line at the information desk.

He blotted his forehead with a tissue, took the bull by the horns and approached the counter.

The woman smiled at him and Andrew tried his best to relax. Give off peaceful, calming vibes. "Um, hi. I'm, ah, looking for books on black magic or—or maybe witchcraft. They should be close together, right? In terms of proximity? I mean, that would make sense, wouldn't it?" Rushing ahead without waiting for an answer. "See, I have this, uh, situation and I need to find out more about spells and stuff. Like I said, uh, witchcraft, black magic, voodoo, whatever you have. D'you know if there's anything like that or..."

She shook her head. A pleasant-faced woman with short, silvery hair. "I'm afraid that's not my area of expertise. However, I think I can direct you—"

"Okay, that's fine. That'd be great. Because this place, wow, it's so *big*. Like a hangar. A person could get lost for *days*." She was tapping something into her computer, search terms, probably. "It's really great, you helping me like this. I need to find out what's going on and, y'know, I figured this would be where to look. Because we need to know if these things are superstition or the real deal. You know what I mean? So we can protect ourselves. People might be up to no good and, y'know, you have to be careful."

He was babbling. He needed to stop. She didn't seem to be paying much attention anyway. That was a relief. She took a slip of paper, wrote down some numbers. "Try your luck there. If you can't find what you're looking for, our resource person will be back soon, you can ask her."

Andrew stared down at the numbers she'd given him. Mumbled his thanks and moved off. He drifted about the main floor awhile, looking for the right section but it was hopeless. He couldn't get his bearings. Circling past the desk for the third time, he saw the woman talking to someone else, helping them with an inquiry. He got the feeling she was deliberately avoiding looking his way. He paused, his eyes skipping from the escalators to the front doors. Stuck the slip in his pocket and walked out.

Then things got sketchy and imprecise. He had no clear recollection of what he did next, only an impression of making an aimless circuit through the downtown core, barely cognizant of trivialities like traffic and other pedestrians. He must have slipped into some kind of fugue state, one that lasted until he found himself sitting on a bus bench near the library. At least a couple of hours had passed.

The ride home seemed to jar and rattle every bone in his body and he felt nauseous when he finally stumbled off. He walked with his head down, his vision confined to an area a few feet in front of him. The sun seemed unnaturally bright and a headache was throbbing just behind his eyes.

There were symbols scratched in chalk on the sidewalk in front of his building. Not words, not letters. *Symbols.*

Indecipherable, obscure, meaningless to all save the one who'd inscribed them. They hadn't been there when he left. Andrew swayed, the world tilting, gravity shifting. He wrenched open the door, made a beeline for the stairs. Outside his apartment, dropping his keys, retrieving them, fumbling with the lock, panting by that point, desperate to get inside...

It was bad, bad as it had ever been. The pills weren't working. No effect, even at twice the regular dosage. Cast them out, flush them down the toilet. Rid thyself of their toxic poisons.

He couldn't concentrate on a book or the week-old newspaper he had lying around. His TV only got two channels (cheap bastards even begrudged him cable). Half the time only one worked. The bunny ears were fucked and he was never sure he had them wired up right.

Andrew paced, endless miles down a road to nowhere. Up all that night, the next day too. Didn't go out. Didn't even bother turning on the lights. The phone only rang once. Likely a wrong number. If anyone had come to the door, he wouldn't have answered.

His mind awhirl. Going over everything, looking for patterns or clues. The fetishes and symbols. Signs and portents. You just had to know where to look for them.

And that night, confirmation.

The late show was a golden oldie called "The Curse of the Demon". Black and white, made in the 40's or 50's. Dana Andrews was the only actor Andrew recognized. At first it seemed cheesy and he almost switched it off...until he realized what was going on and that, in fact, the movie had particular relevance to his ordeal. He started paying closer attention. The plot focused on the struggle between Dana Andrews' (Andrews/Andrew?) character and a modern day black magician who dispatched his enemies by slipping them enchanted runes, ancient spells that summoned a murderous, blood-thirsty demon.

Just like that, everything fell into place. Andrew could have wept with relief and gratitude.

Of course! It was *so simple*. And it almost exactly paralleled his own situation. He was snared in a web, the plaything of supernatural forces. That *oppression*…it was part of being bewitched or spellbound or whatever you called it. Nothing else came close to explaining what had been happening.

And now that he knew what was going on, there were steps he could take, counter-measures and such. He settled onto the couch and finally, after nearly forty-eight hours, closed his eyes and slept.

Not surprisingly, his dreams were fantastic, harrowing: things clutching at him, hissing shapes in the close dark. He didn't want to look at their faces. They had removed their flesh masks and were hideous to behold. They pursued him, threw themselves at his feet like penitents, beseeching him to *look* at them, their horrible, twisted countenances…

-Today Corey yelled to me and when he came running up, I saw he was wearing a t-shirt with a strange logo—asked about its meaning but he seemed vague/evasive. Crashing headache descends almost as soon as he leaves—coincidence?

-colored strings and ribbons wrapped and tied around trees for no apparent reason. Interviewed city worker but gained no satisfaction. Called city hall, consigned to voice mail hell. (Follow up later!!!)

-jet contrails, smoky patterns in the sky (air borne inscriptions/incantations)

-more rune-like symbols out front, copied some of them (last ones erased)

Scanning the roster. Each entry innocuous, in and of itself. But viewed collectively, worrisome.

The black coil notebook never left his sight. It helped clarify his thoughts but it was also a liability. He fretted about it falling into the wrong hands. What they would do to him if they suspected how much he knew.

Essential questions:

-who is behind this? who can I trust?

-what are the limits of their influence? what are my options?

-what can I do to protect myself?!!!

He didn't take any chances, used an outside phone to make the call. Terry Cullimore. Why hadn't he thought of him sooner?

Cully made group tolerable. Chronically misbehaving. The scourge of the "facilitators", fearlessly lampooning their New Age, feel good claptrap. A fat, feral Oliver Hardy. Bitter as a mouthful of lemons.

"I'm not here because I need *healing*, dearie," he informed Jeanine, the female half of the dynamic duo leading the Wednesday night sessions. "I'm here because I'm too fucking stupid to live and too much of a coward to die." Most of the others got bent out of shape by Cully's antics but Andrew found him refreshing. After one particularly godawful evening—Jeanine and Phil weren't happy unless they reduced at least one participant to tears—Andrew made a point of approaching him and striking up a conversation.

"What can I say?" Cully shrugged. "This is complete horseshit but it's the price you pay for being a fuckup, so why bitch and moan?"

Andrew couldn't have put it better. They went out for coffee a few times but it never quite clicked. Cully (he answered to nothing else) was a walking encyclopedia, one of those people who kill at *Trivial Pursuit*. He'd keep tossing things out, doing set routines you could tell he'd performed a million times. In two minutes he could explain the theory of relativity so even a moron could understand it. But before you had a chance to say anything, he'd be off again. If there had recently been an earthquake somewhere, he'd tell you all about plate tectonics and if the waitress mistimed her approach, include her in the lecture as well. A consummate showoff and social retard. Fun to hang around with for a while, but wearing out his welcome all too soon.

The group sessions ended in the fall and Andrew still hadn't heard when or if they were starting up again. He hadn't seen Cully in *months*.

The payphone was at a service station several blocks from his apartment. They arranged to meet at the Westgate Mall food court.

"Sounds like you're on a cell or calling from outside," Cully, never missing a trick.

"I'll explain later…"

Cully's appearance caught him by surprise.

"Don't say anything," he warned, swinging up to the table, at least fifteen minutes late and huffing like a chimney. He was on crutches because the circulation in his legs had gone to hell. "Fucking diabetes," he snarled, once he'd struggled into a plastic chair that barely accommodated his bulk. He had to be at least thirty pounds heavier. *At least*. "Doctors say they might have to whack off my feet. Both of them." He regarded Andrew morosely, all the bitterness squeezed out, sadness and self-pity filling the void. "I'm a fucking mess, Andrew. Rotting away piece by piece."

Andrew commiserated, offering to buy him lunch to help raise his spirits. Went to one of the nearby kiosks, placed an order for his ailing companion. Extra large *everything*. Some things never changed.

The food seemed to rally Cully, restore some of his old spark. He started ragging on Jeanine and Phil, who (in his view) weren't qualified to coach a girls' volleyball team, let alone dole out what passed for therapy these days. "Imagine putting those two twits in charge of a bunch of emotional cripples. Talk about the stupid leading the blind. Remember the trust exercises? I thought I was gonna *puke*." He had devoured a triple burger and large fries and pounded back a pint of cola on top of that. If his diabetes didn't kill him, his heart would.

"Yeah, pretty pathetic. Listen, Cully, I wonder if I can pick your brain about something." Cully nodded, sucking at the dregs of his drink, the racket drawing the attention of nearby tables. Social skills not his strong suit. Finally he was done.

"Sure, Andrew. Shoot…"

Andrew had thought long and hard about what his approach should be. There was no reason to suspect Cully was implicated and yet one couldn't be too careful. Some people are unwitting pawns of larger forces.

He decided to call it a "working theory". Completely hypothetical. Make it an intellectual proposition. Appeal to Cully's vanity.

Question: could certain powers, possibly of a supernatural nature, be called upon to affect the course of human lives? If so, was it conceivable that some people, *adepts* or *witches* or whatever you chose to call them, might use these powers to exert their will over others?

Cully was cautious, but receptive. "There *could* be something to that, sure. Religion comes from our fear of the unknown, combined with our curiosity, our desire to understand the forces that made us. Science, magic, superstition...maybe it's all entwined. I've read stuff on quantum dynamics that's closer to mysticism than science. No shit. In a quantum universe, literally *anything* is possible. So if a butterfly flapping its wings in Illinois can cause a cyclone in China...hey, who knows?"

Andrew wasn't sure he followed Cully's reasoning but it *sounded* good. "I want to show you something." He unwrapped the tissue paper, revealing his prizes. "I found these in my building. That one right outside my door."

Cully didn't touch them at first. He stared at the little figures for some time, then nudged them with the tip of his finger. "They look like they were made by a kid."

"There's more." Pulling out his notebook, pointing to the symbols he'd copied from the front walk. "Do these look like anything to you? Maybe a language or—or a *message* there, do you think?"

Cully studied them, his expression thoughtful. Reached for his drink, shook it. His eyes were tired; ill health and pain had aged him. Even his skin looked sick, dry and scaly. "This is really strange shit. Kinda creepy." He picked up the broken fetish. "Is that human hair?"

"I feel so *bad* sometimes. Like there's something lying in wait for me, just around the corner. It never goes away. I'm wondering if *this* maybe isn't part of the explanation."

Cully went back to the notebook. "There's a crescent shape and some of these others seem familiar. And this one...an *ankh*, maybe?"

"What's that?"

"Egyptian. One of their sacred symbols. Like a cross."

"So it definitely *means* something," Andrew pressed. "There's an intelligence or a—a will at work."

Cully sat back, weighing his response. "I *guess* you could put it that way. Can I have this page?" he asked, then went ahead and tore it out anyway. Now *he* had the only copy.

Andrew's unease returned. *Cully? Could he be part of it too?*

He waited two days. Three days. Back to the service station, but Cully wasn't answering his phone.

-*Cully / disappeared.*

-*advertisement for local church—Sunday sermon: "The supernatural at large in the world"*

-*today a bird smacked my window, hard enough to crack the glass*

-*mood very black: OPPRESSION*

It was Paul who broke the news. Tuesday morning, 9:30, the two of them crammed into his office, smelling each other's breath. "You were acquainted with Terry Cullimore, right? From group?"

Past tense.

Post mortem.

Terry's gone.

"What happened?" His throat drying up. Because he already knew. The symbols. Cully must have deciphered something. A death rune. Intended for Andrew, rerouted to an innocent party. Poor bastard.

"Well…ah, there's no easy way of…it was suicide, I'm sorry to say."

Andrew felt something inside him come unmoored. "Suicide…"

Paul seemed uncomfortable. Not emotionally equipped to provide solace or comfort. Hardly the cuddly type. "Yes, I'm afraid so. Very sad, obviously. I spoke with Terry—well, not very long ago, as a matter of fact. He had some hard decisions to make and was facing surgery, possibly life in a wheel chair."

"He told us he was too scared to kill himself. That it wasn't an option."

"It seems he didn't take his own words to heart."

Or he wasn't acting of his own free will.

For his part, Paul was already putting Cully behind him. A lost cause. Another client who didn't make the cut. Casualty of war. Only Terry Cullimore's name would never show up on a wall or monument, remembered and commemorated for all time. His battle had been a private one, his death squalid and lonely, lacking the necessary *esprit de corps*. "Sorry to be the one to tell you…"

Later that night, hunched over his notebook:

1) Terry Cullimore was killed by mistake.

2) I am responsible for his death.

3) Now almost certain Paul is part of it too.

Inez Delgado asked him if he'd seen Pilar. She described her daughter, held her hand waist high to demonstrate her diminutive size. Andrew said he hadn't, started to walk away, then doubled back. "Inez?" She turned toward him, her face expectant. "Do you and Pilar ever do crafts?"

"Crafts?" Head tilted in puzzlement.

"Yeah. Make little things. Toys and, uh, decorations."

"Mebbe. I don't know whachu mean. Like sewing?"

"Just wondering. She seems like, y'know, such a creative kid."

Andrew watched her, alert for any hint of deception. But she played it cool. Blameless? Or demonstrating the skill and duplicity of an accomplished liar? He wondered…

. . .

The fetish dolls were gone.

He was certain he'd left them on the kitchen counter. And then he knew what must have happened.

The fire alarm.

It had gone off again that morning and everyone in the building who happened to be home went out to see if it was the real thing this time or just kids again. Including Andrew. Leaving his door wide open, his attention distracted for a critical two or three minute interval. Long enough for one of their minions to slip in and steal his most valuable evidence. It was a devastating setback and Andrew stood in his living room, fists clenched, trembling with fury and self-recrimination...until something else occurred to him.

They knew.

Maybe Cully talked before he died or Inez had guessed the real purpose of his cross-examination. It was possible he'd given something away to Paul. The various scenarios made his head spin.

He was a marked man. He had no doubt whatsoever that his enemies would use whatever means necessary to avoid exposure to the rest of the world. Their web of control had to be preserved at all costs.

There seemed to be no recourse but to hide out. Crawl into a deep, dark hole and pull it in after him. The good news was thanks to his lifestyle no one was liable to take much notice of his absence. No job, no girlfriend; social services paid the bills and a phone call postponed his next appointment with Paul.

"Sorry, I think I'm coming down with something. It's really knocked me on my ass."

Paul pretended to care, told him to pop in when he was feeling better. It bought him some time but sooner or later he was going to have to go out for food and essentials. Unless he wanted to be reduced to wiping his ass with sheets torn from his handy notebook.

-dreams too terrible to record. Bleeding eyes/huge faces leering from the sky

-2:32 a.m. Loud outburst in the street (man howling like a wolf/laughter)

-Doris Day in the late movie (when times were purer/before the shadow fell)

-4:45 Furtive sounds in hallway/someone creeping past

-open the Bible at random—Acts 3:14-16 (!!!!)

-possibility of securing weapon (gun?)

It went on for pages and pages.

Andrew managed to stretch it out to eleven days. Eleven days shuttered up inside three small rooms. Watching TV 'til he was bored senseless, spending the rest of the time checking the windows, peering down at the street from several different vantage points. Pacing endlessly. Sleeping only intermittently. And then not at all.

Supplies ran low. He ate cereal with cold water instead of milk. Went without bread and eggs (the first things devoured); used dish soap for shampoo...but was finally forced to concede defeat when he scraped the last thin streak of margarine off the side of its plastic tub.

Venturing out cautiously. Cracking open the door, peering into the hallway. The coast was clear. It was going to be all right. He'd sneak out, grab a few things from Lang's convenience store, just enough to tide him over, then scamper back here, free as a bird.

Except Pilar Delgado was at the bottom of the front steps, on her hands and knees, scratching away with a dry, white finger of chalk. Andrew watched her from the doorway, his mood darkening to a murderous hue. Hating the little bitch for being a part of it. Inez had undoubtedly initiated her, served as her mentor. His thoughts chaotic, indecipherable as he pushed through the door and started down the steps. He knew something was about to happen but it was like he was separated from himself, a mere witness to what was transpiring.

Pilar was seven or eight. A bright, cheerful child. Not bashful, looking up at him with frank interest. "Hi! Wanna play with me?"

Andrew stared at her, then his eyes ranged along the numbered squares stretching up the sidewalk. No arcane symbols or runes. *Hopscotch! She's playing hopscotch!* Suddenly the sun came out, street sounds and birdsong flooded back in and he smiled, patting her head. "Not today, sweetie. Maybe some other time."

Pilar isn't one of them. Turning so he could wave to her again—

Lowering his arm when he spotted the 8 1/2 X 11 sheet taped to the bus shelter, looking crisp and fresh compared to the other announcements and posters plastered around it.

Lost dog. A Shih Tzu answering to the name "Angel". Reward offered.

Shih Tzu...An-drew. (They were getting sloppy, far too obvious.)

Andrew, the lost angel?

Was it a warning? Or a jeering taunt?

That wasn't all. He was certain he was being followed, under surveillance. The little hairs on the back of his neck prickling. Passing a billboard with most of the lettering worn off, leaving: "*...fear...security*". The panhandler he was sure he'd seen somewhere else. A blue van with no windows. And then a passing car, trailing music from its open windows:

"*...wooo-hooo, witchy woman...she got the moon in her eye...*"

This was wrong. All signs pointed toward imminent danger. He should turn around, run back home. But the store was right *there*, he could see it, so he kept going, against his better judgment. Inside, it wasn't as bad, he didn't feel so exposed. Until he noticed the camera, bolted to the wall, panning slowly over the narrow aisles, alert for suspicious behavior. *No matter where you are, someone is always watching...*

He found most of the items on the list, decided to dispense with the rest. Syrup? He'd make do with honey.

One guy ahead of him in line: middle-aged, suit and tie, fancy briefcase. Flirting with the cashier even though she was young enough to be his daughter. Wanting to know what time she got off work. There was a camera behind the cash register too. With a stern warning to shoplifters underneath.

185

Andrew browsed the rack of tabloids, one headline catching his eye: "Coven Exposed in Cincinnati". Next to that, a rag with a cover story celebrating the latest serial killer, "The Priest", who left his victims' heads in churches. Stuck on pulpits, arranged so they were facing parishioners.

He felt sick, repulsed by the growing power of evil, the terrible, corrupting influence it had on human affairs. The rest of the world unaware of what was going on right under their noses. Unaware or indifferent, it amounted to the same thing.

Andrew unloaded the items from his plastic basket and the girl, who was dumpy but quite pretty, started ringing everything in. She had black fingernails. That bothered him. And she wore too much makeup for someone her age.

He decided he needed to say something, make conversation. Eleven days alone will do that to you. "So…what do you think about all this witchcraft and demon stuff they're always going on about. This crap…" Indicating the tabloids. "Crazy, huh?"

She raised her shoulders. "I think it's *cool*."

He stared at her. "But…"

"Evil's cool, man. Who wants to be *good* all the time?" He couldn't believe what he was hearing. The businessman had left the store. They were alone and terrible things were afoot. "John Lennon is right, God is just a concept. But the Devil, he's the real deal." Beckoning him closer. "You wanna see something?" She took a quick look around. Slid off the stool and leaned over the counter, sweeping the hair from the nape of her neck.

There was a tattoo, just below the hairline.

An eye. Flawlessly rendered. Looking right back at him.

"That's my third eye. It sees all."

She straightened, nonchalant. But this time they had seriously miscalculated. The challenge or, more precisely, the *threat* was too brazen to ignore and he felt compelled to act. Let them know they couldn't toy with him any more.

The steak knife was in his waistband, Andrew had secreted it there just before leaving his apartment. It was in his waistband and then it was in his hand *and then it was leaping at her*, the thin, sharp blade biting and slashing and tearing and gouging...and the whole time there was this grim satisfaction that *finally* he was striking back. On some of the footage caught by overhead cameras, he seemed to be *smiling*. Bowdlerized versions played over and over again on the news and proved to be popular fare in cyberspace as well, downloaded and viewed by the morbid and curious millions of times.

It was an open and shut case. Andrew's lawyers advised him to cop to insanity, so he fired them. He informed the presiding judge he would conduct his own defense. In an impromptu press scrum convened on the courthouse steps, the girl's family accused him of grandstanding, exploiting her senseless death.

He sympathized with their position but a full-blown trial granted him a public forum to expose what he insisted was a dangerous and insidious plot. In the meantime, Andrew told the court, his life was in grave danger, his enemies anxious to silence him before he could disclose their closely guarded secrets. He demanded special provisions for his safety, causing an embarrassing spectacle in the courtroom when that request was summarily denied.

Eyes in the Sky

THE GUARD'S NAME was Chorney.

It was printed on a triangular badge pinned to the tunic of his spotless, meticulously pressed uniform: *A. Chorney*.

A for Al or Anthony or Andrew.

A for pompous, over-efficient *ass*.

"May I see your identification, sir?"

Seething at the delay, Pete dug into his pocket and produced his credentials, waiting as the burly soldier took his sweet time, examining the laminated card and accompanying photograph with exaggerated care. "Can we move it along, please, Corporal Chorney? You know who I am. And right now I'm running late, so if you don't mind…"

Chorney gave him a withering look. "It's *Sergeant* Chorney, Mr. Vukovich. Since February. Three stripes, see?" Showing Pete the hash marks on his sleeve, giving him ample time to count them. "And they call you folks *watchers*, huh?"

As far as their routine went, it was a pretty typical exchange. The guard was insolent but he was also the size of a defensive tackle and could kill him with one flick of his little toe. So Pete held his tongue and kept his temper, grinding his teeth until at last Chorney passed back his I.D., snapped him a mock salute and sent him on his way.

He kept meaning to lay a formal complaint against the jerk but somehow never got around to it. Not sure what, if anything, would come of it and reluctant to rock the boat. To be honest, once he passed beyond that last checkpoint and entered the egg-shaped inner chamber, he rarely gave Chorney—or anything else from the outside world—another thought.

By then, his mind was preoccupied with other, far less mundane matters.

* * *

The air in the RVC was dry and none too fresh. It smelled of sweat, cheap cologne and over-worked machinery.

Reese sauntered past. "Welcome back to Weirdo Central," he offered by way of a greeting. That was Reese. The man was an enigma, the wild card in the deck. A petty criminal and chronic gambler. He made all kinds of extravagant claims, bragging about how when he was on a real tear he couldn't lose. The right card or die *always* popped up, like he'd willed it. As far as Pete could tell, Reese's main talent appeared to be an innate ability to annoy just about everyone in the vicinity. General Murray referred to him as "our resident misanthrope" and cut him some slack for the sake of the program. But there were whispers circulating that he was hanging on by the fingernails. His scores woefully low, his intel obscure and frequently contradictory. Not good.

Tonight the RVC was bustling, a full complement of watchers along with the usual support staff and requisite military types. No one below the rank of Major. General Philip J. Murray, their sponsor, mother hen and avenging angel, was present, conferring with his junior officers. The program was *his* baby and its success or failure weighed heavily on his career prospects. From the expression on his face, he was definitely feeling the strain.

Pete's attention was drawn to a group off in one corner. They were gathered, three deep, around a television set, a big Motorola someone had wheeled in and parked by a convenient wall outlet. Technicians, mostly, two of them wrestling with a troublesome antennae, another playing with the controls, trying to get better reception. More and more people came wandering over, jockeying for position, vying for a good viewing angle.

Pete went to see what all the fuss was about. On screen, a commentator was talking to a bespectacled man wearing the patient expression of a long-suffering saint. He noticed Reese, shouldered his way closer. "What's going on, Tom?"

Reese grinned mirthlessly. "Tonight's the big night. Those crazy space boys are giving it one last shot. That's von Braun, selling more snake oil. He just got finished explaining how this one's got new, improved engines, performed perfectly in every test run."

Pete scowled. "Won't those idiots ever learn? Every single one of their death machines blows up and *still* they keep wasting taxpayers' money."

"But this is *it*. If their latest rocket-propelled coffin doesn't perform as advertised, they've shot their wad. And this time they ain't sending up no damn monkey."

Right on cue, they cut away to a shot of the interior of the command module, jerky, crackling footage of a suited figure, strapped in, immobile, listening to the countdown along with the rest of them. A fine specimen of American manhood, selected for his physical stamina and steadiness of nerve; the best of the best, secured to a sacrificial altar, pointed at the stars.

Pete felt sick, knowing what was about to happen but helpless to do anything to prevent it. At least tonight would be the end of it. A brave man wasn't dying in vain.

Everyone around them was talking excitedly, some of them even laying bets, morbidly predicting how far the craft would get before becoming the world's most expensive firecracker. General Murray had to bark for silence as the countdown approached zero and switches were engaged, chambers flooded with volatile fuels, intermixing, channeled downward with tremendous force. The people in the room gasped as flames poured from the base of the rocket, streams of bright energy erupting from its powerful engines. Pete watched along with the others as the supporting clamps and restraints fell away and the craft began to ease up from the launch pad, fighting the stiff bonds of gravity, rising with reluctant grace.

"It a miracle!" A woman next to Reese cried, clutching his arm. "He's going to make it!" Reese caught Pete's eye and winked.

"Not in a million years!"

Pete thought about the man in the metal capsule. They told him he would be a hero, exhaustively trained him for this moment. Half killed the guy in their efforts to find out if he could withstand the physical and mental rigors of life beyond earth.

Stuck him atop a device so complex no one man could understand it. Ten thousand different people drawing up plans, conferring on the science, spending a couple of billion dollars in the process...but if you asked any single one of them how it worked, you'd get nothing back but a blank stare.

But it *wasn't* working, that much was immediately clear. The bullet-shaped craft had barely cleared the gantry and was already looping back on itself, metal crumpling and then, inevitably, a massive explosion, billowing gouts of yellow-orange fire that consumed the spacecraft, launch pad and anyone unlucky enough to be within two thousand feet of the blast zone.

Viewers in the RVC reacted with horror, recalling that there was a human being in the fiery heart of that inferno, a man who likely suffered a great deal in the few seconds it took him to succumb. Some of the women were weeping and everyone was smoking cigarettes, looking grim. But not Tommy Reese. He appeared unmoved by the tragedy.

"So much for Smilin' Al," he quipped. Roth, one of the twerps from Recon, glared at him. "Hey, I ain't cryin' over spilled milk. Remember when Sputnik went *kaputnik?* At least the Russkies had the decency to cash in their chips right then and there. Not us. We gotta spend *another* billion bucks and charbroil a good American boy, *just to prove rockets don't fly!*" People were nodding and through the throng, Pete caught glimpses of von Braun, looking shell-shocked, trying to explain what had gone wrong.

"Well, everyone, we're back in business!" A lusty roar greeted the announcement.

Pete drifted off, not interested in celebrating what amounted to the official end of the so-called "space age". *Schadenfreude* wasn't his cup of tea.

"Sickening, isn't it?"

Marla Dunbar stood a short distance away, so small and undemonstrative you hardly noticed her. Achieving invisibility at will, a faculty he secretly envied. The others called her "the mouse" and were always taking little digs at her, but he liked Marla. She seemed like the real deal to him, unlike Reese and a few more he could name. That was the problem with this business: it was hard to tell the charlatans from those who genuinely possessed the gift.

"You thinking about that poor astronaut? Whazzis name?"

She shook her head. "I mean how smug everybody is. Building reliable rockets with our present technology is virtually impossible. They still haven't perfected fuel mixtures and many of the alloys are untried or—"

He headed her off at the pass. "You don't have to convince me, kid. I got nothing against those rocket jockeys. Brave men...they'd have to be." He resisted the urge to pat her head. "But Reese is right: what we just witnessed was a—a pointless exercise and we lost a good man for absolutely no reason. Now explain to me how that makes any kind of sense."

She looked glum. "They're saying that's it. Now the President will be forced to cancel the program."

"About time too." Then he softened his tone. "They've been wasting vital resources on a lost cause. It's time to divert those funds into programs that have proven worth, that yield reliable, real world data."

"You sound like our fearless leader," she muttered and he realized she was talking about Murray.

Pete blushed, embarrassed and somewhat nettled. "I'm no super patriot, all right? I have a job to do and I do it. It's thanks to people like you and me that our nation can sleep safer at night. Is that such a terrible thing?"

She gave him an odd look, like she was trying to decide if he was kidding. "Oh, Pete," she sighed, "how can you can talk like that? Surely you realize..." But she stopped herself. Touched his arm and walked away, head down. Acting like she'd just met a man who still believed in the Easter Bunny. Trying not to pity him but, at the same time, recognizing that he was too far gone to help, his delusions too deeply rooted.

He didn't have much of an opportunity to ponder whatever was eating Marla. Mulvaney, his PA, was signaling him from over by his cubicle. A meticulous man who wore a watch on each wrist, Mulvaney hated it when Pete was last one in. Claimed it made him look bad. Occasionally tried to lay a guilt trip on him but Pete wouldn't bite. Mulvaney did a quick check of his vitals, thumbed back his eyelids, examined his pupils. Aware of doors closing around them as the other watchers took their posts.

"No alcohol or illicit drugs in the past twenty-four hours?"

"Nope."

"Any changes in your physical health?"

"None."

Only then did the PA relax. Switching the clipboard to his other hand, he clapped Pete on the back. "Nice to have you back."

"I was only gone three days. Not much of a holiday."

"No rest for the wicked."

"At least I got to see the sun."

"Anybody else around?"

Pete grimaced. "They must have cleared the beach. Had it to myself for as long as I wanted it."

Mulvaney laughed. "Without broads? No chicks in bathing suits? What's the point?" Then he saw Pete's face. "Er, sorry, Pete. I guess it's, y'know, national security or whatever. Can't take any chances."

Pete stepped past him, jerked open the door. "Thanks for being so understanding about it," he cracked.

Slamming the door behind him to punctuate his complaint.

He brought home another headache, a real doozie this time. Aspirin wouldn't touch it and two gin and tonics only made it worse. Pete was reduced to getting an ice pack from the freezer and gingerly resting it on the back of his skull. A spot the size of a quarter throbbed with each beat of his treasonous heart. In desperation, looking for something to distract him, he turned on the TV.

Two channels came in reasonably well but he wasn't sure how much of it was edited and doctored before it got to him. Did that sound paranoid?

But I'm their golden boy, they wouldn't mess with me, would they? Would they? General Murray is a good man, the one person who's believed in this program all along. He had to put up with a lot of crap, endure the taunts of "voodoo science" and, meanwhile, the space nuts were collaborating with Nazis and passing off science fiction as science fact. Murray heard about people like me, recognized the possibility for a whole new branch of human endeavor and now look at us! The guardians of the frontier, the first line of defense against the Red hordes. Ever vigilant, fearless and omniscient, never allowing our enemies a chance to sneak up on us again...

It had been a good night, he knew that. He handed over his notes and watched as Colonel Frers, Murray's adjutant, scanned the raw data, his expert eye quickly plucking out the best nuggets. Finally, he looked up at Pete, grinning wolfishly. "Those Commie bastards. Thought they'd pull the wool over our eyes. Got it into their stupid heads that if they snuck around at night we wouldn't notice. Real smart, doing it under cover, using rail lines." Tapping the sheaf of papers. "But you can see, it's plain as day: they're massing troops near the border, threatening ol' Tito again. Telling him in no uncertain terms to start toeing the party line, or else."

"D'you think they're bluffing? Is this a genuine threat or are we getting our socks in a twist over nothing?"

The Colonel, who had somehow missed action in both theaters of operation during the previous war, gave an impatient shrug. "Who cares? It'll give us a chance to demonstrate our level of preparedness, or lack thereof. Goose those boys up on the Hill, come appropriations time. Besides, with the Ivans, you don't want to show weakness. Gotta let 'em know we're out there, eyeballing them, our finger on the trigger." He hurried away to brief his superior. It was the kind of intel guaranteed to get the old man's juices flowing.

So orders would go out, troops placed on alert, a few pawns moved about on the great checkerboard known as Europe. Would it amount to anything? Secure the peace by alerting the godless Bolsheviks that their schemes had been uncovered and they should tread carefully, the eyes of the Free World were upon them? It was a dangerous game, hide and seek with global implications.

Sometimes, when he was having trouble sleeping, Pete told himself he was helping maintain deterrence, averting a calamitous clash between the two super-powers. There were nights, increasingly rare, when he could *almost* bring himself to believe it.

Nobody wanted another war. Not really. The man in the White House, the brass at the Pentagon, the Reds and their minions and *apparatchiks*, these weren't stupid people. They knew the score. And most of the time they played by the rules. After all, there were certain formalities to be observed. Two societies, divided by history, language, ideology; two armies, poised for war. You had to strike a fine balance. Know when to call and when to fold. Sometimes things got tense. On the other hand, the on-going state of crisis quelled dissent and solidified popular opinion. Which simplified governance and helped keep their respective populations in line. It also fed endless streams of dollars (and rubles) into military-industrial combines that measured their worth in billions and corrupted every single politician they touched, left, right and center.

It was up to the spies and watchers to keep everybody honest.

Ludmilla's beloved Sergei was killed during the assault on the Japanese home islands in October, 1945. The war was supposed to have been over by then. They should have been married, preparing for the arrival of their first child. There would be ample food and little Tatyana (her choice) or Fyodor (his) would never want for anything. Their children would grow into a bright future, educated in the finest universities, traveling around the world, experiencing many diverse cultures, representing a new generation, with exciting new ideas...

At Potsdam, the Americans promised to produce a miracle weapon, a device so powerful, they assured Comrade Stalin, that a single demonstration would convince the Japanese to sue for peace. But two test runs in early August finally forced the Americans to admit that their much-vaunted super weapon had fizzled. A billion dollar bust. Scientifically unsound, wholly impractical. A much-ballyhooed fiasco it would take the imperialists many years to live down.

And so, while MacArthur pored over plans for "Operation Downfall" and Truman dithered, spooked by the massive casualties an invasion of the Japanese mainland would incur, the Great Helmsman acted. Two hundred and fifty thousand Russian soldiers splashed ashore near Otaru and one of them was Sergei. *My first hours have been charmed*, he wrote later, *while others drop around me, I carry on without a scratch*. He didn't paint a very romantic view of his fellow soldiers. That fateful morning, half of them were drunk and the landing craft awash with sick, everyone desperate to be off, even if it meant wading out into machine gun fire.

They landed largely unopposed and the Soviet juggernaut sped swiftly inland, whipped on by a leadership that wanted a *fait accompli* before the Americans got wind of what was going on.

It was a brutal, ugly campaign, no quarter given on either side. "I can't write in detail of some things," one of Sergei's notes went, "but let us just say that old scores are being settled." No one could forget the disgrace of 1905, the Czarist navy, grown fat and complacent, relentlessly pursued and pummeled, out-sailed and over-powered by the crafty Nips. "The yellow man will pay the price for his aggression and cruelty."

One of the last letters she received from him and it was nothing but patriotic platitudes. It didn't sound like Sergei at all, the confidences and intimacies they had exchanged, the risks they'd taken together and damn the consequences!

Finally alerted to what they were missing, the Americans began a horrific aerial and naval bombardment of Japanese targets, including major population centers. It was the kind of total war they had perfected, along with the Brits, in the skies over Germany. These, of course, were the same Yanks who had waited until the last moment, with the German army literally at the gates of London, before declaring war and launching a counter-invasion, appropriately enough, from Plymouth. Too bad Churchill was already dead. He always put great faith in his American cousins. Refusing to believe they would betray him...

The drunken old fool.

All the histories and accounts Ludmilla read were unanimous on one point: the Japanese defended their homeland with a ferocity and determination that shocked their adversaries. They died *en masse* rather than surrender, and that went for civilians as well as soldiers. Even after the high command conceded defeat and the Emperor abdicated, many Japanese refused to capitulate. The fighting was savage, barbaric, rural farmers brandishing sharpened bamboo stakes, city-dwellers erecting barricades, fighting house to house, yard by yard.

The Japanese propagandists had done their job too well, the ordinary men and women thoroughly indoctrinated, imbued with a contempt and fear of the invading horde, the atrocities committed by enemy soldiers feeding the jingoism and xenophobia that helped sustain and legitimize the Japanese insurgency.

The Great Patriotic War in the East finally wrapped up in the spring of 1947. There were still isolated pockets of resistance, militarists and right wing crazies refusing to acknowledge the hopelessness of their cause, exploding the occasional bomb or ambushing the odd motorcade. But those incidents became more and more infrequent; the damage, it seemed, had already been done.

For all intents and purposes, Japan had ceased to exist. What little that remained after years of incessant bombing and warfare was jointly administered by the USA and USSR, but neither side had any great desire to govern lands scoured and depopulated by armed conflict and its handmaidens Famine, Disease and Death.

The Allied coalition tried but it was simply not possible to feed hungry multitudes in the ruins of Europe and, at the same time, provide for their Japanese wards. There were shortages: medicine, shelter, even basic foodstuffs.

Asia would never forgive or forget America's role in what happened next. Who knows what the final death toll was? It was classified a state secret, as were the locations of many of the mass graves.

But the Motherland had taken no part in that dark chapter. Moscow, as Comrade Stalin assured the world with a foxy smile, did not have imperial ambitions. Such things were in direct contravention of the revolutionary spirit. She couldn't remember the exact wording but it went something like that. While the Americans struggled to feed and shelter the Japanese with winter fast approaching, the Union of Soviet Socialist Republics withdrew all combat soldiers, leaving behind only a few advisors and diplomats, perhaps a spy or three. And what did they ask in return? Oh, nothing much, the Kuril Islands and a few other innocuous lumps of rock, for purely strategic purposes.

Another great coup for the Father of All Nations, the Red Tsar!

She glanced at her watch, an expensive Swiss model, a gift from Colonel Laptev.

Who knows of my lavish tastes.

Further on that subject, a new *Beriozka* shop had recently opened on Blavatsky Prospekt. Very chic. She'd heard from an unimpeachable source that all the diplomats' wives shopped there, which told her everything she needed to know.

The lift was out of order again and on the way downstairs she encountered her next door neighbor, Rejdak. A revolting specimen of manhood and, it seemed, utterly smitten with her. So far she had managed to ward off his attentions but one had to be careful. You could never tell who might be a *stukach*. Every building had at least one and probably more. The fat old *telkas* downstairs wouldn't hesitate to denounce her the first chance they got. It wasn't wise to have too many enemies. And so, as much as she loathed herself for it, she pretended to be flattered by his advances, tried not to recoil as he fawned over her.

"Such a lovely wrap," he crooned, referring to a beautiful sable stole that she would be paying for, as the joke went, until either Stalin died or a Pole was elected Pope. Not Russian made, *Scandinavian*. An impulsive, stupid act on her part; her state stipend was generous but hardly accorded her the disposable income required by her roving, acquisitive eye. She couldn't bear to watch him stroking the gorgeous fur with his greasy fingers. At last she was able to extricate herself with a half-hearted promise to get together at a later date. Hurried down the poorly lit stairwell, her heels clattering on the treacherous steps.

A black Zil was waiting outside, one of the new models they'd recently introduced. Her driver was a thick-headed Georgian with a deplorable accent that reduced even the briefest exchange to a mime show as they struggled to make themselves understood.

When they passed Blavatsky Prospekt, she rapped on the glass partition but he ignored her. The dark sedan sped along a lane reserved for those on official business, making good time. She tried not to sulk over missing a chance to pick up some authentic American blue jeans. He took her directly to the Ministry. She had to show her pass three times before she could report to her immediate supervisor.

Some cruel bureaucrat had assigned Vasili the smallest office in the building. A converted broom closet. She could barely get through the door; poor, fat Vasili, meanwhile, all a hundred and fifty kilos of him, was wedged in so tight behind his desk he couldn't rise to greet her. Its surface was a debris field of half-eaten food and mounds of stained paper. It was said that he lived at the desk for *months* at a time, terrified he might miss a call from the Inner Sanctum. It could come at any hour, day or night. The Boss was a notorious insomniac.

"The Americans have been buzzing about," he informed her without preamble. "I think it's time we fed them a little more candy..."

An after hours visit from General Murray couldn't bode well, could it? And yet Murray was courteous, perhaps even a trifle deferential, waiting for Pete to step back and admit him to his quarters. Surely if he was in trouble, he would be *summoned*, called onto the carpet for an official dressing down. No, something else was up. This encounter was definitely "off the record".

Murray was looking about, taking in his simple living space, a small, rectangular compartment hewn from billion year old rock and about as welcoming as a cave could be. "Not much for decorations, are you, Pete?" They glanced at each other and laughed. The walls were pretty much bare, except for a couple of pinups and some Impressionist thing with a spray of flowers a neighbor had donated when he first moved in.

The General sank into a creaky rocking chair but Pete was too jumpy and anxious to sit down. "Can I get you anything, sir? A drink or…?" Surprised when his guest nodded, hurrying away to comply with the request. *What the hell*, he thought, pouring two fingers of a decent scotch Ferris had given him for Christmas. Shortly before trying to seduce him. Who would have thought he leaned that way? He hadn't taken kindly to the rebuff either, accusing Pete of being "confused". Talk about the pot calling the kettle black…

Murray accepted the glass, sipped, nodded his approval. "Good stuff. Thanks, I needed this."

Whoops, Pete perked up, *here it comes*.

But the General seemed distracted, his eyes roaming about the room. "You need more homey touches, Pete. Knick-knacks or what have you. I know this place isn't much, but we're worried you have a tendency to be…what's the word? Morose?"

"Been talking to the shrinks again?" Pete guessed.

"Ah, those guys are all the same," Murray snapped. "Hell, I know the score. It can't be easy for you people, cooped up here, cut off from the rest of the world. No one will ever know how much this country owes each and every one of you. We try to make it bearable for you but there's only so much we can do. That trip to Florida. The idea was to get you outside but we—we overdid it on the security end. Next time will be different." He stood, came over and rested a friendly hand on Pete's shoulder. Coming from the General, it was practically a hug. "I want you to know," he continued, his voice husky with emotion, "I'm doing my best for you. You people are my eyes in the sky. Especially *you*, Pete. You're in a class of your own."

Pete nodded, barely acknowledging the praise. More concerned by the tension on Murray's face, the strange vibrations he was giving off. "Is something wrong, General? I appreciate what you're saying but—"

"You're my ace in the hole," General Philip Murray rasped. "As long as I've got you, the rest can go to blazes!" He spun about and marched back to the rocking chair, retrieving his drink. Now Pete really *did* have to sit down, in an orange armchair purchased from an officer unexpectedly transferred to Nome. A steal of a deal.

"Is the program in trouble?" And this time he hit it right on the nose, he could tell from the way Murray reacted. "That's it, isn't it? Some of those bastards have never accepted us, don't put any stock in what we do, you've said as much yourself. No matter how much we give them, it's never enough. The nuts and bolts boys, refusing to abandon their rocket ships and robots. God, I despise those people!"

Murray was nodding. "There's some truth to what you're saying," the three star general admitted. "Our enemies are deeply entrenched. And they've got powerful, influential allies. There are some in the scientific community who think—"

"Discredited hacks! The other night proved it. They're finished and they know it."

"They aren't going away, Pete. They're like sharks, constantly circling, sniffing for blood."

"It's always been like that," Pete reminded him. "All the data we've passed along, right from day one, the disasters we've helped avert and the so-called intellectual elite *still* treat us like a bunch of charlatans fleecing bumpkins at a county fair."

The General appeared uneasy. "Well, sometimes we've made it easy for them."

"What do you mean?"

"There have been complaints about the quality of our intel. There are perceived...inadequacies. Questions are being asked at the highest levels. This is just between you and me, understand?"

Pete felt queasy. "Are they saying the material is fake or—"

Murray's face was grim, ashen. "It's their view that lately there have been more misses than hits and too many of the reports they've been getting have been *vague*, of little value, strategically speaking."

I knew it, Pete said to himself. *Fakes, phonies and fools, the entire bunch*. And now the whole house of cards was threatening to come tumbling down. "You sound like you're half-convinced yourself."

The General straightened, his attitude defensive. "I read the reports before anyone else. They cross my desk first. And, I must confess, I've been troubled by some of what I'm seeing. While *your* sessions are remarkably rich in detail, their accuracy beyond question, some of the other watchers have been...less diligent in their efforts."

Pete tensed. "Which ones?" His guest didn't seem inclined to share that information. "Then I'll tell you. Reese, for one. I spotted him as a flim-flam artist right from the start. Ferris is another, I'll wager. The little creep couldn't tell a column of tanks from a hill of termites." He glanced over at Murray to gauge his reaction and was startled by what he saw. "Who else? Good God, General, do you mean to tell me—"

"I'd barely give *any* of them a passing grade," his superior growled. "Not from what I've been seeing recently. At first I chocked it up to a variety of factors, including over-work. Maybe we were pushing you too hard. So we scaled things back, created more down time. If anything, it's gotten *worse*. You're the only one still delivering quality intel. The rest..."

"What about Marla?"

"No better than the others." Murray's voice bleak, condemnatory. "Two weeks ago, we were ordered to cooperate on a clandestine test—"

"Oh, no." Pete buried his face in his hands but Murray continued without pause.

"We directed you toward a certain installation, asked for your input."

"Good God, General! You actually sanctioned this?"

"*I didn't have any choice.* We had people on the ground, first hand reconnaissance. Some of our best men and women risked their necks getting the goods. It took a ridiculous amount of time to arrange and coordinate but we managed it. You and your colleagues were given a number of maps and photographs and asked very specific questions. It was near a Naval base. Novo-something-something."

"I remember. I said it was nothing. ONSV." *Of no strategic value.*

"It was, in fact, a dairy farm. Quite a successful operation, by Soviet standards." Murray winced at the memory. "Your colleagues failed to recognize its utter lack of significance. Their reports indicated the facility was either a training center for elite troops, or possibly the testing ground for advanced aircraft *or* perhaps a disguised radar installation. There were other, even less likely possibilities..." He waved a hand dismissively. "We knew there was nothing there because our agents told us so. Only one remote viewer out of the whole lot refused to bite. What does that say about the effectiveness and reliability of our program?"

"But as we've explained," Pete's voice rose, reflecting his growing alarm, "sometimes weather conditions and—and atmospherics screw things up. You start seeing stuff that isn't there, ghost images, reflections, or—or—" Sagging back into the armchair, feeling like someone had let the air out of him. "Wow, I can't believe this is happening, that after all this time I still have to rationalize what we do."

Murray was sympathetic. "I know. Look—"

Pete pounded the arm of the chair with his fist. "Damnit, sir! Our President got elected in large part because he accused his predecessor of allowing an 'ESP gap' to develop under his watch. The Russians have been tapping into the powers of the human mind for years now. We know that and we've seen some of the manifestations—"

"No use, Pete," the General favored him with a wan smile. "You're preaching to the converted. And if all of our watchers were as accurate and trustworthy as you, we wouldn't have this problem." They sat forlornly, silently, and during that interval, the General finished his drink and set it on the table beside him.

"So...where does that leave us? On probation? Needing to prove ourselves all over again?"

Murray leaned forward. "I had to do some house-cleaning to hold off the wolves. Show them that we value accuracy and reliability as much as they do. The

Joint Chiefs meet Thursday and that's when I'll tell them about Reese and Ferris."

"Just them?"

General Murray shrugged. "For now. But the others will have to pull up their socks." He rose, brisk and haughty once more. "One thing about the military is that we expect results. It's the closest thing to a meritocracy this country has."

"So you'll be speaking to them, laying down the law?"

Murray straightened his tie, tried to smooth some of the wrinkles from his uniform. It had been a long day. "I'll merely remind them of the expectations this country places on them. You're the vanguard, the early warning system we rely on to keep tabs on a dangerous and relentless enemy."

"Now who's preaching?"

Murray gave him a sour look, rapped on the door and waited. There was a guard stationed outside 24/7. Young killers with boyish features and cool, fearless gazes. They might be under a thousand feet of granite, hidden away in a redoubt somewhere in the mountains of eastern Wyoming, but the powers that be weren't taking any chances.

Not as long as they still retained some hope for the project.

Not as long as some of them still *believed*.

Predictably, the episode with General Murray had a dampening effect on the rest of the evening. Pete endured a hellacious bout of melancholia and self-abasement, feeling lower than any time he could remember.

It seems like everything is coming apart and it's up to me to step in and hold it all together. Maybe it's better to let it go, own up to the charade. I'm tired of carrying the load...

His personality verged on the depressive at the best of times. Probably had something to do with his rotten childhood (most things did, these days).

Sad Sack, Maureen, his last girl friend, had dubbed him. A funny, pert little thing from the secretarial pool. Active and exciting in bed. A girl who loved a good time. Nonetheless, this was also the same girl who confided to him that should the facility ever fall into enemy hands, the entire staff had orders to shoot the watchers.

He didn't believe her until she showed him the gun it was mandatory for her to carry at all times. A compact, nickel-plated .38 that fit neatly into her purse. "I'm a crack shot too." Her face serious; definitely not kidding around.

That was Maureen and before that there was Susan and before that sultry Annie and before that...*uh*...

Well, never mind. There weren't that many and they never seemed to last long. One woman he ardently pursued for weeks finally owned up and admitted that she was *afraid* of him, convinced he could read her mind. No matter how much he protested, tried to explain his gift, she wouldn't have any of it. Turned out many of the other girls felt the same way she did. Frankly, as far as most of them were concerned, Pete Vukovich was a complete *freak*.

"No offense meant," she hastened to add. "And by the way, you should shower more often. That would help too."

Good grief.

Most nights he spent alone, in his rocky dungeon, watching TV or reading a book snagged from the facility's impressive library. Currently, he was working on the latest Irwin Shaw novel, which was turning out to be saltier and more fun than he'd expected.

But he didn't feel like reading tonight and nothing on television appealed to him. Flipped through his record collection but it was an exercise in futility.

They're going to shut us down.

Terrified by what that signified. No job, no livelihood, nothing to fall back on. General Murray had plucked him out of his second year of business administration. He'd read a flyer on the campus bulletin board, volunteered for a study devoted to extrasensory perception. According to Dr R., he'd graded considerably higher than the curve and continued to do so in subsequent tests, a consistency that dazzled researchers.

Pete did particularly well with the Zener cards and they never did figure out his shtick. Most of the researchers wore glasses and, depending on the light, the way they sat, he could see practically every card they were holding. So right away he was a fraud. Or just plain lucky. Even when he was guessing, completely winging it, he scored well.

Cynics might say he was a master of the "cold read"—that is, attuned to body language, allowing his interlocutors to give themselves away via numerous twitches and "tells". A carnie huckster or "spiritualist" knows the routine. It's all about closely observing your subject, noting the subtlest change in their demeanor, knowing when you've scored a hit.

The program is in danger.

I've got to do something.

Right now he was making just over nine hundred bucks a month (after deductions). Not exactly Andrew Carnegie-like numbers maybe, but hardly chump change. Especially when he didn't have anything to spend it on. Most of his salary went straight into a savings account. If this whole thing fell apart, that would likely be the extent of his severance package and pension. The armed services not exactly known for their charity. Especially when failure and public humiliation were involved.

He couldn't let that happen. He'd speak to some of the others—Marla and Dale Fedoruk and the Hyslop woman. *Make sure we're all on the same page. They're a good bunch, not show-boaters like Reese, curse the man. I'll sidle up, drop a few names, at least get them looking in the right places.* He had a hunch that was one of reasons General Murray had popped in and unburdened himself. As the star attraction, the wunderkind, it was his job, nay, his *duty* to make sure his compatriots understood what was at stake.

They'd gotten cocky, that was part of it. Assumed their masters would always trust them and act in good faith. Now they'd been tested and found wanting. They had critical ground to win back and only a limited period of time to do it. He was determined to take whatever actions were necessary to maintain his position here. It may not have seemed like much on some days, but to Pete Vukovich this little hole in the mountain had become something like a home.

Bare walls and all.

* * *

From an accompanying note, scrawled by the unit's zampolit, *one R.K Lozanov:*

"Comrade S.V. Kharlamov acquitted himself admirably and died like a soldier."

What did that mean? *Curled up in an agonized ball, screaming for his mother? Dangling in a dozen unrecognizable strips from blood-drenched tree limbs, pulverized by a merciless artillery barrage? Freezing to death in inadequate clothing, refusing to allow his Kalashnikov to be pried from his fierce grip?*

How many ways are there for a soldier to die?

Mulvaney was signaling frantically, jabbing at his watch. Dale Fedoruk and Sylvia Hyslop broke from the impromptu huddle, waving to each other as they made their way to separate cubicles. Marla gave Pete's arm a quick squeeze, not meeting his eyes. Complicit, but still retaining enough decency to be ashamed. He watched her trudge off.

"You're cutting it close again," Mulvaney complained.

"You're a ninety-two year old grandmother locked inside the body of a thirty year old worry-wart," Pete fired back.

"Giving the others a pep talk?"

"Nah, just getting a line on the World Series—wanna know who's gonna win?"

Mulvaney started to say something, then thought better of it. You could see it in his eyes: *these esper types have a weird sense of humor.* Held the door open for him, waving Pete into the six by eight foot cubbyhole. Bidding him "clear skies and good watching", as ritual dictated, Mulvaney then closed the door and left him to his business.

Pete liked the lights kept dim, he told them it aided concentration. Actually, it made it easier for him to catnap, especially on nights (like tonight) when he was more than a wee bit hung over. He'd been hitting the sauce pretty hard of late and who could blame him? He was worried, fretful, hardly sleeping, heading for a nervous breakdown if he wasn't careful. Bearing the weight of the entire program on his skinny, hairy shoulders. Not only that, now he was conspiring with his co-workers, slipping them intel right under the noses of their superiors. Not exactly standard operating procedure.

But it couldn't be helped. They needed success, they needed hits, they needed solid data on what those sneaky goddamn Russkies were up to and they needed it *pronto*. He glanced down at the map they'd left for them, a detailed representation of some place near the Manchurian border. *Useless*. Time to put on a show.

Plucking up the phone, ad-libbing: "I've got a…*um*…hunch. Pull me up Kazakhstan. Make it snappy." Aware that outside people would be scurrying around, rushing to comply with his request. Sure enough, less than a minute later there was a knock at the door and a breathless techie handed him the requested map. He spread it out on the small table, bent forward intently, searching: "Semipalatinsk… Semipalatinsk…" *Where the hell is it*? It was supposed to be in eastern Kazakhstan. She told him to look for the Irtysh River…

He tapped it with his finger. Back to the phone: "Semipalitinsk area. Find out if our people over there know anything about a big—uh, like a factory. Lots of chimneys. Mountains of coal piled around it but it's not a power plant. That's just window dressing. Get me a better map and I think I can pin it down."

Three hours later, he'd had enough. He called Frers. "That's it," he told his controller, "I'm tapped out. Running on empty."

Frers consulted with someone nearby. "C'mon out," he told Pete. "The Chief says you've already given us enough to keep us busy for the next month."

Pete hung up, leaned back in the chair. He'd done his part. Hopefully the others had stayed on script. *Because it wasn't too late*. He had a sense that if they all worked together it might still be possible to pull their fat out of the fire.

When he left his cubicle he was smiling and for the first time in weeks wasn't nursing a vicious headache.

A little black bird whispers that Khrushchev is out, his intrigues discovered and exposed. Bundled into a black maria and carted off to Lubyanka, dispatched with a single bullet to the back of the neck.

Beria is now heir apparent and why not? He's privy to all the Boss's secrets, a confidante going back to the old days. *If you want to know where the bodies are buried*, the old saw went, *ask Lavrenti Beria. He'll show you where to dig and even offer to sell you a shovel...*

"Remarkable, absolutely remarkable," General Murray murmured, scanning the pages before him. It was a transcription of Pete's report (perhaps typed up by the delectable Maureen). The General looked up, beaming at him, and all at once Pete got an inkling of what it felt like to win a national spelling bee. "What I find so mind-boggling is how much *detail* you perceive. It's like you're right there on the ground."

Pete squirmed modestly. "I have to say, tonight the reception was unnaturally clear. I could even make out unit insignias. That's unusual, even for me."

"You're certain about the submarines?"

"Slipped out of Murmansk, trying to hide in the fog. I even wrote down the names of their commanding officers." Murray's face was alight with excitement. His faith restored, a true believer once again. "Show *that* to the lads in the Pentagon," Pete urged him. "And tell them they'd better get someone to Semipalatinsk, there's big things going on out there."

"I can't wait to see the look on Lindgren's face." Murray clapped his hands together, rubbing them vigorously. "This is amazing stuff. *Exactly* what we needed. Jesus, Frers said it was good but I had no idea." He pushed a button. "Get me a flight to Washington." Snapping off without waiting for a response. All that braid and ribbon on his chest allowing such liberties. "I hope this is as good as it seems. It looks Triple A to me but—"

"Nothing to worry about. The DoD will take one look at it and fall all over themselves."

"I hear *Herr* von Braun is trying to weasel his way back in through a side door. Assisted by a few sympathetic Congressmen—"

"Von Braun is yesterday's news, he just won't accept it. They were given every chance to prove their science worked. Hell, they never got the V-1 off the drawing board and now we know why!"

"What it comes down to is *results*." General Murray indicated the pages in front of him. "And this is the kind of solid, verifiable material that will put us in the free and clear again. I know for certain the President's on side. Did you see that article in *Time*? His wife admitted they sometimes hold seances at the White House. Trying to conjure up the ghost of Lincoln. Or maybe Tom Dewey—"

"What you mean is this will buy us more time." Murray shrugged at the correction but didn't deny it. "But we still need to deliver more consistently. We need to know what the Russkies are up to before they do. That's what we were hired for."

"Getting rid of Reese and Ferris might be bad for morale."

"—*or* it might be a wake up call, light a fire under the others."

Murray's eyebrows shot up. "You think they've been slacking?"

"I *know* they have. And I know they can do much better. Matter of fact, I guarantee it."

Murray chuckled. "You're a tough customer, Pete. No wonder you're our number one guy."

"You place high expectations on us and it's our job to deliver."

General Murray glanced at his watch, the significance of the gesture obvious. "I'm glad you understand."

"Off to see the brass?"

Murray appeared more at ease than he'd been in *weeks*. "In awhile. First, I'll take a peek at what the others came up with. Correlate their findings and see if any patterns emerge."

"Hope you're pleasantly surprised."

"Me too, Pete. Me too."

* * *

Ludmilla told them to play Debussy and there was a long pause before someone stuck their head inside and whispered that there was no Debussy to be found. The implied message being that Debussy's music had fallen out of favor and perhaps it was best not to mention his name again on the off chance someone might overhear and, well, y'know. *Wssst!* (Accompanied by a throat-slashing gesture.)

They settled on Schubert.

Death and the Maiden.

She closed her eyes and the music helped transport her, drew her out of herself.

My dearest one:

They did not even grant you the dignity of a grave. Your body dumped like waste somewhere in the Sea of Japan. I received your personal effects, a few odds and ends, and was promised a small pension. I slept and had terrible dreams. Imagining your final hours...

Those were dark days and I've spoken of them to no one. Convinced I was going mad and not caring one way or the other. When I wasn't sleeping, I was propped upright in a chair, staring into nothingness and gradually feeling it seeping into my body. And then one day experiencing a sensation I dimly remembered from childhood: sliding out of myself, drifting away like a balloon on an endless tether. At first, visiting old friends and distant relatives, some in places I had never been. Finding myself moving invisibly above fields and forests or great tracts of desert, hurtling over rippling, blue-black oceans. And all the while dimly aware that part of me hadn't left my small suite of rooms, a thin, silver thread leading back there, a lifeline to guide me home...

General Philip Murray was euphoric. The reports from the other watchers, while not up to Pete Vukovich's standards, showed real improvement over previous sessions. *Every single one of them* zeroed in on Semipalatinsk. Which was unusual, to say the least, it wasn't often there was that kind of consensus. Where the hell was Semipalatinsk and why hadn't it come to their attention sooner?

I'll bet Frers knows where Semipalatinsk is, he reflected glumly. *Bastard is a real whiz kid at geography.*

211

He was pretty sure Frers was the rat in the works. Someone was leaking raw intel, the stuff he hadn't had a chance to clean up. Had to be Frers. For a mere colonel he had a lot of well-heeled connections. Friends in high places. Ambitious as hell too, you could see it in his eyes.

Is he after my job? Hopefully he has bigger fish to fry than that. Phil Murray was happy being a career officer, serving with honor and quiet dedication. The remote viewing program was his brain child and, as far as he was concerned, his crowning achievement. The benefits of *psy* warfare could no longer be denied. The proof was right here in front of him.

Frers knocked and poked his crewcut head inside. "Still here?"

"Looks like."

"Give 'em hell in Washington."

"You bet."

Frers hesitated. "Everything okay, sir?"

"Sure, sure. Just savoring the moment."

"You deserve it. This is your baby."

The praise seemed genuine and the General found himself unaccountably moved. "Well...thank you for saying so, Ken. I appreciate that."

The colonel fired off a quick salute and departed.

Murray felt a rush of shame. Even Frers had his moments. *One thing this job has definitely taught me,* he acknowledged, gathering up the relevant papers and stowing them in his leather attaché case, *compared to a genuine article like Pete Vukovich, my psychic powers don't amount to a hill of beans.*

Pete always had an inkling, a shiver of anticipation that presaged one of her visits. Maybe there was something to this ESP crap after all. Or perhaps you could chalk it up to good old-fashioned intuition.

Usually they met once a week and there didn't seem to be a preordained day. Always after eleven in the evening, but never later than midnight. Just an outline at first, a human-shaped figure sketching itself out of thin air, gradually filling in, acquiring depth and texture, a face he recognized, eyes he had come to know well...

He was constantly amazed by how *real* she looked. Three dimensional and perfect down to the last pore. It was easy to forget she was a mere projection, albeit a projection that could speak and interact...and beguile. She asked questions and responded in kind. They had long conversations and for once he could be himself, with no walls or defenses. Her company, her *presence* came to mean more and more to him as the months wore on.

Ludmilla.

"How are you, Peter?"

"I'm fine. Wow, this is a treat."

"How do you mean?"

"You were here only the other day. Remember? The suspicious factory in Semipalatinsk?"

"Ah, yes..."

"Don't you find it draining? It must take a lot out of you."

"I enjoy my time with you. And so for me it is worth it."

He smiled. "You look wonderful, as usual. Very...life-like. It's like you're right here with me."

"Don't I wish." There it was again. Not just a casual flirtation, she wasn't like that. On a few other occasions she'd let her guard down. Once their business was dispensed with they often spent an hour or so chatting, discussing matters completely unrelated to the crucial issues of the day. He came to understand that loneliness was a universal affliction and that even in a closely monitored, totalitarian society a person can feel utterly isolated, cut off from others of her kind.

Before long he learned about Anton, the man she had loved and lost in the Far Eastern campaign. Most Americans didn't know anything about that war (it wasn't exactly the nation's finest hour). There were no movies made about it, no great victories to celebrate. The Russians had borne the brunt of the casualties and deserved a lion's share of the credit for bringing the Second World War, at long last, to its bloody conclusion.

Anton had been a sailor and a brave one. He'd gone down with his ship somewhere off Sakhalin Island. A simple buoy marked the spot. Stalin had stopped by to lay a wreath. It promptly sank to the bottom, joining the majority of the crew.

"You gotta admire the old bastard," he cracked when she related the story. "He's, what, pushing eighty and still going strong."

She flinched, as if dodging a slap. "You must not speak of the First Secretary like that. Not even here, as we are now."

He laughed. "I'm *praising* the old murderer. He's out-lasted them all. Roosevelt, Truman, Dewey, Nixon—"

"Still, one must always be careful…"

Her caution and reticence were understandable, considering the system under which she lived.

Ludmilla's face was rather plain and flat, though her features were pleasingly arranged and proportioned. Her hair was stylish, shaped by professional hands. Her clothes reflected expensive tastes. She stood very straight and spoke precisely. He asked her once if she came from aristocratic stock and she insisted such things did not exist where she lived. He wasn't sure he believed her.

She wanted to know about the reaction to the latest batch of material. Was the General pleased? Did he seem convinced of its veracity? Pete did everything he could to reassure her. Their plan, despite a few bumps in the road, was still fully operational.

Viewed from another angle, losing Reese and Ferris was a blessing. They were weak links, never having learned to feed back exactly what their handlers expected to hear. After awhile they started coasting…until someone got wise to their game and now they were out the door. Good riddance.

"In the end," Pete summed up, "what it comes down to is that *General Murray* believes. He automatically dismisses anything that doesn't agree with what we're doing here. If we're wrong, it's an aberration; when we're right, it's vindication."

"Then we must make certain you are right more often than you are wrong." He raised his glass to that and saw her frown. "I think perhaps you are drinking too much, my dear."

"I think you're right...my dear." He set the glass down. "The problem is I'm *lonely*, Ludmilla. I crave company but I can't seem to fit in. There's no one...aw, forget it. It's too hard to explain."

Her eyes found his. "No, I understand. I, too, have been alone for a long time. It is not...natural."

He shook his head. "No, it isn't."

They looked at each other.

"Peter, this is not me. I am not real."

"You're real, you're just not *here*."

She laughed and he joined in sheepishly. "You are a good man."

"But you still love Anton." She couldn't look at him. Widowed so young, deprived of the love of her life. Poor kid. "And you're right not to betray him." She lowered her head, unable to speak. "His memory, what he meant to you, deserves a decent period of mourning. I admire your devotion. I hope one day somebody loves me that much..." He meant it too.

"Peter..." Her face had changed. No, it was the same, only lit differently. An *internal* light source. Good Lord, she was beautiful. "Do you really mean that? Is it possible that you, of all people..." She was crying, the tears so real he wanted to reach out and brush them away. And then take her in his arms. His heart *ached* for her.

"Oh, heck, I thought you knew. I'm a romantic from *way* back."

For the next half hour they kept it light but Pete could tell something had changed between them. Anton no longer hovering in the background, temporarily banished to parts unknown. Time and loneliness were gradually working their magic. She was still young and vital, a woman in her prime. Deserving of another shot at love.

It was hard saying good-bye. Her gaze lingering, even as she faded away.

He blinked, scarcely believing his luck. Was it conceivable? Could she be falling for him? A beautiful, desperately unhappy war widow who, by the way, could bi-locate at will, zip ten thousand miles at the speed of thought and show up here, smack dab in the heart of the most secure fortress on the planet?

It was hard picturing it working out. There were cultural differences to consider and the whole distance thing would put a crimp on any relationship. The physical aspect would have to be addressed at some point. But there was no denying they had some kind of affinity for each other. He and Ludmilla *clicked*. Improbable, illogical…but there it was.

At least it's something to wish for. My impossible dream.

Because in all honesty there were days when the energy required to maintain the subterfuge nearly overwhelmed him and he wanted nothing more than to crawl away and die. On numerous occasions he'd seriously contemplated suicide and found it brought him a measure of comfort knowing it was available as an option. He figured he could hang himself if it came right down to it. Or wrestle a gun away from one of the guards. Maybe Chorney, the big jerk. Wouldn't that be something? The star of the show checking out with *his* cannon. Boy, there'd be some kind of sweet justice to that, don't you think?

Sergei. Milaya moya. Angel moy.

I'm sorry. There was a moment—only a moment, I swear—when I almost lost you. Listening to him talk, watching his face. Knowing he was alive, somewhere in the world. Alive and in the flesh. I thought…I imagined…

But the Americans are liars. I swore I wouldn't let them fool me again. It was because of them and their duplicity that you died.

They took you from me, Seryozha, and now I am making them pay.

Second Sight

for Richard Matheson, Charles Beaumont & Jerome Bixby

THE SIGN SAID *Welcome to Zephyr, Enjoy Your Visit* and Walt, keen-eyed as ever, wondered: "Why just *visit*? Why not *stay*? As in, 'Enjoy Your Stay'. Do I detect a certain amount of, shall we say, passive aggressiveness among the local natives?"

Cheryl signaled, slowing as she approached the turnoff. A filthy half-ton barreled past them on the left, the vehicle's massive bulk eclipsing their little Civic. Traffic had been heavy most of the way; it was a relief getting off the highway. Her neck and shoulders were stiff with tension and, on top of that, her stomach was acting up, doing nervous back-flips now that they'd finally reached their destination.

Moving days are always hell.

"Creeping Jesus," Walt muttered, untangling his long, skinny, white legs and levering himself up straighter in his seat. "*This* is the reason we drove all the way out here, on what has to be the hottest day of the year, with *no* air conditioning, listening to bad commercial radio and smelling each other's farts? Oh, my *Gawd*." Cheryl waited for the rest of it. "It's even worse than you described it. This is the place that time forgot, honey. I'll bet you five bucks our new neighbors are something right out of 'The Addams Family'. Look at that fine specimen of humanity. Any uglier and he'd have cloven hooves. In-breeding, dear," he nodded gravely, "that's what gives them the heavy, mongoloid features. Around here, everybody's kissing cousins, if ya know what I mean..." He finished with the theme from 'Deliverance', plucking imaginary banjo strings *bee-dee bing bing bing bing bing bing bing*.

Actually, he was taking it much better than she'd expected.

"I'm glad you approve," she kidded him but he was having none of it, giving off all sorts of heavy vibes as he sullenly eyed a looming grain elevator. "Walt? *Walter*...look at me." He complied, reluctantly. "We were together on this, right? In total agreement. We *needed* to make this change. We couldn't keep…" She glanced at him, finishing the sentence with her eyes.

He understood, relenting, reaching over and patting her thigh. "Hey, we're a unit, you know that. All for one and one for all."

"I'll admit our new home on the range will take some getting used to but let's try to keep an open mind, *hmmm?*" They passed a gas station that looked like it belonged in Mayberry and ahead she could see a cluster of stores and businesses. "I have to turn up here somewhere, I'm sure of it. Can you find that map I drew? I think it's in my—"

"*Main* Street?" He squawked in delight. "Is this supposed to be *Main* Street? The *main* street? The main drag? The—dare I say it?—downtown sprawl? Or uptown, depending on which direction you're facing, I suppose."

"You're raving, dear," she admonished, only half-listening, "try not to frighten the children." None of the buildings in the business district were new, a single parallel row of shops dating back to at least the Second World War. The effect was charming, rustic. Unless your name happened to be Walter Everett Boyko.

"Greatgodalmighty." His tone was reverential as he eyed the old-fashioned wooden storefronts. "Does that actually say…it *does.*" He turned to her, his eyes as big as softballs. "Do you see it? *Look!* 'Bert's General Store'. You're seriously suggesting we live in a town where they still have something called a *general* store?" He slumped in his seat, temporarily overcome, unable to take in any more.

"And a bakery," she pointed out, "and a barber shop, complete with pole, and churches that actually look like churches—"

"Enough," he groaned, covering his face with his hands, "I think I'm going into culture shock. I demand that you turn this vehicle around and take us back to the 21st Century *at once.*"

"Are we there yet?" The Divine Miss Em squawked from the backseat. "Me 'n Gloria hafta go Number *Twooooo.*"

"Uh oh, in that case we'd better shift into emergency mode. Hon, dear, sweets, would you *please* get out the map, I need to know where to turn." Cheryl

218

idled along, trying hard not to fume while her husband, oblivious to her mood as ever, kept up the snide comments and what *he* thought were witty observations.

"Shouldn't we stop off at the *general* store first maybe?" he suggested, hefting her purse and pawing through it ineffectually. "Get some milk, bread, eggs, a chaw of tobaccy maybe—"

"*I hafta go Number Twooo,*" Emily repeated, louder, a tyrant demanding to be heard.

"Sweetie," Walt said, shifting so he could see her, "you'd better not wake up your feral brother with your grousing or else I'll—I'll—" He scooched up his face, baring his teeth and making his fingers into claws but she insolently heeled the back of the seat, refusing to be mollified.

"He's already awake," she replied, grimacing, gesturing toward the adjacent car seat, "and he *smells*. I think he just—"

"—hey—hey—hon, *LOOK OUT*—"

—*everything happens in slow motion, shuttersnaps of frozen instants, each individual moment lovingly framed and presented for her personal appraisal. Mercifully, she has been granted a point of view that places her well above the action so she watches with interest—and absolute detachment—as the woman driving makes several almost simultaneous, split second decisions, wrenching the wheel, stomping on the brake with both feet, the seatbelt tightening across her chest and shoulders, arresting her forward momentum. Walt is half-turned toward her, still trying to warn her and already and forever far too late.*

At that point she understands there can be any number of possible outcomes: she sees them, laid out before her like a fanned deck of cards. In many versions, something resembling a human body somersaults over the hood of the car, its spine broken, legs and arms going out like spent fuses.

But not this time, this life. The car has merely brushed him, incidental contact, leaving him dazed but very much alive.

She is aware of all of this, knows even before the vehicle comes to a complete halt that everything will turn out fine—however, she is equally certain that something has fundamentally and irrevocably changed. By avoiding one destiny she has only succeeded in placing them directly in the path of another.

Then it's like God twists the volume knob and—

"—crazy, idjit motherfucker just came wandering out—"

"Emmy? Dylan?" Cheryl ignored Walt's tirade, fighting with her seatbelt so she could get turned around. Emily was rubbing the back of her head and building up to a good cry.

"Mom-*meeee...*"

"It's okay, sweets," she said, reaching for her while at the same time ascertaining that Dylan was still safely trussed in his car-seat, puzzled by the commotion.

"Hon? Kids?" Walt's voice prodded. "Everybody okay?" He caught her eye and she bobbed her head once. "Then I guess I'll go see if that guy's all right. Maybe you should pull over and park." But as soon as Cheryl tried to let go of Emily, the little girl clung to her, blubbering to make her point. "Gimme a break," Walt grated, stiff-arming his door open, "it wasn't *that* bad, for Chrissake." He slammed the door and Cheryl glared at him as he stalked away, so cold and uncaring.

She caught Emily under the arms, hauling her into the front seat and holding her close, absorbing her fear and helplessness. Freeing one hand, she adjusted the rearview mirror so she could see him, the man she had come within a few parallel universes of killing—

—his body flung, tossed, arms and legs flopping bonelessly—

She shook it off, while in the mirror Walt confronted him, waving his hands, demonstrating his flawless diction and impeccable logic to a disheveled individual who appeared quite intoxicated. He kept reaching out and holding on to Walt's shoulder to steady himself.

But then he turned—not Walt, the other guy—and looked toward the car and for a few seconds he and Cheryl stared at each other and she got this sudden flash—

—pain, fathomless reservoirs of sadness and grief pervading his entire being, a dark rainbow of violets and turbulent blues surrounding and enclosing him—

The pair were soon joined by five or six other people, with a good many more on their way as news of the near-accident spread. Shop-keepers, dowdy matrons, grubby mechanics, children of all ages, everyone appearing genuinely concerned, gathering around, checking the condition of the tipsy pedestrian before turning their attention to Walt. Now *he* was the one doing the listening and he made a great show of it, nodding politely, shaking hands and managing to smile despite the fact that he was still seething, high on adrenaline, *his* aura spiking bright orange and crimson.

Two young guys—big, strapping lads—started helping (more like escorting) the unfortunate man across the street but he pulled away from them, calling something to Walt, and it must have hit home because all at once her hubby was radiating cozy pastels and nice, pacified earth tones. Walt watched him lurch off and she watched Walt, witness to his bafflement. He chatted with a few more people, waved and sauntered back to the car.

"He'll live," Walt announced, dragging the door shut. He leaned over and tried to tweak Emily's nose but she turned her face away. *Take that, Daddy.* "And can I assume the same can be said for the Boyko clan?"

"What was all that about?"

"Hmm?" He was turned around, waggling his eyebrows at Dylan, pulling faces.

"The big pow-wow with the kissin' cousins back there."

He brushed it off. "Aw, it was nothing. Just getting acquainted. Apparently the guy you—we nearly offed is some sort of local character. A complete wino but, well, you saw it. Half the friggin' town comes running, everybody wanting to know if he's okay. Which he *is*, by the way, not a scratch on him. His name is Henry something and I guess..." Then he was looking at her, *really* looking, and what he saw made him reach over and stroke the side of her face, a tender, consoling touch. "Everything's *all right*, hon. Honest. No victim, no crime. And *nobody* blames you." She loved him unreservedly again, this warm, big-hearted, generous man. "What about us? Let's hear the casualty list."

221

"We're fine," Cheryl said. "A bit worked up, that's all. Would you—" At first Emily resisted the transfer but as soon as Walt took her, she buried her face in his chest and cuddled.

All is forgiven.

She was about to put the car into gear when she remembered something else. "What did he say to you afterwards? When he turned back and—"

"What? Oh, that." He looked abashed. "I think he gave me a blessing or something. He said I had a good heart and—uh—something about serving the light. He was sort of slurring so I didn't catch all of it."

"I saw him…" Remembering. Shivering. "He looked like such a wreck."

"Definitely got a few miles on him. Kind of a tormented Monty Clift type. Hollow cheeks and big, dark circles under his eyes. One foot in the grave…" Curious: "Um, what are you looking for?"

"The map, kemo savvy." Within a few seconds she plucked out a slip of folded, lined paper. "We'll find the house first," she decided, goosing the accelerator, "I *must* get out of this car." She slouched over the wheel, pausing at each intersection to read the signs. "It's got to be somewhere down here. There was a lumberyard—*there!* I think that's it. So this is…Davin, that's right, and we should be able to take this, then make a left onto Pangman—"

"Whatever you say."

"You get lost in airports," she reminded him.

"Don't be impertinent."

"And…those people…they weren't mad or anything? *You didn't tell them who I was, did you*? Please tell me you didn't, Walter."

"*No*. Believe me, everybody could see how pissed the guy was, he smelled completely *rank*…" He patted her arm. "No, love, I'm telling you, if you didn't have such great reflexes, that dumb, drunken asshole—sorry, kids—would be pushing up the daisies."

"So what's his story, do you think?"

"Like I said, he's either the village idiot or the mayor's illegitimate son…around here, maybe both. But one thing's for sure and that's thanks to your superior driving skills, he'll live to see another day." He snickered. "A day he will no doubt spend on a variety of intellectual and cultural pursuits, perhaps exploring the meticulously detailed novels of Proust, for instance, or—"

"You are *such* a snob. Hey, I think this is Pangman. This is our street, chicks and ducks." She felt light-headed, almost queasy. *Now* it was real.

"How charming." Walter, the Voice of Doom.

Some kids were playing hockey in a driveway, the smallest one stuck in net, as befitting someone of that low social caste. A flabby, shirtless man was rolling a lawnmower out of his garage…while an old woman knelt in a flowerbed, weeding and lovingly grooming what appeared to be a small, private pet cemetery. "You realize we'll have to buy a gun and string garlic around all the doors and windows."

"Be nice," she chastised.

"I *won't*," he simpered.

"You've got to stop looking at this through the arrogant, jaded eyes of a natural born city slicker. You must learn to adapt your inflexible ways…or die."

"Children, your mother just threatened my life."

"Gloria says she's hungry," Emily stated matter-of-factly to whoever might be interested.

Walt gave her a squeeze. "You tell Gloria that she is the completely imaginary playmate of a lovely little girl with blue eyes and knock-knees and therefore her opinion doesn't carry a whole lot of weight."

"Twelve eighty-one. This is it. The green one. Well, sort of green." Her heart was sinking faster than the *Titanic*. "I thought it was…it seemed a lot more…oh, well, at least it's got a nice big yard."

"*Yes!* The neighbors drive what appears to be a hearse," he crowed. "That's five bucks you owe me, shweetheart. *People are strange…*" He sang and up and down the block dogs started barking.

"Yuck," the Divine One sniffed, "our house looks like puke."

"Yes, my dears, but it's home for the foreseeable future so let's put on our happy faces and try to grin and bear it, shall we?" She turned to Walt. "Mr. Kissoon told me on the sly we can get this place for a real steal. Maybe we should think about it. We could borrow the down payment from my folks, grow some roots, become part of the community. You could join the local chapter of the Loyal Order of Water Buffalos."

He wasn't amused. "You are describing the scenario of a nightmare. Already I find myself positively pining for civilization, with its noise and heightened stress levels and 7-11's and live sex shows. I want our children brought up right, *damnit*." He thumped the dashboard for emphasis.

"Don't forget," she warned, "there've been lots of school closures, cutbacks. Finding a teaching job *anywhere* is getting harder and harder. I'm a thirty-one-year-old art teacher with no Master's, nothing going for me but my good looks and charm. We may be here," she paused, letting it sink in, "for a long, long time."

"Stop it," he said, reaching for the door handle, "you're scaring me."

The house wasn't much better on the inside, its interior stale, the rooms small and, despite the best efforts of previous tenants, cell-like and claustrophobic. There were larger, older dwellings occupying lots on either side of theirs and, as a result, the house would likely remain dark and oppressive during the brightest days of summer. The aforementioned former occupants had tried compensating for the perpetual gloom with color, lots of color, a *riot* of colors. Hues of choice ranged from limey greens and rosy pinks to blistering yellows and livid whites. When the lights were turned on the effect was hard on the eyes and Walt made a great show of staggering from room to room, arms flung out before him, screeching that his retinas had been seared and threatening to sue for damages.

As he groped sightlessly along a nearby wall, Cheryl gritted her teeth and wrote 'paint & wallpaper' at the top of her list in VERY LARGE LETTERS.

"Christ, this place is positively Neolithic. Like living in a network of caves."

"Our stuff will be here tomorrow," she reminded him. "It'll help make it seem more like home." She stared at the scuffed, scarred hardwood. Wrote down 'rugs and/or carpet remnants'. "It's not so bad, is it?" she asked, knowing that it was and not looking up in case her disappointment showed. "I mean, we'll make do, won't we? To me, this is like a new start, a second chance. Maybe it'll help, y'know, put the other stuff behind us." The wording deliberately oblique, coded, for his ears only. He went over, slipped his arms around her. Emily left the room in disgust. Cheryl raised her face and they kissed, softly, and then more deeply, moving closer until they were in a tight clinch.

Luckily, Emily wasn't around to see this. She detested overt displays of affection.

"You still got it, kid," he mumbled in her ear. "Still the hottest woman I know. Truly a yummy mommy."

"You, suh, have the manners of a common swine-herder." Her nipples were tingling and a rather conspicuous hard-on pressed against her bellybutton.

"Har," he said, swooping down for her throat. "Grrr, argh, *hmmm*..."

"You tempt me with your sweet words, sir," she cooed demurely, warding him off, "but...there's the small matter of unloading the car, going for groceries, starting dinner, getting the kids settled..." He gave up, deflating in her arms. "*But*," she surreptitiously cupped his balls to gain his attention, "after we put the wee ones to bed, I'm yours for the taking. Just you, me and a sleeping bag, what do you say?"

"You bring the gerbil, I'll bring the mayonnaise."

"Pervert."

"Gimme more smooches."

"Sure thing."

"Mom-*meeeee!*"

"What is it this time?" Her lips and chin burning thanks to Walt's cactus-like stubble.

"There's no toilet paper...*and Gloria 'n me gotta go poooooooop!*"

"Shit." Walt sagged against her.

"I think she's about to. Emmy, go ahead and do your business, I've got kleenex in my purse." She pushed him away...gently. "Do you mind taking Dylan with you? I'll write a list and that'll give me time to walk through the place and figure out what goes where. Oh, please, honey, *please*, *please*." She looked so damned pathetic he had to laugh.

"No problem." He leaned in close again and they touched lips...and then tongues, grinding against each other, neither of them wanting to be the first to break contact.

"What's going on here?" he murmured.

"A taste of things to come." She grasped his shoulders, pointed him toward the door and sent him on his way with a swat on the butt. "Now, g'wan, get out of here and take that nasty son of yours with you."

"Yes, my Queen..."

Once Walt had wrestled Dylan, *aka* the poster boy for T.W.A. (Toddlers With Attitude), out of his car seat and *into* a shopping cart, the rest of his task should have been relatively simple.

Except...whoever stocked the shelves at Bert's General Store was either seriously schizoid, or else they had a helluva sense of humor. There wasn't the slightest hint of order apparent: foodstuffs and hardware supplies and toiletries and automotive parts were scattered seemingly *at random* throughout the establishment. The canned peaches were on the opposite side of the building as the canned pears; coffee at the front, filters in the back; baby food here, diapers there, with spark plugs nestling up—rather obscenely, he thought—next to tampons and kitty litter.

"Jesus, Dylan," he *sotto voced*, "this is it: consumer hell. Trapped here for all eternity, doomed to roam these accursed aisles in search of—" he checked the list, "raspberry jam, toilet paper, light bulbs and *Life* cereal."

Dylan nibbled on a digestive biscuit, his brow furrowed. Jeez, he was really bearing down, it almost looked like he might be...

...like he was...

Uh oh.

"Aw, no, Dylan, *no...*" Well, it had finally happened. Code Brown. The Doomsday Scenario. There was no question of trying to ignore the problem, this had to be dealt with *immediately*. Except there didn't seem to be any public washrooms. *And* he hadn't remembered to bring an extra diaper with him. Dylan bounced up and down in the cart, cackling like an evil troll. And then the smell hit him, a rank, foul, infernal stench that almost overcame his usually stalwart gag reflex. *Hope nobody lights a match.*

The important thing was to stay calm, avoid panic and evacuate the premises as soon as possible. He had located most, well, *some* of the stuff they needed and the rest could bloody well *wait*.

"Okay, buddy," he told his noxious charge, "we're outta here. Gone with the wind."

He pulled up to the single (!) checkout counter and hurriedly began to unload his groceries with one hand, while keeping a firm grip on Dylan with the other. Every time the little twerp tried to swing a leg out of the cart, Walt pushed him back down. Which, understandably, didn't go over too well with His Majesty. The kid had the pipes of Caruso and the temperament of Stalin. Walt estimated he was *maybe* a minute away from a fit of major and possibly even calamitous proportions.

"How are you doin' today?" the cashier (he had already secretly dubbed her 'Marge') asked, so polite, so jovial...and so blissfully unaware of the looming danger. She began ringing in his purchases, taking her sweet time, smiling at Dylan, foolishly exposing her throat.

"Doing fine, thanks." Cripes, now the kid was banging his forehead on the side of the metal cart. That *had* to hurt. "Uh, how about yourself?"

"Can't complain." She held up a plastic yogurt container slick with Dylan's spit. "You happen to notice the price on this?"

"Shit—shoot, no, I didn't."

"That's all right. I'll make an educated guess." She punched some buttons on a vintage National cash register and he found himself grinning like a dope. *Small town*

227

life, he thought, but he must have *said* something because she was looking at him expectantly. "Pardon me?"

Or maybe she's psychic and picking up on your pissy big city attitude and now you'd better—

"I was, ah, thinking that in the city you'd be on the blower, getting a price check and, uh, y'know, how laid back everything seems in a place like this, compared to what I'm used to, all the hustle and bustle and—y'know what I mean?" It never failed, whenever he was the slightest bit nervous or caught off-guard, he raved. Even Dylan was staring at him.

She smiled gamely. "Well, my dad owns this place," she confided, "so if I'm wrong, he can take it out of my allowance." They both laughed. Then Dylan laughed just because they did. "Aren't you the cutest thing." She reached over and pinched one of his enticingly plump cheeks, somehow emerging with all of her fingers intact.

"Oh, this isn't a human child, ma'am," he told her, unable to help himself, "he's a changeling, a creature of the nether regions." Right on cue, Dylan growled at the woman. "You have no idea what it's been like. Last week he ate the family cat."

"You don't say," she replied. "Well, I don't believe it, you must have the wrong boy."

"No, ma'am, it's true and DNA tests confirm as much." Whispering: *"He's not like us."* It just kept rolling out of him. She probably thought he was stoned or a head case.

"Aw, he's not that bad, are you, honey?"

"Oh, it's terrible, ma'am, just terrible." Now Dylan was imitating a Komodo dragon, his favorite creature, real or imaginary. Snapping at the air, glaring at them with cold, reptilian eyes. "The EPA has certified his poop as toxic waste. It has to be sealed up in oil drums and dumped at sea like raw plutonium." *Shut up, Walter, right this second, you're making a goddamn fool out of yourself.*

Just then the bum came in, the one Cheryl had nearly reduced and recycled. He appeared no worse for wear, passing by them without so much as a nod of acknowledgment, listing slightly to compensate for the roll of the Earth as he made his way toward the rear of the store. They heard him give a wet, phlegmy hack and glanced at each other.

"That guy," Walt fumed.

"What, poor old Henry? He's a good soul, never you mind."

"Yeah, I know all about 'poor, old Henry'." Walt finally admitted defeat and lifted Dylan out of the cart. The smell was unbelievable; it was only a matter of time before the kid started attracting flies. "Take my word for it, Henry there is lucky he isn't roadkill right now. I'm talking about the world's ugliest hood ornament..." She frowned and he immediately recognized his mistake and tried to backtrack. "Oh, by the way, I guess I should explain. I'm Walt...Walt Boyko. Hi, there. Uh, my wife and I—" Unfortunately, Dylan chose that moment to lash out with his sneaker, catching Walt right in the balls, almost doubling him up. "Shit! *Jesus Christ, kid!* We, ah, sorry about that, we nearly hit Henry with our car as we were coming into town today. Just, y'know, an hour ago. *Wow.* Boy, that *hurt*..."

"So *you're* the ones," she said, pausing as she bagged the last of their purchases.

"Yeah, it happened just down the street. He walked out from between some parked cars and my wife—y'know, fortunately she's an excellent driver—she was able to react in time. Otherwise, it could have been, y'know, a lot worse."

"*Thank goodness he's all right,*" 'Marge' said, barely resisting the urge to cross herself, carrying on like they were talking about some kind of latterday saint. Just then St. Henry emitted another tubercular hack and every milligram of Walt's sympathy went out the window.

"It almost would've served him right," he said, feeling cranky, nuts throbbing, imagining stepping in some of the creep's sticky, green gob, puddled on the floor next to the Ritz crackers, booster cables and stationery. "A few days in the hospital might keep him off the sauce for awhile."

"I guess," she said, her intonation odd. When he glanced at her he saw that her face had gone rigid with indignation. While he tried to think of something to say, she rang up the total. "That'll be thirty-four sixty." He gave her some bills, meekly accepted his change.

"Uh...thanks." He started away, stinky Dylan in one arm, three bags of groceries dangling from the other, wanting only to get out of there as quickly as possible—

"Mister? Excuse me?" He turned back and she was holding out a fluttering strip of paper. "Almost forgot your receipt." He took it from her, nearly dropping it when she drew back her hand to avoid touching him.

"Thanks. I—I'll be seeing you, I guess. We...literally just moved here. This afternoon. Like I said, maybe an hour ago. My wife got a job teaching at the elementary school...great gal, I'm sure you'll really... okay...all right then..." She wasn't paying attention to him and Dylan was trying to chew the buttons off his shirt. Time to go.

He pushed out through the door, knowing in his heart that soon it would be all over town what an obnoxious jerk the new teacher's husband was, foul-mouthed and mean-spirited to boot.

Not the first impression he'd hoped for.

"At least we're only renting," he reminded Dylan as they pulled out of the parking lot. His son was jabbering away to himself, bored, poopy, momentarily harmless. The kid was some kind of freak of nature, barely a year old and already meaner than Mike Tyson and craftier than Machiavelli. The day would come when the name Dylan Robert Boyko would resound in the annals of history. Walt's worst case scenario had the kid winning the Nobel Prize for Physics...and delivering his acceptance speech from Death Row.

The following morning around eight the moving van arrived and a pair of troglodytic mutes—"Jed" and "Tommy" according to their embroidered coveralls—started unloading all of their worldly possessions. The two movers never communicated beyond the level of shrugs or grunts. Walt claimed he saw scars: their voice boxes had been surgically removed. Cheryl shushed him...and then couldn't help sneaking a peek when one of them walked by.

Well, at least they worked fast, bringing the stuff out of the truck at a trot, even Walt's sadistically heavy book boxes. The pots and pans ended up in the bedroom and their headboard on the kitchen counter but Cheryl didn't complain, happy just to have everything arrive in one piece.

After the movers brought in the last box, she slipped them twenty dollars, getting them out the door and underway before Walter discovered that the cover on his printer had somehow gotten cracked in transit.

Once the dynamic duo left, the Boyko clan started unpacking and organizing, hanging drapes, putting together beds, *etcetera, etcetera.*

"Fun work," Cheryl called it, although the others soon discovered it was anything but.

It wasn't long before the harsh regimen began to take its toll. First, Emily complained that Gloria felt sad and ignored, then Dylan proceeded to register his disapproval by climbing up on the dining room table and leaving his (full) diaper in his great-grandmother's crystal fruit bowl.

And then Walt got in on the act, carping about his supposedly chronic back problems. After enduring it for as long as she could, Cheryl snapped at him and he snapped back...

It ended up with the two of them walking away from each other, going to separate rooms to cool off, neither of them sure what had happened, confused by an anger with no apparent source.

He found her in the "master" bedroom, wrestling a dresser into the closet to make space for their queen-size bed. Came up behind her, placed his hands on her shoulders, gently guiding her to the window, which overlooked a pretty decent-sized backyard, with a gnarly, old elm tree...and their daughter, the one they had made together, dancing and hopping about, buck naked except for a dry, fan-shaped leaf somehow stuck to the middle of her chest.

They laughed until they cried.

That night they had the best sex they'd had in *weeks*. As they fucked, the house came to life around them, shifting on its foundation, the walls growing ears and the mirrors eyes. Cheryl could feel the scrutiny as she straddled him but paid it no mind. She had been raised in a fundamentalist Christian home, taught to believe in the existence of spirits and angels, accustomed to invisible presences and curious ghosts.

Keeping Dylan away from the stairs proved next to impossible. It was like Hillary seeing Everest for the first time. He easily cast aside any barriers they erected and screamed like a scalded peacock when they stuck him in his playpen to prevent him from climbing.

"I think it's either let him have his way or else nail his feet to the floor," Walt remarked, leaving unstated which of the two alternatives he personally favored.

"He's bound to fall and kill himself."

"True," he admitted, "but it's the only way he'll learn."

It also kept him out from underfoot and let them get some work done. And for awhile everything would go smoothly, everyone assigned a duty, scrubbing or toting while Dylan joyously risked life and limb on the steps. But it seemed like every time they got some momentum built up, something would interrupt them, a neighbor coming by to say 'Hello' or a visit from the meter reader or Dylan finally taking a spill serious enough to warrant attention. It just didn't seem like anything was getting *done* and Cheryl could feel herself winding up tighter and tighter.

Finally, around lunch time, everyone converged in the kitchen and Walt and Emmy started complaining about the sandwiches she'd cobbled together and Dylan was hanging onto her leg and slowly but surely sucking her into his solipsistic universe...and within a split second Cheryl just *lost* it, rattling a wooden spoon around in a saucepan to get their attention and then banishing everyone (Walt included, and maybe Walt *especially*) from the vicinity until her mighty wrath cooled and she could be trusted around sharp knives again.

After her mini-tantrum, everyone seemed more willing to pitch in. Walt took on a larger share of the load, lifting, hammering, inventing tasks for Emily, giving advice and, for the most part, the Boyko family observed an unspoken moratorium on whining. It took them most of the week to make the place livable but finally even Walt was forced to concede (quote) "I guess it isn't *that* ugly a hovel". Remarkable progress indeed.

There was still a lot of work to be done—God, look at the *floors*—but never mind that now. She had to admit it: she was starting to fall in love with their love shack...and was feeling downright soft and squishy toward her big lug of a husband as well, and went to tell him—

—finding him upstairs, at the end of the hall, a silhouette in the doorway of the smallest of the three small bedrooms. His ancient oak desk was one of the first things out of the van and he personally made sure the tongue-tied movers set the heavy brute *exactly* where he wanted it, away from the window, against a blank wall, facing north. The room was half-full of boxes containing his books, computer, files, stereo and CDs...along with his toys and magic fetishes: *Star Trek* figurines and plastic models, thumbtack-nibbled posters of John Lennon, Led Zeppelin and Marlon Brando shedding bloody tears and promising *Apocalypse Now*. And Walt, standing on the threshold, looking in at the mess with an expression on his face that said so much to someone who'd known him as long as she had.

"It's going to be great, isn't it? A whole room to yourself."

"Yeah," he said, both of them aware that having an office, a space to call his own, had been a major selling point and quite possibly what had tipped the scales in favor of the move to Smallville. "So, um, you need help with anything?" The enthusiasm in his voice was completely underwhelming.

She hesitated, thinking about the kids' room, the bookshelves, the painting and puttying and at least a hundred other jobs, big and small...that all of a sudden no longer seemed so pressing or critical. "No, I'm all right. Listen, here's a radical idea: why don't you take the rest of today and start getting your office organized?"

He gaped at her. "You're sure? That would be okay?"

"Sure. You've been great and I want to see you spoil yourself, you deserve it. I'm okay for awhile. I'll finish in the kitchen. I can handle that. Go in there and get to it." It started out as a hug but then he pulled back and kissed her, putting everything into it, a kiss that could've melted lead. "Thanks, babe." He rubbed his hands together, eager to begin. "I really appreciate this. Just having everything out of those bloody boxes would be a start."

"Hey." She held up a hand. "You don't have to explain. This is important to me too. To *all* of us. We need to get you back on track. Then I'll know we've...put everything behind us. Once you start writing again, that's the key."

He shook his head in wonder. "What did I do to deserve a great chick like you?"

"And make sure you shave before coming to bed tonight. Confucius say: 'Man with smooth cheeks gets the girl, but the bearded one whacks off alone'."

When she was gone, he went inside and closed the door, his first priority already clear to him. "Need some music to work by." Hendrix. Somehow he knew it had to be Hendrix. And, he reflected as he plugged in his Yamaha portable stereo, if he could find the right box and a lighter, he had the fixings for a joint that would lend the occasion a certain spiritual significance...

"How late were you up last night?" Cheryl inquired at breakfast the next morning. Right away he got the feeling that she knew *exactly* what he had been doing, that his mind was an open book, one of those cheap, lurid thrillers with a bosomy blonde on the front. Then again, he'd also read somewhere that prolonged cannabis abuse can lead to clinical paranoia and bizarre thought patterns.

Walt slipped off his glasses and rubbed his puffy eyes, buying time. "I dunno. Um, one o'clock maybe? Not sure."

"And, so? Was it fun?"

"Yup," he confirmed, grinning sheepishly. "Uh, I need to get more bookshelves—Em, take your fork out of your ear, please—and a desk lamp and it's smaller than a freakin' cubbyhole, not to mention dark and stuffy and hotter than Hades...but other than that, what can I say? It's *perfect*."

"Can you break away from it for awhile? I'd like to finish the kids' room today and maybe decide what gets dumped in that dungeon of a basement. By the way, your daughter says Gloria saw a salamander down there and I found mouse poop under the sink." She casually plucked an elasticized booger out of Dylan's nose, wiped it on his bib.

"No problem. We'll start with the rugrats' room, get to it as soon as we're done eating." Emily was off in another world so he reached over and dug his fingers into her ribs, unerringly zeroing in on her 'tickley spot', which only he seemed able to find.

"Dummy daddy, dummy daddy," she chanted, fighting him off and giggling through gaps in her teeth that Dr. Walz, their dentist back in the city, planned on building his whole practice around.

"Emmy, you know you mustn't call your daddy a dummy," he told her, trying to sound stern.

"Your father's right, Em," Cheryl concurred. "Everyone knows he's retarded."

"'Tarded daddy, 'tarded daddy—"

"Thanks," Walt acknowledged. "Oh, when I was going through the stuff in my office I came across a box of my books. I was thinking I should donate some copies to the local library." Suddenly suspicious: "There *is* a local library isn't there, sweetums? Precious angel?" She didn't answer right away and ignored his growing dismay. "I'm *waiting*. No bookstore is bad enough but in the name of God, woman, *tell me there's a library!*"

"You're chewing the scenery again, dear," Cheryl cautioned.

"Answer the question, harlot!" he thundered.

"Yes, there is a library," she allowed.

"Praise be to Allah!" He slumped forward onto the table and wept while the rest of them looked on, unimpressed.

"But I wouldn't get my hopes up, I'm told it's pretty tiny." She waited an appropriate interval. "As in minuscule."

"Faithless woman, you have delivered us unto Philistines!" He disconsolately slurped his orange juice.

"I wonder what the Philistines will say when they read some of your, shall we say, *spicier* work. I can think of a few stories that are bound to raise eyebrows in a town this size."

He set down the glass. "To which are you referring? The carnal knowledge with a dead cat story or the man-eating vulva piece?"

"They're both pretty naughty."

"Vulva, vulva, vulva," the Divine One sang out.

"Wubba, wubba, wubba," Dylan bleated.

"Walter," Cheryl sighed, "look what you've started now."

Once the house was more or less in order—well, everything except the basement but who was counting *that*—it was time for Cheryl to start thinking about school.

She managed to sweet-talk someone at the office into giving her a set of keys so she could get inside and prowl around, assess the state of her art room, pausing every now and then to mark her territory.

It was still two weeks until school started but Walt could tell she was revving up, writing lesson plans, painstakingly plotting out her classes, trying on what Emily called her 'teacher clothes'. Walt thought she was too tense and tried to talk her down, joke her out of it, but made little headway. She spent more and more time at school, getting her space ready, organizing her files and scrounging up what she could in the way of resources.

She *seemed* all right.

Almost like her old self. Nervously anticipating the start of the school year, over-preparing to bolster her confidence. A great teacher because she cared so much about her job. Her students. But *she* had adjustments to make too.

"There are almost no computers in the entire school," she marveled at one point. "There's an old one in the main office, looks like an antique, and a couple in the library but they're both out of order."

"A school without computers. A town without pornography or a visible drug problem. Have we slipped back into the dark ages?"

"I know, I kind of like it." She switched so Walt could do her other foot. After eight or nine hours of running back and forth, her arches were holy terrors, but he could work wonders with those strong, skinny fingers of his.

"You *like* it? No computers, no cable, no wi-fi, lousy cell phone coverage—I still can't get over our 1950s-era telephone. Thing must weigh five pounds. Took me awhile to remember how to dial a number. *Dial*, Cheryl."

Her eyes widened. "But isn't it *neat*?"

Sometimes it was like they were on two different wavelengths.

As far as his work went, the less said the better. Walt kept telling himself he always had difficulty adapting to a new environment. And moving away from the city had been hard, it had seriously disrupted his normal, strictly regimented existence and that was bound to play havoc with his creativity.

But the words would come…eventually. In the meantime, he puttered about his office, read, paced, arranged and rearranged his books, listened to music and took *a lot* of walks. At least once a day he would stick Dylan in either the stroller or backpack, seize Emily firmly by hand and they would all make like an ordinary, happy family, out for a nice leisurely stroll around the neighborhood.

Maybe it was just his super-heightened state of awareness (Cheryl had other terms for it), but there was something about Zephyr that just didn't seem *right*.

Start with the whole retro, act-like-the-Information-Age-never-happened thing. No one wandering around with a phone stuck to their ear and where were all the iPods and gadgets and frantic text messaging back and forth?

Once he passed the ball diamond and saw an actual, for real baseball game in progress. Nine kids on each side, at least a dozen interested spectators watching from wooden bleachers behind home plate. City kids didn't play baseball any more. It was too slow. Basketball and the occasional drive by shooting provided much more of an adrenaline rush.

237

Zephyr, he noted, was a very *clean* town, everything giving the appearance of having been freshly scrubbed that morning. No litter, lawns trimmed, houses well-maintained, fences painted, gardens weeded…

Was it real or an amazingly detailed movie set?

If it was all for show, the locals played their parts to the hilt. Walt couldn't get over how friendly folks were, the waves of passing motorists, the amiable nods of fellow citizens. People were constantly stopping and introducing themselves, welcoming him warmly and doting on the kids.

But…were they trying maybe a wee bit *too* hard to achieve a semblance of normality? The homey chatter about the farmer's market and harvest fair and winter carnival, everyone urging him to take his children skating when the new rink opened in the fall—a facility built, he was proudly informed (over and over again), by an all-volunteer workforce, with funds raised locally, not so much as one thin dime of government money.

They certainly were inordinately proud of the ugly fucking barn. If only they knew: he absolutely *hated* ice sports, a loathing that perhaps could only be fully appreciated by those who, like him, possessed not a smidgen of natural grace or coordination.

Yes, it was all very convincing and superficially consistent.

But there *were* anomalies.

Tim and Terry, for instance.

"Tim and Terry?" Cheryl asked.

"Tim and Terry," he confirmed.

She smiled sleepily. "Tell me about Tim and Terry."

"Tim and Terry run the local garage," he explained as she wrapped herself around him, a warm, aromatic embrace. "Tim and Terry are also identical twins. Identical down to every mole and freckle. In fact, they look so much alike that even *they* can't remember who's who any more, which makes it quite hard on their wives, I'm told."

"You're making this up," she suggested.

"I am *not*. One of them has a tattoo—"

"Well, that should settle it then—"

"—*but* they can't remember if it was Tim or Terry who had it done."

She yawned. "That is completely mad."

He thumped the mattress in frustration. "That's what I've been trying to tell you! This town, as average and wholesome as it may seem on the outside, is home to some major league whackos. Tim and Terry? They're merely the tip of the iceberg. Wait until you go by the, yes, *butcher* shop. Then you'll understand what I'm talking about. And do you know they still rent Beta videotapes at Bert's? Like, a whole shelf full."

"I think I'm starting to like this place," she sighed. "Seriously, Walter, I can live without cable and all that other crap…everything seems simpler here, slower."

"And that's *good*?" He was incredulous. "Denied the conveniences we've come to know and expect? Transported back in time to 1968? Zephyr isn't just a backwater, darlin', it's like this giant, county-sized bubble of—of—"

"Sweetie, I'm really, really *tired*." He took the hint, reached over and turned off the lamp. "Sorry," she mumbled, "I was at school all day and it really pooped me out. There's only one stupid photocopier and since I'm the newbie, guess who's lowest on the totem pole?" Sigh. "I feel like it's my first year of teaching all over again."

"Don't sweat it, doll. You need your hair stroked?"

"Oh, Walter, you're so—"

"And in return for this selfless act, should you wish to reciprocate with some kind of oral gratification involving—"

"*Aughh*! Get that thing away from me! *Walter!* There's an ugly, one-eyed lizard in bed with us!"

There was a play park three blocks from the house so he and the kids often walked over there right after Dylan's (brief) afternoon nap. Usually there were other people around, parents keeping watch over their children, old fogies looking on from benches. Walt made a point of sauntering up to them and introducing himself, turning on the charm, complimenting their repulsive offspring, doing a few routines, getting them laughing and loosey-goosey. He had to admit that for a misanthrope he had a real knack with people, even complete strangers, a way of quickly gaining their trust and confidence (apparently Ted Bundy was similarly gifted).

But after three or four trips to the park he'd learned frustratingly little about his adopted community, other than a bit of local history (nothing remarkable) and some general background on its leading citizens (mostly businessmen and lawyers). He found Zephyr to be, as could be expected, a conservative place, its citizens inward-focused, hard-working, evincing only passing interest in current events, definitely parochial in their outlook. The kind of people who probably thought Creationism should be given equal time in the science curriculum and corporal punishment restored to instill more discipline and fear of authority. He couldn't fault them for their friendliness and tried not to hold their backwardness against them...but the lack of bookstore thing really galled him and he made a point of telling them so.

"I mean, not so much as a decent news stand...that's pretty bad."

"There's the library," was the standard reply to that particular thrust. This from people who, when pressed, freely admitted that they hadn't set foot inside the town library in years, if ever, confining their "reading" to the sub-literate regional newspaper—"*Two-headed calf born at Hadley area farm*" and "*Digging a well? Consult the Water Witch (Guaranteed Results!)*"—or the latest *Farmers' Almanac*. As for tackling a work of fiction or, God forbid, a *poem*...might as well suggest they take up Attic Greek.

One afternoon, Walt decided enough was enough, the time had come to pay a visit to the place, see for himself how it measured up. He took along his two published books as peace offerings, intending to introduce himself as Zephyr's new resident artist (even willing to appear modest and unassuming, if the need arose).

He had envisioned a small, red brick building, filled to capacity with leathery tomes by the likes of Zane Grey, Helen MacInnes and Daphne DuMaurier. He was given directions to what turned out to be the original town hall, a First World War-era structure with white pillars and a Latin inscription over its entrance that likely translated into something analogous to "Work Makes You Free". The library occupied *part* of the main floor.

It was, ah, not terribly large, its rather diminutive size accentuated by leaning shadows. The window shades were drawn, the lighting of the low-wattage variety (to put it kindly).

At first he didn't think anyone else was there. He stood inside the door, holding Emily's hand, Dylan in the backpack but still capable of inflicting injury. Every so often he would lunge forward and either yank Walt's hair or hook stiletto-sharp fingers in his ear canals. It was like giving a piggyback to a wolverine.

Walt took a deep breath. "*Ahhhh.* Smell that, honey?" He looked down at Emily. "You know what that is?" His darling daughter refused to take the bait. "Book dust, my dear. The holiest, purest substance in the known universe. Why, just a gram of it will—"

"Gloria says she's bored," she moped, hovering between petulant and surly. "Gloria says it's stinky in here."

"Well, Gloria can take a hike," he retorted. "Let's have a look, see if there's anything worthwhile."

"But there's nobody here," Emily argued, "maybe it's s'posed to be closed."

"The door was open. This isn't like the big city, honey. You're probably on the honor system. But there should at least be a volunteer..." He spent the next ten minutes alternately snorting and giggling, the selection of books confirming his worst suspicions. There didn't appear to be a "New Release" rack and the "Biography" section consisted of kiss-and tell books about the British royal family.

Emily pretty much summed things up: "This place *sucks*."

"Well," he said, plucking a Nelson Algren collection off a nearby shelf, "some people see dung and others diamonds." He glanced around. "But, confidentially, I'm afraid I have to agree with you." Just then Dylan went for his ears again, this time intent on drawing blood. "*Yow!* I think we're done, we might as well—" He paused.

Because all at once he knew with eerie certainty *they weren't alone*, someone else was in the library, a presence that barely registered, like a soft breeze after an interval of stillness. Otherwise, he or she was virtually undetectable, careful not to betray themselves with a rustle of clothing or incautious footstep…

Right away Walt's imagination went to work:

—no clothes, she's naked and ancient, white hair down to her knees and a skinny, emaciated husk of a body. The book dust preserves her and renders her immortal even though she'd give anything to die. As we move down the aisles, she spins and pirouettes, always keeping out of sight, watching us from between shelves, peeking over books. We never get a direct look at her, only a glimpse of that white hair, movement on the periphery of our vision. Because she shuns the company of others and lives in a dream world of her own making, lying between cool, papery covers beside Sir Lancelot one night, Heathcliff the next—

"Daaaaddyy, let's gooooo…."

"Ma'am? Sir?" He sounded like he needed to pee. He cleared his throat, tried again: "I'd like to borrow a book if I may." He received no response.

They went to the checkout desk, where Emily drew his attention to a sheet of foolscap wrinkled with damp. There were columns of names and titles and he was pleased to discover the library was fairly well-frequented, despite its spotty collection and dingy atmosphere. The last borrower was Ina Phelps, who'd checked out a book the previous day. The title caught his eye: *The Heart of the Master* by Aleister Crowley.

Hmmm.

Walt signed out the Algren collection, leaving everything precisely the way he found it. He decided to hold off donating his books, at least for now. He could feel the gaze of the phantom librarian on them, then smelled the sacrilegious smoke. Watching them and puffing away on a cigarette. *Let's hear it for customer service.*

"Thanks, you've been a big help!" he called, letting Emily lead him toward the door, meanwhile grappling with Dylan over a book on *Dianetics* the fledgling Scientologist had swiped from somewhere.

Emily was quiet for the first part of their trip home. Finally, she looked up at him, her expression *very* serious. "Daddy, was that place haunted?"

"All libraries are haunted, sweetie," Walt answered firmly and she perked up.

"*Really?* Libraries are haunted? Who are the ghosts?"

"Writers," he answered, "still waiting for their last royalty check."

The Boyko family's 'alternative' lifestyle raised eyebrows around town.

"You mean she teaches over at the school and you stay home and mind the kids?" Randy, the young teller at the bank, couldn't get over it. He looked like an Eagle Scout, buttoned down, nicely groomed, no earrings, piercings or visible tattoos.

"Sure. Neither of us is big on daycare and I work at home anyway so why not?"

"Guess that makes you a kept man," the teller joked but Walt wasn't offended.

"Cheryl's always been the primary wage-earner in our family. She works so I can stay home and write. Every so often I'll get a grant or a workshop gig and that helps but we're pretty much a one-income family. We support each other, like when she said she wanted to come here to teach. We were, uh, fed up with the city, all the crime and craziness, so when this job came along, we figured why not? Zephyr is only a mere three hundred miles away from everything I hold sacred and essential to my spiritual and emotional well-being—"

Cool it, Walter.

"And you say you're a writer? What kind of writing do you do?" Unfortunately, there never seemed to be a lineup at the bank so there was no way to duck the inquisition.

"A bit of everything. Short stories, poetry, some radio plays—"

"But you have kids," Randy said, "how do you find time to work?"

"Sometimes it's tough, like if they're sick or we've got a Yeti-sized laundry pile. But, you know, you make the time. I'm a writer and that—that's what I do.

I'm also a father and I have to look after those responsibilities too. I'll admit, it can be a real balancing act." Randy seemed to accept that but their domestic arrangements were likely the subject of more than a few discussions on coffee row.

Or, maybe not.

The reputation small towns had for being hotbeds of shameless gossip and cruel innuendo was, it turned out, completely unsubstantiated. From his sources at the park, Walt heard little in the way of juicy tidbits (the torrid affair a certain married lawyer was carrying on with a popular waitress, the dope ring at the high school, the wife swapping and swinging and who was into what and so-and-so on medication and the next door neighbor who was a secret souse, etc.).

Instead, he got an earful about the weather, poor crop prices, the proposed property tax hike and, inevitably, the community's pride and joy, the brand new skating rink.

Occasionally, someone would mention "poor old Henry" or "that poor soul, Henry". Their sympathy quite touching considering he was nothing more than your basic, garden variety bum. Wasn't he? There had to be *some* reason people cared so much about him. Maybe he was a war hero or something; served with distinction, discharged with honor, wounded beyond saving.

Actually, it wasn't anything like that, as he eventually found out.

What happened was, he had to get away from the house, relax, do *something* to take his mind off the total lack of inspiration. So he grabbed the kids and—

Picture a clear, gorgeous Saturday morning and our beleaguered hero has decided to take his children for (yet another) walk, whether they like it or not. The mood is somewhat testy as they proceed down the block, Emily kicking and scuffing the ground resentfully, Dylan upright and alert in the stroller, regarding the world about him with malign intent.

Not long into their excursion, our trio spot Doris Wakaluk, age seventy-four, struggling up her steps with two bags of groceries. Walt, temporarily unhinged by the beauty of the day, gallantly offers to relieve the grand old dame of her burden. Little does he realize that Miss

Wakaluk is, in reality, a clever, scheming sorceress intent on luring the unsuspecting family inside.

Some time later, he wakes from a reverie to find himself seated at her kitchen table, sipping tepid tea and listening as she talks about Henry. He tries following what she's saying but after eating God knows how many of her highly addictive shortbread cookies, he is experiencing a monumental head rush, almost drug-like in its intensity. There has to be something in the cookies because after polishing off three of them, Dylan has slipped into a semi-somnolent state, sunk back in the stroller, an unblinking, witless gaze. The Divine Miss Em, meanwhile, sulks in the living room, refusing to eat or have anything to do with them. Walt makes one last, valiant effort at breaking free of whatever has him in its thrall, interrupting her as he struggles to impose some sense on it all...

"So what you're saying, ah, Doris, is that Henry—"

"He's got the *sight*, dear, as I just explained. You wanted to know how he ended up the way he is, well, that's it, don't you see?" She was pouring more weak tea into his dinky china cup. His renal system was on the verge of shutting down in protest. "Have another cookie, dear."

"No, I, ah, couldn't possibly." Recoiling as she thrust the plate of goodies at him. "Um, Doris, getting back to this whole Henry thing..." Trying to stay focused in order to counteract the effects of the enchanted cookies. "You're saying he's got this special power, basically he's able to see into the future—"

"That's right. And anybody around here will tell you the same thing. It's always been that way with the Slaneys, some more than others." She had short, thick fingers with huge, knobby arthritic joints. *The woman must live in almost constant, bone-throbbing pain.* "My mother was good friends with Edna, that would be his maternal grandmother. Edna had it the strongest, I think. She got impressions off things— she'd hold a watch or brooch in her hand and tell you all about who owned it and what their life was like. And she'd do readings, you know, with cards, tell you anything you wanted to know...and sometimes stuff you didn't. I knew Henry's father quite well. Crazy, old Harold. He was a healer and a rain maker. He even claimed he could, what's the word, make things move just by looking at them. I never believed it but some of that bunch he hung around with said they saw him do it. With the Slaneys anything is possible, I suppose."

She leaned in close, too close, he got a whiff of something sour. "Before the war, Harold used to have bad dreams. He said he could see cities on fire and bombs dropping and soldiers marching under a crooked cross. But the worst nights, the nights he'd wake up screaming, was when he dreamt about big chimneys behind barbed wire, long lines of people being killed and burned to dust." She sat back, pleased with herself. "Now how could he have known about that if it hadn't happened yet? According to *science,* it shouldn't even be possible."

"So Harold had this 'sight' thing too, like Henry?" Walt tried not to let his incredulity show.

"Well, not *exactly* like Henry, no." She thought about it. "Henry isn't nearly as strong as Harold, for one thing. It's the drink and dope, I guess." Pursing her lips in disapproval. "Such a shame. And by the look of things, he's going to be the last of his line too."

"He's not married? No brothers and sisters?"

"Not a one." She got up, turned on the kettle for another (*Ah, Christ, no!*) pot of tea. "After he's gone..." She seemed bewildered, unable to get her mind around the notion.

"I see," Walt commented, wishing he'd brought a notebook along. "And I take it nobody's studied him, ah, under controlled conditions, tried to scientifically measure—"

"This isn't about science, Walter," she reminded him. "I already told you, it's *bigger* than science."

"So you feel there's a religious component involved."

"Call it what you will, call it what you will. All I know is that it isn't *natural.* And that's not all. I could tell you some other things that I guarantee would make your hair stand on end..." She paused, clearly willing to elaborate but in need of encouragement.

"Come on, Doris," he coaxed, "I love a good story. And you've got a fresh pot of tea going so let's hear it." *Ah, the sacrifices one makes to satisfy a morbid curiosity.*

Maybe she wouldn't have been nearly as forthcoming if he wasn't such a *nice* boy with two adorable children (*ahem*), who'd helped a lonely widow lady in her hour of need. Or it could be that she was just a back-biting busybody who liked the sound of her own voice. Regardless, once she got going there was no stopping her. All Walt had to do to hold up his end of the conversation was raise his eyebrows or nod his head occasionally, letting her know that her tea hadn't killed him yet.

She told him that ten summers ago Henry Slaney had started acting crazier than usual, drinking heavily, stumbling around town, muttering under his breath about something terrible that was going to happen. One day in early July he had some kind of fit in the pharmacy and when Ed Duguid bent down to make sure he hadn't cracked his skull or swallowed his tongue, Henry opened his eyes and said—

—her voice acquiring a husky, *spooky* quality: "He said, 'Ed, along about the fifteenth we're gonna have us one Christer of a storm. I keep picturin' this big funnel cloud and buildings and animals flyin' by. It's the Keller place, I can tell'. Ed hollered for his wife to call for help but then Henry got up and started for the door. Ed tried to stop him but Henry can be an ornery S.O.B. so he figured it was better to let him leave under his own steam." She sipped daintily at her tea, waiting for the inevitable questions.

"So did it happen? Was there a storm?"

She nodded. "Yes. Only it was the *sixteenth*." She smiled. "Henry isn't perfect, farthest thing from it sometimes, but he has his moments. As soon as the weather showed signs of getting really bad, the Kellers vamoosed. Some of their neighbors too." She topped up their cups. Walt's bladder was snare drum tight, a slopping reservoir of sweet tea. "You ever see a twister, Walt?"

"Only on the news."

"They move like they're alive, like they have a *purpose*. I remember that day. The sky was black as can be. And the air still, not a sound. Then, all at once, you could hear it coming, this awful wailing. It passed to the north, screaming as it went

247

by. Unearthly. Scared the bejesus out of me. Worst storm I've ever seen but it spared the town, just like Henry said it would. And the Kellers, well, they rebuilt and went on and that's all there is to it." She crossed her arms, daring him to challenge historical fact.

"It's an incredible story, Doris," he allowed. "Like something right out of the Twilight Zone."

"Except it's true," she insisted. "Check the newspaper, ask anybody and they'll tell you. And you'll find out lots of other things Henry's done over the years. There's people walking around today that wouldn't be if he hadn't told them to be extra careful. He sees things up here," she tapped her forehead significantly, "the worst things you can imagine: tumors and suicides and car crashes, fires and farm accidents. People he knows, friends and neighbors, dead or dying…" Shivering. "So I guess we shouldn't mind if he takes a nip every now and then."

Make that a quart…

"So he sees these things," Walt, seeking absolute clarity, "he sees events *before* they happen and then he—what? Tries to warn people?"

"When he can," she nodded. "But sometimes he gets mixed up and sometimes he's just plain *wrong*. And it's nobody's fault. The Lord works in mysterious ways."

He managed to hide his smile behind the rim of his teacup.

"Daddy, let's *gooooo*," Emily emilied from the doorway. This was an old woman's house, nothing to amuse her here, not even any TV to keep her occupied (a prehistoric console set gathered dust in one corner of the living room). She had spent the last few minutes applying that thoroughly disgusted and pissed off look on her face, he could tell.

Walt gave their kooky hostess an apologetic glance. "When her grandma asked her what she wanted to be when she grew up, Emmy told her 'The Queen Of England'," he said, by way of explanation.

As she saw them out, Doris told him to drop by again soon. "And next time be sure to bring your wife along."

"Right, we don't want the neighbors getting the wrong idea." He winked at her.

"Oh, pshaw," she said, closing the screen door behind them.

"That ol' lady sure talks a lot," Emily grumbled as they started up the sidewalk. "I thought I was gonna fall asleep an' wake up twenny years from now."

Sometimes the way she put things really astounded him.

"As you grow older, dearie, you develop two characteristics that help you deal successfully with the elderly: a tiny amount of patience and the butt muscles of an African elephant."

"Huh?"

"Never mind. You want to stop at the store on the way home, get a popsicle or something?"

"Yeah! Popsicle! Popsicle!"

"*Shhh!* You'll wake up—"

"Poppy! Poppy! Poppy!" Dylan shrilled from the stroller, suddenly wide awake and raring to go. Walt scowled at his daughter as she skipped and ran ahead of them, oblivious to the horror that had just been roused from its fitful slumber.

Classes started the first Monday in September.

Right away they settled into a morning routine that (with some fine-tuning) would likely stay in effect throughout the school year. Walt rose first and got breakfast started while Cheryl showered and dressed. About the time she was applying what little makeup she wore, Emily was pounding on the door for admittance. Which was Dylan's cue to announce himself with a few well-chosen yowls; Walt, who'd lost the coin toss, went in and released him from captivity. The family convened at the dining room table for a raucous meal, punctuated by flung bits of food (Dylan) and lots of silly banter (everyone else).

"These eggs look like they got throwed up," Emily complained, poking at a runny yoke.

"Throwed up fresh this morning," Walt confirmed, digging in with gusto.

"Jooz! Jooz!" Dylan screamed.

"Here you go, you little Nazi." Cheryl handed him his plastic Bugs Bunny glass. He slurped noisily, pausing to belch like a dyspeptic hippo. And was pleased by the appreciative ovation he received from the rest of his family.

"What's on for today?" Walt asked.

"There's an assembly first thing and that's when the sacrificial virgins—I mean, *new teachers* are introduced. We take our bows and then it's registration, followed by complete mayhem for the rest of the day. My homeroom is a major disaster area and I *still* can't find the textbooks I'm supposed to be using for Social Studies. I suspect another teacher is hoarding them. Do I: a) approach him directly or b) sneak into his room and steal them behind his back?" She paused to consider her dilemma. "Why I'm even teaching something like Social Studies is a whole other story and I haven't even touched on the fact that my principal seems to have developed a fixation on my left breast..."

Walt reached for her hand. "It'll be all right. You know what you're like. You get yourself all worked up and think you're going to completely bomb and everyone will hate you and realize what a rotten teacher you are...and it turns out the exact opposite. They fall in love with you because they can't help themselves. You're an inspiration and a born teacher."

She squeezed his fingers. "Thanks. You always make me feel like a star. I'm sure it's just nerves, like you say. My first day back in a classroom since..." Meeting each other's eyes, an instantaneous rapport. Her hand felt hot in his. "I *need* to do this, Walter. Teaching is my life. It's the only thing I've ever wanted to be and to have that taken from me..." Dropping her gaze. Leaving the rest of it unsaid.

He was barely breathing. Knew what she meant, what she had to be thinking about at that moment. Reliving.

"You can do this." She raised her eyes. Something passed between them, surging through their joined fingers. "You *can*."

"Why are you whispering?" Emily whispered.

250

Which did the trick, breaking the tension. But Cheryl wasn't quite done. "Being off so long and then moving here, it's like I'm starting all over again. Having to be *on* every single day. Standing there, staring at a room full of students who expect me to be brilliant and all-knowing and—and *interesting*. God," she groaned, "I'm exhausted already."

"You'll be fine," he vouched. "You're always like this at the beginning the school year. A complete wreck. But you get through it."

"Yeah, but now I've got the added pressure of knowing I dragged you away from the city and your bookstores and second run theaters—"

"—and, meanwhile, we'll be paying our bills and living cheap. It'll take awhile but we'll manage—*I'll* manage. I promise. Once I start writing, we could be living on the far side of the moon for all I care."

Which was what she had been waiting to hear. Leaning forward, kissing him, violating Emily's strict prohibition against public displays of affection. "That's why you're my man," she said and smiled for real. "But you're right. It won't be long before we're settled in and everything's back to normal. And, honest, Walt, I've got a good feeling about coming here. This was the right decision, I'm sure of it. Mommy's just being a big drama queen," she added, for Emily's benefit. She raised Walt's hand and placed it on her cheek, pressing her lips to his wrist. "Thanks for the pep talk, coach."

"Just go in there and win one for the Gipper, kid."

"Gloria 'n me never know what the heck you're talkin' about," Emily complained and couldn't figure out why they were laughing at her again.

After Cheryl left for school, he herded the young 'uns into the living room to watch TV (still the best babysitter yet invented). They couldn't find anybody locally to hook up their cable so he fell back on the tried and true, sliding in "Milo and Otis" and leaving them to it. The breakfast dishes could wait; he snuck up to his office and started going through the bits and pieces he'd sweated out the night before, keeping the door ajar in case one of them should somehow meet with foul play in his absence.

Unfortunately, he was still bunged up, creatively speaking. He had trouble even *beginning* something, concentration flitting away after a few sentences. There was no continuity, no flow. He was reduced to scribbling poetry, or perhaps more accurately *poetic fragments*. Whatever you called it, it definitely wasn't his preferred medium of expression.

One of the pieces wasn't bad but the other two were just too fucking *precious* (to quote the great Chrissie Hynde), totally contrived and utterly lacking the random precision good verse should have.

His friend Sean was right: he wasn't even a poor man's Allen Ginsberg. *Yuck.* He remembered Meister Burroughs' advice and was tempted to take the offending pages and bury them in *someone else's* trash. Settled for tearing them into itty-bitty pieces.

As he pondered the surviving fragment, he could hear a commotion break out in the living room.

"Dad-*dy*! Dylan keeps tryin' to push me outta the chair."

"If he bugs you again tell him—"

"Ouch! Dyl-*an*!"

"Daddy's going for his ax, Dylan," he yelled. "Now I'm putting on my hockey mask! You'd better run!" He started to cross out a word but something stopped him. He tried again and the same thing happened. He did his best to clear his mind, read it through once more from the beginning. And came to the conclusion, at least for the time being, that it wasn't *completely* awful and might even have some merit.

He left the snippet untitled and made a mental note to show it to Cheryl later. He bent over it, scanning it one last time. "Not bad, Boyko. Undoubtedly evocative, perhaps even mildly diverting."

But will anyone understand it?

"Daddy?" Emily, standing in the doorway, wearing Face #6, The One That Will Not Be Denied. "Dylan won't leave me alone an' I seen that show a hunnerd times."

"Wait! Wait!" He clutched the sides of his head. "Don't tell me, don't tell me, let me guess: you're bored?"

"Bored, bored, *bored*," she stated emphatically.

"*Triple* bored? *Ohhhh noooooo*!" Walt shook his fist at the heavens. "Have you no mercy? Can you not see how this child is suffering?"

She was used to his antics. "So can I go outside and play?"

"Sure." Then he caught on. "But what about your darling, sweet baby brother?"

"He has to stay in," she said firmly.

"You, um, wouldn't want to look after him for a few minutes more, would you, angel? You, who are my sunshine of my life, the apple of my eye, not to mention the very fruit of my loins...no?" He saw how determined she was, felt himself bending to the force of her will, unable to resist her. "Okay, go ahead," he agreed, "but make sure you stay in the yard."

He took his yellow legal pad and favorite medium point pen and went down to the dining room. He couldn't see Dylan but their one and only arm chair had been dragged to a strategic position in front of the TV, the Beastie Boy entranced by the adventures of a curious cat and pug-nosed pup, out of his hair (hopefully) for at least the next half hour.

Perfect.

Walt had no idea how long he had been scratching away when he heard the back door slam and the squeak of sneakers on linoleum.

"Daddy?"

"Hmmm...?"

"Daddy, that smelly ole man tole me—"

"Oh, yeah?" He was *sort of* listening, but mostly concentrating on committing to paper the contents of his disjointed brain. Proceeding, predictably, in fits and starts. Stream of consciousness scrawls and navel-gazing private investigations...most of it crap of the first order.

"He tole me to tell you—"

"Honey, *later*, okay?" He stuck out his hand and sort of nudged her. *Go away.* "Daddy's busy right now. So go and—and find something to do with yourself. *Now.* Scat." His voice betraying some of his frustration. Later, he would undoubtedly pull her aside and apologize for his brusqueness but she also had to understand that he had a job to do, damnit.

"But Dad-*dyyy*, he tol' me to tell you to watch the baby. He said that to me an' he was scary an' me an' Gloria ran." Emily whimpered and tried to cuddle in closer and just then Dylan coughed or wheezed, a small, odd sound from the other side of the high-backed chair.

Walt finally surrendered to the needs of the moment, raising the pen, turning to his daughter. "*Who* was this, Emmy? Sorry, kiddo, but could you—" From the living room, a muffled *bump-bump-bump*. Walt half-stood but couldn't see over the chair, which was framed in flickering light, a weird, strobe effect.

"A old man," Emily repeated, losing patience with him. "Gloria 'n me were playin' an' he *scared* us. We were by the fence an' he came an' tole us about the baby, to run inside and—an' now I'm scared and Gloria won't stop screaming—"

bump bump bump

Walt got up from the table and headed for the living room, his guts tying themselves into cold, slippery knots, balls instinctively drawing up closer to his body. Coming alongside the chair and there was Dylan, the sweetest little boy from the Eighth Ring of Hell you were ever likely to meet—

—purple bulging cartoon face gaping silent shrieking Munch mouth floppy livid tongue grotesque swollen bug-eyed pleading miniature arms legs thrashing kicking spastic convulsions driving his head into the back of the chair causing the

bump bump bump

Walt's throat closed up in sympathy and it was like he was strangling along with his son, gasping for a few sips of air, enough so that he could scream, scream for help, scream in despair, scream for—

"—baby, baby," Walt whispered. Standing there, looking down at him, unable to move, not knowing what to do if he *could* move, scared, alone, *useless*...

Then, all at once, it was like a whole other person was taking over and this guy was a man of action—*ta ta-ta taaaaa!* He snatched Dylan from the chair, slinging him up to his shoulder, pounding his back with the flat of his hand, trying to *save the baby save the baby O Jesus Christ Almighty save him*! "—I'm here, shhhh, daddy's here, don't worry, daddy will—" He fell into the chair, pulling the twisting, bucking child across his lap, hitting him again, three good, hard thumps. "—daddy, daddy will—will—*EMMY!* Emmy, call somebody! Get on the phone and call somebody—"

"—don't know how, daddy, don't—" Baffled by the ancient rotary phone, holding out the heavy bakelite receiver, flustered and beseeching.

"DIAL IT! DIAL FUCKING NINE-ONE-ONE!"

"—*scared,* daddy, help me—"

"Dylan!" He flipped his son over, trying not to look at the bursting face, pressing with his thumbs where he thought the diaphragm was, pushing hard enough to bruise but only succeeding in hurting the dying boy more. Then it was back to his shoulder and walloping him again *do I use the Heimlich no not on kids this young but if nothing else works then then then daddy will save you baby daddy's here daddy will—*

Walt heard him gag, felt a shudder and something hot and wet spewed down his back. Dylan sucked in a breath, just a tiny, pipsqueak of a breath, but that was followed by another one and *another*…within a minute he had enough of his wind back to expel a soft, keening cry that seemed to recognize and articulate, with wordless perfection, the importance of what had just taken place…and what had nearly been lost.

Walt held Dylan and cried along with him. He could hear Emily in the kitchen, struggling with the telephone, in a state of near panic and thought to himself *well, what doesn't kill you makes you stronger,* but it was false bravado, futile and stupid. He should have known from previous hard-won experience that you were never safe. Not in this world. Things happened, and not always for the best.

But you just kept going.

* * *

Walt spoke first to the school secretary and did okay, not babbling *too* much, managing to sound, for the most part, reasonably sane and composed. When Cheryl came on, he was able to provide a fairly coherent account of what happened, although he found himself downplaying how scary it had been, for her sake.

Yes, definitely a close call but Dylan was fine. Let's see, right now he was tearing up and down the hallway, gouging chunks out of the hardwood floor with the metal Tonka truck Grandma Grace had thoughtfully purchased for him, having the time of his life. No indication of trauma or damage of any kind. Nothing to worry about, everything hunky dory—oh, and, by the way, was it possible for her to, y'know, book the rest of the day off, come home and kind of take over and, ah, did she happen to remember where the *happy pills* were, y'know, the ones Dr. Cameron was good enough to prescribe for emergency situations…

As soon as he hung up he got a whiff of raw, undigested baby puke and peeled off his t-shirt to escape the worst of it. He could feel the residue drying on his skin, encrusting his back in a sour scab.

He looked, of course, but couldn't find whatever it was the kid had put in his mouth. Something dug up from under the cushion. Probably swallowed it, the turkey, which meant they should keep an eye on his BMs for the next couple of days in case a family heirloom showed up. Or the license plate off an old Studebaker. With Dylan, you never knew.

When Cheryl got home, the three of them were in the living room, watching (for therapeutic purposes, she supposed) a video of Emily's last birthday party, filmed in the distinctive jerky, verité style of the great cinematographer and *auteur* Walter Boyko. The kids hardly reacted to her but Walt waved lazily, quite stoned by the look of it.

After giving Dylan a good smooching up, squeezing him until he almost succumbed a second time, Cheryl sat on the couch beside her heavily sedated husband, taking the usual readings and not liking what she was seeing.

"Hey there," she said and he laid a grateful head on her shoulder.

"Any griping from your boob-fixated principal about having to leave?" He groaned. "Shit, can you believe it? Your very first day. What can I say, honey..."

"Forget it. It was just registration. Besides, everybody was really nice about it. I explained what happened and right away they arranged for someone to cover for me." She kissed his forehead. "Sorry I took so long. I got it into my head that I wanted to make you a really fabulous dinner, so I stopped by the butcher shop for some ribs—"

"—*oh, God*—"

"Walter, those people...they're complete *freaks*. That one guy, it looks like he files his teeth, did you see them, they're these little, sharpened *nubs*." Shuddering.

"Um, honey," he broke in, "I have to be honest with you: in my present condition those dudes are the *last* people I wanna be thinking about."

She hugged him. "Okay, how about this, we forget about the ribs for now and slip upstairs and—"

"Are you sure I deserve it?" Finally getting to the crux of the matter. "After all, it was because of my negligence—"

She wouldn't let him finish. "Don't you *dare* go blaming yourself for what happened, you hear me? I know that's what your nasty brain chemistry is telling you but *stop it*." She saw the children twitch at the sharpness in her voice but then their attention was drawn by something onscreen.

"Look! *Look!*" Emily squealed. "Dylan's pretendin' to pee on Grandma!" It was priceless footage but this was more important.

"Who else can I blame? God, for designing an esophagus that fails to meet safety standards?" He seemed very far away, a speck on the horizon. "Hon, you should have seen me. I was totally tuned out and—and not minding the store like I should have been. And it haunts me, I have to keep asking myself: what if Emily hadn't kept pestering me? What would have happened if that Henry guy hadn't showed up and—"

"*Stop it, Walter*," she commanded, slapping his chest. "As far as I'm concerned, you're a hero in every sense of the word. And while we definitely owe Henry our thanks, we're also very, very proud of *you*—aren't we, Emily?"

"Yeah," she agreed, not tearing her eyes off the boob tube, "whatever."

"Poor Emmy," Walt said, "there was daddy yelling and swearing at you 'cause he was so scared." He sounded miserable. "Daddy's sorry, honey." His voice cracking.

Dylan soon nodded off but Cheryl didn't take him up to his crib. Instead she wrapped him in a crocheted afghan and sat with him in the rocking chair, staring down at him, his sleeping, dreaming face.

She watched Walt clear his papers off the dining room table, listened as he trudged up the stairs. He'd gotten very quiet and that wasn't a good sign. She hoped this wouldn't lead to one of his big time downers. If that was the case, she knew from experience that it could get bad, it could get very bad indeed.

He closed the door to his office, shutting himself in or them out, she was never sure which it was. From his point of view he probably thought he was protecting them. Facing his demons alone.

But all she could think about was how much she needed him at that moment, his presence, the strength and courage it gave her. Didn't he realize that he wasn't the only one with demons to contend with, jeering voices that denounced and accused?

A few minutes later, Cheryl heard him come back downstairs. As he passed the living room, she called out to him, softly, trying not to wake Dylan, who had commenced to snore.

"Yeah?" He stood in the doorway, giving off ominous plumes of black and purple.

"How are you doing?"

"Fine. Just getting a drink. I'm gonna be, um, upstairs awhile."

"Working on something?" Pressing a bit.

He deflected her parry with a shrug. "More like thinking things through."

She relented. "Don't overdo it. Save some of that brain power for when you *really* get writing again. It's coming. Any day now, I can feel it."

"Yeah, well..." She could tell he wanted to say something offhand or clever, let her know he was all right. Instead he came over and kissed her, surprising them both. She watched him rub his cheek against their son's feathery hair and then—this was totally strange—he stuck out his tongue and *licked* the top of Dylan's head. She thought it was maybe the sweetest thing she had ever seen.

"So are you—" Changing her mind. "Well, just so you know, I'm planning something special for later on and you're the guest of honor. I'm gonna cook my bigga hero a great bigga mess of Greek ribs and then I'm going to..." She had to mouth the rest of it and he blushed at her raunchiness.

He kissed her again and started out of the room.

Emily was watching her younger self blow out five birthday candles, getting every last one. All the relatives and invited guests were clapping, gathering around to congratulate her. Off to the side, Cheryl beamed proudly. Dylan was about two seconds away from slamming his fists into the cake and pelting everyone in the vicinity with gobs of pink icing, the family's trusty camcorder capturing the ensuing scenes of carnage and pandemonium, preserving them for all time.

Walt averted his eyes from the cruel footage, trying to get out of the room before—

"Oh, Dylan," Emily clucked, while her party guests sought cover from a fusillade of cake bits, "Gloria says you're such a *boy*."

Emily reported that Walt would be down in a few minutes. "He almost dint hear me. I kep' knockin' an' knockin'."

"What was he doing? Did it look like he was working on something?" Cheryl tried not to sound anxious.

"Nah, he was just sittin' there. Listenin' ta music 'n stuff."

He still hadn't appeared by the time the food had been portioned out, everyone seated at the table. Cheryl was miffed but decided to go ahead with the meal and leave him to whatever he was doing.

She made them hold hands with her and close their eyes, offered some words of blessing. Of *protection*. Just as she finished, Dylan spoke up and said, clear as a bell: "Gob blef be!"

Walt, who had been loitering in the doorway, laughed along with the rest of them. He came in and took a place at the table directly across from Cheryl, examining the food in front of him with apparent interest.

Hmmmm, maybe Mom's right, sometimes prayers really do *get answered.*

She wanted to tell him how glad she was to see him. What a wonderful husband and father he was and how much she admired him for what he had done. But Walt wouldn't meet her eye and kept casting glances at Dylan, his face registering intense, immeasurable love—and something else as well, a darker aspect that she was quick to recognize (and dread).

Cheryl resolved then and there to do whatever was necessary to help all of them put the episode behind them and prevent any lasting psychic harm.

The kids seemed fine, no visible signs of trauma. It was *Walter* who worried her the most, him and his deep, dark depressions. After the attack (no, dear, say the word, *rape*), he was the one who had the most to work out, the emotional spikes and undirected rage requiring therapy and, for a time, some pretty serious medication. It was around then that his writing started drying up.

She'd needed a change of scenery but so did Walter, as much as he might deny it. The city had come to represent danger and lurking menace. Too many people running around like the man who'd done such terrible harm to her, her family. Walt's sense of helplessness made him furious and that kind of anger, unless addressed, released somehow, might well eventually tear them apart. She couldn't allow that. But she had her work cut out for her. She'd have to use all of her feminine wiles, seduce him, flatter him, cajole him, baby him…help him see the world wasn't *all* bad.

Doris Wakaluk called it "white magic". Doris, it turned out, had taught Social Studies for thirty-eight years and had taken a special shine to the Boyko clan, Cheryl in particular. Once they met, the two of them got along like a house on fire.

According to Doris, white magic was a woman's best friend and had been since, well, since *forever*. "I use it all the time," she confessed, "and no one's the wiser. I hear someone's sick or feeling low so I'll take them over baking and goodies. A sprinkle of this, a pinch of that, and before you know it, they're right as rain again." Cheryl was eager to learn more and Doris knew why. "You have an ancient heart, dear. You're one of *us*, I knew it the first time I met you." She smiled. "Of course, there's plenty of men who claim we're *all* witches underneath." They laughed, toasting each other with their teacups.

And so after the butcher shop (*yikes!*), she had driven to Doris's place, arriving unannounced, hesitant at first, not sure how to ask—

"Anything for dessert?" Walt used his fork to pick at the bits of oregano lodged between his teeth.

"Well," she started to say but—

"Mommy an' me made cookies!" Emmy, playing the spoiler, yet again.

Taking his cue, Dylan started chanting "*Cook-ie! Cook-ie!*", keeping it up until the others joined in, creating a head-ringing racket.

"*Quiet!* I'll get them, all right? Just *be quiet.*" The din abated, but only slightly.

Once in the kitchen, Cheryl deliberated only a moment before picking up the tray of cookies and returning to the dining room.

Offering them first to Walt, somewhat flustered maybe, nearly forgetting the silent invocation. Then she went around the table, moving clockwise, serving Emily and finally Dylan, making sure to kiss each of them afterward, as Doris's recipe stipulated, consoled by the knowledge that it was for their own good.

Afterword

WHAT PLEASES ME MOST, I think, is the diversity of voices. By some fluke, the collection opens with four consecutive first-person stories. But each protagonist/narrator is so different, I felt comfortable leaving the roster as it was, certain that readers wouldn't mind.

The tales are not arranged chronologically, but according to an arcane, esoteric logic I cannot elaborate on due to space constraints.

The usual collision of genres, I'm afraid (I have little respect for time-honored boundaries). Ranging from mainstream fiction ("Boys", "Matriarchy") to suspense/horror ("Printed Matter", "Daughter") to science fiction ("Strays", "Eyes in the Sky") and _____ (sub-genre yet to be named, situated somewhere between slipstream and old-fashioned tall tale).

It's been a long time since my last collection and I think the nineteen stories making up *Exceptions and Deceptions* show real progression in terms of technique, the unity of theme and content, etc.

Soon I'll be turning fifty, a peak time for writers. And there is some evidence that in the past few years I've come into my own, finally arrived as an artist (independent or otherwise).

Well, it's been a long, fraught apprenticeship. I've definitely earned my spurs. Now on to bigger and better things...

Exceptions and Deceptions is my latest love letter to the printed word, a volume that exalts the power of language, its unique and inimitable ability to describe our most terrible and sublime dreams and somehow, magically, bring them to life.

March, 2013

Story Notes

"Boys" At first glance, a tame choice to lead off the collection but there are subtle forces at work in the tale, layers within layers. The three-sided relationship intrigued me, a shared past that still impinges on the present. A relatively "easy" story to write and, surprisingly, it sold very quickly as well, to a Canadian literary magazine.

"Daughter" As an author, I don't like to play favorites but there's something special about "Daughter". It came quickly and I felt completely possessed by the young narrator, intimately experiencing her plight. Only three drafts to wrap it up and it remains, a decade and half later, one of my very best tales. The voice consistent throughout, the narrative grim and believable. Still gives me a shiver when I read it. So credible it might be true.

"Matriarchy" Another favorite. A bloodless revenge story (imagine that). There's something about passive-aggressive characters that fascinates me. Mother and son have been taking it on the chin all their lives. Constantly living in the shadow of more dominant personalities. But karma can be a bitch. The closing lines *hum*, don't they?

"Partners" Inspired by an encounter with a drunken wedding party while in the company of my friend Stacey Shannon. A feeling of melancholy overhangs this one; I think I captured the mood of that evening with some accuracy. I lost Stacey soon afterward, an absence still keenly felt. Thus, the dedication, with gratitude and with love.

"Surrealist World" I'm fascinated by all things Surreal (and that's a mighty big tent). My research revealed a savage, controlling intelligence at the heart of the movement, none other than Andre Breton. He was Surrealism's Pope, Grand

Inquisitor, High Priest and Generalissimo, all rolled into one. I detest bullies and when it comes to creating art, I invoke the immortal words of Van Morrison: *no guru, no method, no teacher.*

"Spies" The first draft was handwritten while observing my teenage nieces and nephews one holiday weekend a long time ago. Recalling episodes of (mostly unrequited) passions from my own adolescence. Combining everything into a charming yarn I'd rather you didn't refer to as a "coming of age" story.

"Among the Invisibles" Originally written for a Canadian short story competition. Perfect tale for public readings. Short, sharp and leaves a lasting impression.

"Strays" Peter Watts, Canada's premiere science fiction author, was an editor at *On Spec* magazine when I submitted this tale for consideration. Peter, clever lad, immediately recognized "Strays" for what it is, a twisted homage to Cormac McCarthy's *Blood Meridian*...the other editors were merely annoyed and offended. Peter protested loudly and publicly; as a result, "Strays" acquired something of a reputation. Dunno why. I just think it's a really fucking cool premise. What's the fuss all about?

"Facing Mrs. Abercrombie" No big epiphanies or road to Damascus-type conversions. A small story about a small woman and her tiny, constricted universe. I'm not asking you to pity her, merely soliciting some understanding. Besides, doesn't she sort of remind you of someone you know?

"Adult Children" One of the oldest stories in this book; I regard it with a great deal of affection. Many folks out there are dealing with the stresses and responsibilities that come with aging parents, moms and pops who are starting to lose their faculties, declining physically and mentally. I have a feeling this piece will resonate with a lot

of readers. Another tale where there's stuff going on below the surface, hidden, treacherous currents, waiting to sweep the unwary away.

"Harold Stensrud Watches the Olympics" Again, there isn't an accompanying message, no dead horse I'm beating. Those seeking epic storylines or earth-shattering disclosures should look elsewhere. But I love ol' Harold, his little secrets and the lengths he goes to in order to retain his dignity.

"Femme Fatale" Older story, one that's stuck around a long time. I don't often write from a female point of view and I won't claim any great talent at it when I do, but I like how "Femme Fatale" turned out, the office environment I created. My belief is that no man/woman is a victim unless they allow themselves to become one. With courage and determination we can overcome many hurdles. That conviction is front and center in "Femme Fatale".

"Printed Matter" So old it just missed making it into my last collection (*The Reality Machine*; 1997). I enjoy its twists and turns, the relationship that develops between the specialty bookseller and his decidedly odd client and admirer. A sense of menace slowly descends...

"The Daddy Monster" Incredibly difficult story to write. A tale that forced me to explore some dark places, locales I hope never to visit again. *This guy is not me*, I kept telling myself as I toiled away, anxious to be done with the damn thing. Because you do, occasionally, resent your kids, the demands they make on your time and energy. It's easy to be transformed into a monster, raging and abusive, inflicting wounds that never really heal. Writing this story was both costly and cathartic. I expect reading it will provoke similar reactions. I apologize if some find it *too* heavy, something of an ordeal. But if I made it an easy read, I wouldn't be doing my job. This is one you're going to find hard to forget.

"Death Threats" Poor guy, he's reached that magic age where you realize the clock is winding down, the Grim Reaper starting to close the gap behind you. I really feel for the narrator. He's wracked by anxiety, a hostage to his fears. But he's kind of pathetic too. The combination adds that extra bit of dimension to his character and renders him all the more life-like and believable.

"The Future" The first (and best) of a quartet of stories I wrote centered around "Conrad Dahl". Conrad's family has a fascinating dynamic and, no, this tale isn't as autobiographical as it seems. Very few of my stories are.

"Bedeviled" Why do people do such crazy things? The loners, the delusional, suddenly erupting out of their docility and savagely attacking the chaos pressing in on all sides. Seeking to silence jeering voices, expose global conspiracies, act as God's personal agents on Earth. Attempting to discern order where there is none, design in the midst of abstraction. A hopeless exercise, doomed to failure. But can you blame them for at least trying?

"Eyes in the Sky" I've been hooked on space and science fiction since childhood. My first heroes were Neil Armstrong and Captain James T. Kirk. I love SF but admit to a lifelong aversion of *science*. Almost a phobia. The complexities of physics befuddle me, chemistry and biology are strictly *terra incognita*. And so, when I approach the genre it's from the perspective of a fan and admirer rather than pointy-headed geek. "Eyes in the Sky" is easy on the science, heavy on story and character. Enjoyed the alt-history aspect as well. Would the world be better off without nuclear weapons or the Space Age? Because the two are intricately linked. Space was militarized right from the beginning. And, yes, army brass did indeed look into "remote viewing". Not sure how long it took them to decide it was without merit. Or the eventual cost...

"Second Sight" The longest tale in the book and, I think, the most personal. It's been in the pipeline for *ages*; first started in the mid-90s. Shelved for five or six years, resurrected at the turn of the century, reworked, put away again. The story seemed to lack something—part of me knew what that something was and fiercely resisted adding it. But the attack on Cheryl explained so much, it was like the tumblers finally fell into place. Once I plunged ahead and made the required changes, progress on the story was swift and assured. Thrilled, at long last, to introduce readers to the Boyko family...and the unusual denizens of Zephyr. The dedication comes from the heart. The three gentlemen in question were huge influences on a young, developing writer. I owe them a great deal.

Cliff Burns is the author of a number of previous novels and collections, including *So Dark the Night*, *Of the Night*, *The Last Hunt* and *The Reality Machine*. He lives in western Canada with his wife, Sherron, and two sons, Liam and Sam.